SECRET LOVE

THE SINGLE DAD PLAYBOOK
BOOK 2

WILLOW ASTER

secret
LOVE

Willow Aster
www.willowaster.com

Copyright © 2024 by Willow Aster
ISBN-13: 978-1-964527-00-0

Cover by Emily Wittig Designs
Photography by Aisha Lee
Map by Kess Fennell
Editing by Christine Estevez

Silver Hills

The Fairy Hut

Jupiter Lane

Luminary Coffeehouse

Rose & Thorn

GROCERY

BOOKS!

Aurora's

Twinkle Tales

Wiggles & Whimsy

Pixie Pop-Up Market

The Enchanted Florist

CAFE

Starlight Cafe

Serendipity

Pet Galaxy

NOTE TO READERS

A list of content warnings are on the next page, so skip that page if you'd rather not see them.

CONTENT WARNINGS

The content warnings for *Secret Love* are sports injury/depression and profanity.

CHAPTER ONE

WALLOWING

HENLEY

I hate it when the alarm goes off during a sex dream.

Lately, that's the only place I'm getting any.

Rumor has it that professional athletes have pussy falling from the sky day and night, and while I've had my share of offers, they do me little good since I've always been a one-woman kind of guy. For years, that woman was my ex-wife, Bree, but when she decided she didn't want to be married to me anymore, I tested out the casual-hookup waters.

Not for me.

Most of the time.

Between football and kids, there's hardly time anyway.

But on mornings like today, when the blue balls are doing me in, I think maybe I should make time.

I'm not suffering from a broken heart. Bree and I are actually good friends. There's just no time to go out and find my soulmate while I'm at the height of my career as the wide receiver for the Colorado Mustangs and raising my three daughters.

There's also no time to wallow.

I take care of my situation in the shower and get dressed quickly. I made the mistake of not stopping by the store yesterday to get my daughters' favorite bagels and cream cheese and I want to make sure they have them before school. They're usually at their mom's during the week, but Bree went out of town, so they're with me.

I knock lightly on each door, making sure everyone's awake.

Cassidy groans when I knock on her door, until I remind her that I need to run to the store.

"Okay, I'll make sure we're all ready by the time you get back," she says.

We set this up last night before bed, and there is nothing my girl loves more than being in charge of her sisters. Lately, she's been a grump of sizable proportions, so I'm celebrating the wins.

"Thanks, Cass," I tell her. "Get up, girls. I'll be back with bagels soon. Love you."

They mutter their sleepy affection and agreement, and I hurry out the door. The parking lot of Aurora's grocery store is nearly empty when I pull in, and I rush inside, hoping I can avoid anyone I know. For the most part, in the small town of Silver Hills, people are respectful of my privacy. The past three Super Bowl wins have changed that somewhat, with people coming up to congratulate me or to talk about certain plays, but it's not too bad.

With the cream cheese in hand, I reach out to grab the bag of bagels and a pretty hand with white nail polish bumps into mine.

"Oh, sorry!" a soft voice says, and I turn to look.

The greenest eyes stare up at me from behind black-rimmed glasses, and for a moment I'm quiet as I take in her dark hair pulled back in a bun, those eyes, and her full pink lips. She's wearing a white button-down shirt, tan dress pants, and a matching jacket...accountant maybe? Something very buttoned up. Sexy librarian comes to mind. Her face is compelling and friendly, a smile playing at the corner of her lips.

"Looks like there's only one bag left of the cinnamon raisin bagels," she says.

"Go ahead. You take it," I say.

"No, I think you were here first. I wasn't paying attention. Those cinnamon rolls up there were distracting me." She points up a few shelves, and I spot the tantalizing cinnamon rolls.

My eyes narrow on them. "Oh, those look dangerous."

She laughs and picks up the package of rolls. "I like to live on the dangerous side." Her eyes are laughing and my heart does a little stutter-step.

Wait—is she flirting with me? I think she might be flirting with me.

God, I'm horrible at this.

I chuckle. "For someone who lives on the dangerous side, you look awfully—" I clear my throat as I wave my hand over her conservative ensemble.

She puts her hand on her hip in mock offense. "Awfully what?"

"Awfully proper," I say, grinning.

"Don't you know you can't judge a book by its cover?" She laughs and my heart does that weird thing again.

She's really pretty when she laughs. And when she doesn't.

"So, what are you...banker by day and cinnamon roll assassin by night?"

She winks and starts walking away, looking back at me over her shoulder. "Something like that."

"Do you have a name?" I call.

"Tru," she calls back.

Tru. I like that.

I'm still smiling, enjoying those long legs and the way her hips are mesmerizing me with that sway, as she rounds the corner.

She peeks her head back down the aisle and I'm caught standing there drooling after her. Shit, that sex dream must have messed with me more than I realized.

"And you are?" she asks.

I blink, loving that she doesn't have any idea who I am. That's rare, especially in this town.

"I'm Henley."

She lifts her hand in a wave. "Bye, Henley."

I stand there for another minute until I remember that I'm in a hurry. I told the girls I wouldn't be long at all, and here I am, dilly-dallying in the grocery aisle and lusting after a stranger.

Not a stranger...Tru.

When I get home, I catch myself whistling, pausing when I hear a racket upstairs.

"Girls. Everything okay? I'm back from the store. Come eat."

Footsteps stampede down the stairs and through the hall,

and when they reach the kitchen, all three girls start talking at once.

"Dad, Cassidy took so long in the bathroom, I almost wet my pants," Gracie whines.

"Audrey was in there just as long," Cassidy says, rolling her eyes.

"No, I wasn't!" Audrey glares at Cassidy.

Damn. I know an argument's been brewing for a while when Audrey snaps back. She recently turned nine and hates confrontation. I think Gracie came out of the womb ready to rumble. At six and with two older sisters, she's already a skilled opponent. And my thirteen-year-old Cassidy, who used to initiate fun games with her little sisters with a sweet smile on her face, is now in the throes of teen hell.

"I don't know why you all insist on using that one bathroom when we have five," I mutter. "You each have your own bathroom."

"It's the pretty one, Daddy," Gracie says.

"And the biggest," Audrey adds.

"I want to move my bedroom just so it can be *my* bathroom," Cassidy says. "*Alone.*"

"Daddy, could you braid my hair?" Gracie asks.

I glance down at her and she looks like she just crawled out of bed. Her light brown hair is sticking up everywhere.

"What have you been doing all this time?" I frown.

"Waiting to go to the bathroom." She holds her hand toward Cassidy like *duh*.

I grumble, pulling out a brush that we keep in the junk drawer, along with some hair ties, and motion for her to stand in front of me. She beams up at me.

"Thanks, Daddy."

"You're welcome, peanut."

I hurriedly brush her hair out and start braiding, while Cassidy and Audrey put their homework in their backpacks.

The braids aren't my finest work, but they'll do. I squeeze Gracie's shoulder and unload the grocery bag quickly.

"How about we eat?" I set the food on the table and turn to grab the plates so they can get started. "We don't have much time this morning—"

The sound of glass breaking and a shriek is followed by more arguing. The hell? I glance back to see what happened, and the pitcher filled with orange juice is now on the floor and on Cassidy's clothes.

Cassidy starts crying and runs up the stairs, and Gracie folds her arms over her chest.

"Stay put, I don't want either of you to get cut on this glass." I get a towel and broom and start cleaning up the mess. "Want to tell me what's going on?"

"Cassidy's mean," Gracie says. "All the time."

I make a face. "Not all the time. She was nice at dinner last night."

Audrey snorts, and again, I look at her in surprise.

"Noted," I say.

Cassidy was just barely tolerable at dinner last night, and we all know it.

Audrey grins at me, and I tug on her ponytail.

"Mom says Cassidy's got big feelings right now," Gracie says, around a mouthful of bagel.

I nod. Bree and I are in agreement about this. I don't know what it's like to deal with the hormones girls do, but my life between the ages of eleven and fifteen were torturous, and Bree assures me it's worse for girls.

"Your mom's right. Cassidy does have big feelings right now. I'll talk with your sister, but let's try to be extra kind to her, okay? When we're struggling with something, it helps when the people we love are gentle with us."

"*She's* not being very gentle," Gracie says, her lips going out in a pout.

Audrey nods in agreement, but when I look at her, her expression turns sheepish.

"We treat people how we want to be treated, even if they don't do the same. Okay?" I wait and there's a long pause before both girls reluctantly agree. "All right. Finish up with breakfast and then go brush your teeth. We need to be out the door in ten minutes."

I get a bagel ready for Cassidy and take it upstairs, knocking on her door.

"Come in," she says quietly.

When I open the door, she's sitting on the edge of the bed in her changed outfit. She wipes her face with the back of her hand and lets out a shaky breath.

"You okay, bunny?"

She stares down at the floor and shakes her head, and I'm ready to fight an army and whoever else stands in my way to make my girl feel better.

"Talk to me. What's going on?" I reach out and take her hand and she clasps it hard.

"I don't want to go to school," she says.

She's usually trying to grow up way too fast and sounds like a teenager most of the time, but now, she sounds like my little girl. The one that used to run and jump into my arms every time I got home, yelling, *"Daddy!"* like I was the best dad ever.

"Why not?"

"Mrs. Carboni hates me. She's so mean. She says I'm wasting her time."

"What? Why would she say that?"

She swallows hard. "I didn't turn in my project."

I gape at her. "Mrs. Carboni is your *English* teacher, right? You're talking about the project you worked on all last week?"

She nods, and a few more tears drip from her brown eyes that are just like mine. I can hardly take it. I put my arm around her, holding her as she sobs, just as Gracie yells up the stairs, "Audrey says we're going to be late if we don't leave now!"

"We'll be right there," I call back. "Cassidy, I don't understand why you didn't turn it in. I looked over that project. Your mom did too. It was good work."

She doesn't say anything and I hand her a tissue from her bedside table. She wipes her face and nose and takes another shaky breath.

"I'll have a talk with her, okay? But you need to turn your project in. Turn it in today and I'll call and set something up."

She shakes her head and says in a much lighter tone, "It's okay, Dad. I'll be okay. You don't need to talk to her. I was just having a freak-out. I feel better now."

I frown. The mental whiplash is too much for me this early in the morning. I'm much better at getting whiplash on the field than I am with the mental gymnastics my girls put me through every day.

"You'll turn in your project?" I ask.

She nods and even musters a grin.

"Okay?" I say, reluctantly.

"We should really get going, Dad. Mom will be so annoyed with you if you make us late."

I stand and stare after her as she hurries out of the room.

"I'm not the one making you late," I call.

She pokes her head back in the door and I see the mischief in her eyes.

"Hurry up," she mouths.

"Trying my patience this morning," I say, shaking my head.

She grins then and I'm happy to see that smile on my girl's face.

We hustle down the stairs.

"Let's go, kiddos." I grab the keys and help Gracie with her backpack. The girls start thumb wars to see who gets the front seat in the Suburban. Audrey wins today, causing a new round of complaints.

I have the cure. No matter how much they argue, when I turn on Taylor Swift, they start singing "Cruel Summer" at the top of their lungs, and all is well.

I drop them off and drive to the gym, still humming to Taylor.

Damn, my daughters keep me hopping.

It felt good to have that small interaction with that woman at the store. Really good. The way she looked me over makes me think I've still got it.

I wonder what she'd think if she knew how chaotic my life is.

Too bad I'll never find out.

CHAPTER TWO

NEW GIRL

TRU

I think about the hot guy—scratch that, he was *all man*—in the grocery store all the way to school. *Henley*. Unique name, but it fits him. He was so tall that even in my heels, he still stood a good five or six inches taller than me. His chest was so broad, I can only imagine how amazing a hug from him would feel. And those chocolate-brown eyes that crinkled when he smiled...I'm still feeling the warmth of those eyes and that smile.

My mom calls just as I'm pulling into the parking lot. I accept the call and her voice fills the car.

"Good morning! I can't believe you're still up. It's past your bedtime."

"Good morning! I was too excited to sleep. A kangaroo was in our yard earlier, and it was the cutest thing, but goodness, those things have a temper on them! It tried its best to kick me, but fortunately, I was fast. Anyway, I wanted to wish you a great first day of school!" She laughs and I smile, a wave of missing her hitting me in the gut. "You're going to be running the place before we know it."

I laugh. "Thanks, Mom. But I'm only the sub, remember?"

"It still counts! You're doing what you've always wanted to do," she says. "And they'll love you so much, they'll *find* a position for you if it's not this one."

"I love you. You're always cheering me on, no matter what."

"Always will, baby girl."

I'm still smiling when I hang up the phone. I think my mom will be calling me her baby girl forever, but I don't mind it when it's coming from her. My ex-boyfriend, Chet, picked up on the nickname, and it grated on my nerves when he said it.

I was a substitute teacher in Boulder for a while, but when my parents moved to Sydney, I decided to find a place I love. I liked Boulder a lot, but it didn't feel like home…especially after my mom left. My parents' moves are always temporary, so unless I wanted to live in a new place constantly, I had to choose where I wanted to land. If they'd stayed in Guatemala, I would've lived there forever. We lived there for two years when I was ten and it felt like home to me. Once we moved from there, I never felt fully settled anywhere.

Passing through Silver Hills over the past few years, I've

thought it seemed like a dream place to live, so I'm hoping to find a more permanent job here and find out.

As I'm getting out of the car, my phone buzzes and I turn the sound off while checking the text.

MOM

I meant to tell you that Dad sends his love.

I stare at the phone for a few seconds. I highly doubt my dad said anything of the sort, but my mom tries so hard to keep up the pretense that my dad and I have a great relationship. We don't.

I'd like to believe that marriage is sacred, but when it comes to my parents, I wouldn't shed a tear if they divorced. Mom's given up several jobs she's loved over the years to follow him. He's moved her all over the world every few years with his job in engineering, and it'd be different if she wanted to move, but she'd love nothing more than to settle down somewhere at this point. It'd also be different if he treated her well, but he doesn't. My mom is upbeat and bubbly and full of optimism with everyone but my dad; with him, she's quiet and subservient and a shadow of herself.

It's heartbreaking to watch.

I decide to not respond to my mom's text. I need to get inside anyway. The hallways echo with the sound of my heels clicking against the floor. Students mill around here and there, but it's not too busy yet. I make my way to the front office and smile when the receptionist looks up from behind her desk.

"Please tell me you're our sub," she says, sounding irritated.

"I am." My grin widens, but it's lost on…Mrs. Davenport, according to the nameplate on her desk. "I'm Tru Seymour," I add.

I show her my district ID lanyard and she nods, handing me a form.

"I'll get your key and you'll be required to wear your lanyard and sign this log first thing each time you're called back...*if* you're ever called back," she says. She looks me over and under her breath, she says, "Good luck in that getup."

Well, that's a pin stuck straight into my confidence balloon, but I think I hide the way I wilt inside very well.

"Let's hope," I say, crossing my fingers.

I sign the form and pay close attention when she tells me how to get to my class. Directions and I don't go together very well.

By late morning, I've already had a sleepy class where the kids barely responded to anything I said, and a rowdy class where they were a little too caffeinated. The class before lunch is a nice balance. The kids are quiet but responsive. The assignment today involves the students reading their favorite passages from their favorite authors. It's part of a project they've been working on. The huge poster boards with pictures, quotes, and facts about their favorite authors are set up around the room, and there are only a few left who haven't done their reading passages.

My finger skims down the page for the next name and I see a red line. I look down the list to see if there are any other red lines, but there aren't any. Those who went before today have already been graded by Mrs. Carboni and the ones who haven't yet are blank. I've left notes on how I think they should be graded, but I'll let Mrs. Carboni put it in her gradebook herself. That's one of those boundaries I typically don't cross as a substitute teacher unless given explicit direction to do so. I skip the name with the red line and we listen to the last two students read. There are still a few minutes left of class, so I circle back to the name with the red line.

"Cassidy Ward? Have you already had a turn?" I look around the room after glancing briefly at the seating chart. She's sitting in the back and I could've guessed who she was without the chart due to her blooming red cheeks.

Her eyes flicker up to mine and I'm shocked to see tears in her eyes. She shakes her head.

"Did you complete the work?"

"Yes," she says softly.

"Okay, let's see it." I smile encouragingly. I'm not sure how Mrs. Carboni feels about late work, but surely it counts for something that she finished the project.

Cassidy stands up and sets the folder on the desk next to where I'm standing.

"I put my poster back there before class," she points to the far right in the back of the room, "and my folder was ready on time—the poster was too, but...I'd rather not do the reading if that's okay."

"Oh, I—" The bell rings, cutting us off, and everyone hurries to leave, including Cassidy.

I flip through her folder, smiling at the pictures Cassidy drew of Margaret Peterson Haddix. I'm a huge fan of MPH's work, and Cassidy captured her perfectly. As I skim through the report, it's also well done, and I walk back to look at the poster when I hear a phone ringing.

I search for the culprit and realize it's the classroom phone too late. It stops ringing right before I get there, and I sit down at the desk, pulling out my lunch bag as I continue looking over Cassidy's report. I wonder why she didn't want to read the passages.

There's a knock on the door and the sound of a throat

clearing. When I glance up, the hot guy from the grocery store is the last person I expect to see standing there. *Henley.* He looks quite different from this morning. His thick black hair is not as unruly, and he's wearing jeans and a button-down shirt, which does little to hide his muscular arms and chest. But the biggest difference is that his eyes are not warmly assessing me the way they were earlier. He's *scowling*, his full lips curled in contempt.

I'm so flustered, I drop the folder on the desk and stare up at him.

"Well, well," he says.

Well, well, indeed, my brain replies.

"I need to have a word with you, *Mrs.* Carboni," he says sharply.

My mouth parts to jump in and correct him, but he doesn't pause long enough.

"Did you really tell my daughter that she's wasting your time?" He shakes his head. "I understand feeling that way sometimes, but that doesn't mean you tell the child that. Do you know how sensitive kids this age are? Apparently, you don't...which makes me question why you are even teaching middle school."

I heat with the reprimand even though it has nothing to do with me.

"I don't know why she didn't turn in her project," he goes on.

"Ah, you're Cassidy Ward's dad."

His eyes narrow, and if anything, he looks angrier. "Yes, I'm Cassidy's dad. Henley Ward." His scowl deepens. "Did you tell more than one student that they were wasting your time?"

One hand goes to his hip and the other drags through his

hair. I get distracted watching his thick hair fall back into place.

"She worked on it all last week and did a great job too. I looked it over myself. I encouraged her to turn it in and will talk with her more about it, but I just wanted to ask you to refrain from speaking to your students that way...EVER. AGAIN."

Who the *hell* does he think he is? Way too many memories of watching my mom be berated by my dad flood through my mind, and I can't tolerate it another second.

His jaw clenches and I jump in before he can say anything else.

"You're one of those parents, I see."

Two spots of color flood his cheeks and I lift an eyebrow.

"I'd probably be the same way if I were a parent," I add. "But you needed to get your facts straight before you waltzed back here and gave me a piece of your mind." I stand up and move around the front of the desk, folding my arms as I lean against it. "Cassidy turned her project in today. In fact, I was just looking it over when you stormed in."

He swallows and those dark brown eyes that looked at me at the grocery store with such amusement and maybe even attraction now simmer with fury.

"I tend to agree—a student shouldn't be told that she's wasting the teacher's time. However," I hold up my hand when he starts to interrupt, "I don't know the context of this statement...what Mrs. Carboni might've been referring to or what might've been said or done to provoke the statement... *since I'm not Mrs. Carboni.*"

His head rears back and he stands there for a few seconds, looking confused. I'd help him out further if my temper wasn't a little spiky itself.

"You're not Mrs. Carboni," he states.

"No, I am not."

A few seconds of silence follow.

"Well, now I feel like a true asshole," he says.

I tilt my head like *you said it, not me.*

"I'm so sorry," he says. "Tru...uh, Mrs.—" He lifts his eyebrows, waiting for me to fill in the rest.

"*Miss* Seymour." I look up at him, not bothering to smooth over this awkward moment.

"I...was out of line."

"You were."

"I hope you'll forgive me." He stares at me for a second and fiddles with the stapler on the desk. His tall, muscular frame makes the classroom feel smaller. "Uh...did you say Cassidy turned in her project?"

"Yes, she did. The bell rang just as she was turning it in."

"Good."

He taps the desk and looks at me through lowered brows. I still haven't seen a wedding ring on his finger, but that doesn't necessarily mean anything.

"Well, I guess I'll be seeing you," he says. He gives me a crooked smile and my iciness thaws somewhat but not entirely.

I nod. "Have a nice day, Mr. Ward." My voice is cool and his smile falters.

"Henley," he says.

"Hmm. You can show yourself out, Mr. Ward."

He sighs and walks to the door, looking at me over his shoulder one last time before walking out.

Well, that was disappointing. After such a fun interaction with Henley this morning, I didn't see that coming.

Growing up, there were times I wished my dad would stand up for me, so I can respect that Henley did that for his daughter.

But a lifetime of being my dad's emotional punching bag cured me of ever taking it from another man.

No, thank you.

I'd rather be single for the rest of my life than ever be spoken to that way again.

CHAPTER THREE

FLOWERS WOULDN'T HURT

HENLEY

RHODES

You forget our meeting?

Running a little late, but I'll be there.

WESTON

Caleb is expecting to see his Unca Hen, so you'd better hurry.

Tell him I'm on my way.

RHODES

You totally forgot, didn't you?

No. I need this meeting. I...I'll explain
everything when I get there.

RHODES

Color me intrigued.

PENN

He's met someone. You have, haven't you?
Have you finally listened to me and Rhodes
and gotten laid?!

BOWIE

Back off. He said he's on his way, and it's
not like we're in a rush to leave. We'll be
here, Hen. Take your time. I am curious
about your answer, though. <Wink emoji>

I snort at their ridiculousness, but I also speed up to just one
mile over the speed limit. The Silver Hills police department
claims to love me, but they don't hesitate to give me a ticket
if I'm five miles over the speed limit on Jupiter Lane, our
main drag.

A couple of times a month, I meet up with the guys who
have become my best friends since we started playing for the
Mustangs. What started out as coffee once in a while with a
couple of single dads on the team, Rhodes and Bowie, has
turned into a necessity in my life. I don't think I'm the only
one of us who feels this way either.

Rhodes' son Levi is such a cute and funny little boy. He's

three now and there's never a dull moment when he's around. Bowie's daughter Becca will be eight soon, and she's a sweetheart. She's smart and adorable and has Down Syndrome. She gives the best hugs and her sunny smile has brightened many of my days.

It's not just Rhodes and Bowie—now there are five of us who get together.

We talk about kids and life and women, not always in that order. Much to the amusement of the only non-dad in the group, Penn, who I guess started coming because of FOMO, we call ourselves the Single Dad Players. Penn and Weston would show up randomly here at the coffee shop or listen in when we were talking on the road, and I swear, fatherhood must be contagious. Weston suddenly found himself with a baby last year, and Penn started tutoring a kid who's in the foster care system and got attached. So after teasing us about our meetings for so long, both of them now show up needing lots of advice. Rhodes, Bowie, and I started writing our thoughts on fatherhood in a notebook aptly named The Single Dad Playbook that we bring each time we're together, but let's be honest—we're all winging it 99.9% of the time.

Case in point: the way I've crashed and burned today.

I walk into Luminary Coffeehouse a few minutes later, still feeling like a prick. I don't know what got into me earlier. I've never confronted a teacher...or a woman like that before...ever. I leave my aggression in the gym and on the football field, and I'd like to keep it that way.

Knowing how hard Cassidy worked on that project and hearing that a teacher made her feel *less than*...it wrecked me. My gut is still twisted in knots over how desolate she looked this morning and how she tried so hard to pretend that she was fine after bawling her eyes out.

She hasn't been herself for a while now. I want her to

know I have her back. I want her to know she can always count on me.

But she'd be so pissed if she knew I talked to her teacher the way I did. I'm fucking pissed at myself.

And it wasn't even the infamous Mrs. Carboni at all.

As soon as I step into the shop, my favorite coffee shop owner, Clara, waves and motions for me to head back to the room where the guys are waiting.

"I'll bring your Solar Latte in a few minutes," she says.

"Thanks, Clara."

I'm hooked on her latte with honey, vanilla, and a sprinkle of cinnamon. Even during our regular season, it's the one thing I'm not willing to sacrifice.

I wave at a few of the regulars. Marv and Walter are here every time I come in, and they usually stop arguing with one another to say hello, but today, I overhear them discussing the Bubbling Brook soup from The Fairy Hut.

"It was inedible last night!" Marv says.

"You're outta your mind. It was delicious, as usual. It's your faulty taste buds. You need to go to the dentist, I keep telling ya," Walter says.

I chuckle under my breath and head back to the small conference room we meet in to avoid interruptions and eavesdroppers. The traffic in Luminary has picked up drastically since we started meeting here, but it's good for Clara's business, and most of the customers are respectful of our time.

When I walk in, the guys are laughing their heads off about something. Caleb is on the floor, playing with a dump truck, and when he sees me, he rushes toward me, his arms in the air for me to pick him up.

"Unca Hen!" he yells.

"Hey, buddy." I pick him up and hold him high in the air.

He waits in anticipation and I toss him just high enough to give him a little thrill…and not so high that it makes Weston nervous.

"Do you feed him snacks on the down-low or something," Penn asks. "He loves me, but not like that."

"He loves all of you," Weston says. He pauses for dramatic effect. "Just Henley a little more…" He laughs when Rhodes and Penn both sock him in the shoulder.

"I mean, I love Henley a little more too," Rhodes says, shrugging. "That goes for you too." He points at Bowie and Bowie winks. We all laugh at Weston and Penn's expressions.

"He's messing with you guys. You know we've welcomed you into the inner fu—effing sanctum…" I correct myself for Caleb just in time. "It doesn't get more loving than that. How's everyone doing?"

I set Caleb on his feet, holding on until he has his balance. He picks up the dump truck and toddles toward me with it. I take the little car out of the back of it and make it ride on top of the dump truck.

"Question is, how are you?" Bowie asks.

"That's right," Rhodes says. "Did the pretty boy get it right?" He nods toward Penn, who grins up at me.

I roll my eyes. "No, he couldn't be more wrong."

Penn's smile drops, and he nods sagely. "You'd look a lot happier if you'd gotten laid."

"Wouldn't we all, wouldn't we all…" Rhodes says.

"I did something so stupid." I groan. "This morning at the grocery store I met someone beautiful, attractive in every way. She was smart, sexy…my game was on point."

One of the guys makes an exaggerated gasp and I look around to see all of them staring at me in shock.

"What?" I frown.

"Just processing the fact that we've never heard you talk about a woman like this ever," Rhodes says, pounding the table when he says *ever*.

"Well, just wait. It's all downhill from here. When I got home, Cassidy told me about her teacher, Mrs. Carboni, and how she told her she was wasting her time…"

"No, who would say that?" Rhodes scowls. "Let me at that teacher."

"I know, I know. I was pissed too. I went over to the school and guess who's there? Guess who's the teacher in her class?"

"*No*, it wasn't her, was it?" Bowie says.

"You're kidding," Rhodes says.

"Yep, she's there in her sexy librarian getup and I went off on her. All the while, so sad that this woman that I was so attracted to this morning is the very one who's told my daughter she's wasting her time. She tells me in no uncertain terms that she understands my feelings….that she would probably feel the same if she had kids, but then in her polite way, she basically told me to fuck off. Get this—she wasn't Mrs. Carboni. She's the sub."

I take a deep breath.

"So I felt like the biggest prick, and I'm still regretting everything I said. Not to mention, it was wasted on the wrong person and that beautiful woman thinks I'm an ass."

"That's nothing a pretty bouquet of flowers won't fix," Penn says.

Weston looks at him like he's crazy. "You clearly don't know women."

"What? They love flowers! I've never given anyone but my mom flowers, and she loves them, but…I just think he should put himself out there." Penn lifts a shoulder. "Let her know he feels bad."

Everyone stares at him.

He throws his hands up in the air. "What? It's a good suggestion."

"Did you find out what she likes? What did you learn about her during the time you talked?" Bowie asks.

"I found out that she likes cinnamon rolls…and cinnamon raisin bagels with cream cheese."

"What are you gonna do?" Weston asks. "I've never seen you excited about anyone like this…you need to fix it."

"It wasn't so much that I felt like I wanted to pursue her…more the feeling that I wish I could…which is new."

"Well, why the hell wouldn't you?" Rhodes asks. "If she liked you this morning, you can win her over again."

"I don't know. She looked excited to see me when I walked in and by the time I left, her iciness was…" I do a mock shudder. "And I don't blame her. I walked in there like an entitled ass and didn't even give her a chance to talk."

"As much as I hate to admit it, Penn is right," Bowie says.

"What is that supposed to mean?" Penn laughs.

"Flowers wouldn't hurt. Send her flowers," Bowie says.

"I can't do that. Where would I send them? The only place I've seen her is at the grocery store and at school—and there's no way I can send them to school."

"Why not?" Rhodes says. "Grand gesture. Don't women love the grand gesture?"

They all laugh and I give them a withering glare until they stop.

"Find out where she lives," Penn says.

"Right, because that's not creepy." My head falls back and I groan.

"Okay, so you can't send her flowers. What else can you do? Let us help," Rhodes says.

"No, the last thing I need is your help. What would you

do, go in there and force her to go out with me?" I say, shaking my head.

"Yes," Rhodes laughs. "Come on, we can be persuasive when we need to be."

"I don't need your help. I need to just let it go. It just sucked because it was..." I trail off and they all wait expectantly. "Forget it. Not worth talking about. It's just been a crazy morning."

"No, you don't need to let this go so easily," Weston says. "Come on, let's figure this out. What else do you know about her? What's her name?"

"Her name is Tru. And I hardly know anything...except, like I said, cinnamon rolls. And she's hot. And she had an upbeat, sexy personality too until I ruined it."

"All right," Rhodes says. "That's plenty to go on. Cinnamon rolls, hmm, well...what's her last name? That doesn't seem hard to find out. We can call the school. I can pretend to be a parent..."

"Oh, no, you don't." I shake my head. "I don't want you getting involved. Her last name is Seymour...and let's talk about something else."

"There's nothing to talk about that's as exciting as this," Penn says.

"How's Sam doing?" I ask.

Sam is a kid that Penn has taken under his wing for a while now. He's in the foster care system and Penn started out tutoring him through one of our charity programs, but they've gotten close over the past year.

"Sam's good," Penn says. "But he's moved into another house again. I'm supposed to see him tonight and hopefully I'll find out more about the new place." He pauses for a second. "So Tru...I like that name, by the way."

"Yeah, me too," I say.

Clara walks in with my drink, and I'm happy for the interruption. I shouldn't have brought up Tru with the guys—they're not going to let this go easily.

"Thanks, Clara. This is exactly what I needed."

"Hey, Clara. We need a woman's perspective," Rhodes says.

"Here we go," I mutter.

"Our old man here met a woman he liked and then he went and wrecked it. What should he do to apologize?" he asks.

"When you're thirty-six, I'll remember to remind you how old you are." I point at him and he just laughs it off.

"You'll still be older, my man," he says.

"You met a woman you like, Henley?" Clara asks, her full cheeks lifting as she beams at me. "You're so sweet, you could never mess it up."

The guys all scoff at that, including me.

"It's true," Clara says, laughing. "But...if you think you messed it up, you could apologize and give her a pretty bouquet of flowers or...a gift card to Luminary." She winks when we all laugh.

"I told you flowers weren't stupid," Penn says. "And I like the gift card idea. Nice touch, Clara."

She lifts an eyebrow. "But really, all you need to do is show her your charm."

Weston points at me, validated.

Clara pats my shoulder and then sighs. "Don't let these amazing shoulders go to waste. Look how happy Weston is with Sadie. We all want that for you."

The guys chime in with their agreement and I chuckle. "Thanks, Clara. I'm happy though."

"Mm-hmm," she says, her disbelief evident.

The conversation moves to other things but keeps going back to Tru. I drink my Solar Latte and play with Caleb, trying to distract myself from thinking of that woman with the pretty green eyes and those full lips. The way she turned from warm and inviting to ice-cold sassiness. Finally, I give up and give Caleb a squeeze.

"I better get going, you guys," I say. "Bree is still out of town, so the girls are staying with me again tonight and I need to make sure we've got everything for dinner before they get home from school."

"You're going back to the grocery store?" Rhodes winks.

"Nah, I think I've done enough damage there today."

"You know what, Henley? I bet it's not as bad as you think," Weston says. "Just turn on that charm the next time you see her and she'll be eating out of the palm of your hand. I've seen it happen way too many times to doubt it."

"I know that's right," Rhodes says. "You're not even trying most of the time, Henley, and women are falling all over themselves to get to you."

I snort. "Yeah, right, when you and Penn are around you hardly leave anything for the rest of us. Not that Bowie or I are interested in all that." I share a look at Bowie, but he's shaking his head.

"I think you will be before you know it," Bowie says, grinning at me knowingly, "and I think her name is Tru."

I laugh and shake my head. "I've made a way bigger deal of this than I needed to. It was no big deal, just sucked that it happened and I feel bad that I was such a jerk."

"I think you'll run into her again," Weston says. "In a town as small as Silver Hills, you'll be seeing her again."

"And if we see her first," Penn adds, "we'll set her straight."

"Don't bother," I groan.

I stand up and give each of them a bro-shake before I leave the room and walk out the door. I never even checked to see the updates in The Single Dad Playbook. It's best I didn't write in there today anyway. So far, today has been a fail.

CHAPTER FOUR

ALL IN A DAY'S WORK

TRU

After I leave the school, with another day lined up in Mrs. Carboni's place again tomorrow, I drive down Jupiter Lane and decide to explore a little bit. It's a beautiful day and I have some energy to kill. A car pulls out, and I take the parking spot in front of a few cute shops and businesses. I peek into the window of Wiggles & Whimsy, delighted when I see the small class of young dancers twirling in their tutus and ballet slippers. There's a small sign on the door, white with polka dots, saying *Help Wanted* in pink block letters. It's the cutest *Help Wanted* sign I've ever seen...also the cutest tiny dance studio. I wait until the class has filed out before I walk inside.

"Hello?" I call out.

A beautiful older woman with slicked-back white hair turns and smiles at me.

"Hello," she says. "You're a new face around here."

"I am! I'm Tru Seymour, and I just moved to town...still trying to find my way around."

Her smile widens. "Well, it's lovely to meet you, Tru Seymour. I'm Jacklyn Toussant, and I'm so happy you stopped in here." She winks and nods knowingly. "You move like a dancer."

I gradually move into fifth position and she claps her hands.

"Lovely form."

"Thank you." I do a curtsy and she laughs, clapping harder. "I saw your sign. What kind of help do you need?"

"Oh, I was hoping that's why you came in! I need someone a few afternoons a week. Evenings really, I guess. Do you teach dance?"

"I'm hoping to get a more permanent position at Silver Hills Middle School, but right now I'm subbing there. And I taught dance for several years during college."

"Ah, it's meant to be." Her eyes crinkle with her delighted smile. "How soon can you start?"

I open the calendar on my phone and we compare schedules for the next week, coming up with a plan for times I can come in. She shows me around the studio and says I can sit in on the next class if I'd like. But I tell her I'll come back the next afternoon to see if I can be more involved in class by the Saturday morning sessions. By the time I leave, she's excited and so am I. Her energy is so positive, it's infectious and makes the challenges of the day fade away.

When I leave the studio and walk down the street a little farther, the happiness that I'm here builds. Silver Hills is such a cute town and the people so far—except for Mrs. Davenport and Mr. Henley Ward—have all been pleasant. Maybe I just caught Mrs. Davenport at a bad time. And I probably shouldn't give Henley too hard of a time since he was defending his daughter, but the fact that he can go from hot to cold so quickly is concerning. I don't need any more people like that in my life.

In the past, I've allowed too many red flags to get past me and I'm done with that. I'm here for a new beginning, not to repeat the same old mistakes.

When I get home and walk from the carport to the side door of the little house I'm renting, I see a kitten hanging out. White and grey and *tiny*.

"Oh my goodness, you're the cutest thing. What are you doing here?" I look around to see if the mother is nearby, but there's not another cat in sight. I walk around the backyard and look in every nook, shining my flashlight under the small deck coming off of the kitchen. Nothing.

"Where did you come from?" I ask.

I reach out to pet her and she comes over and rubs against my hand and then goes around my feet, leaning her tiny body against me.

"Well, I can't resist this. Do you have a collar?" She doesn't. "You're so little. You don't even look old enough to be away from your mama yet."

I pick her up and get back in the car, taking her to Pet Galaxy, a pet store that I've passed every day since I moved here. I didn't realize it, but there's a vet attached to the back of the store. The front is distracting with all the dog and cat toys, pet food, and birds and fish in one corner.

An older man with shaggy white hair stands behind the counter. "What have you got there? What a cutie."

"Isn't she? She showed up at my door this afternoon. Do you think she belongs to anyone?"

"I've heard about a few litters, but I haven't seen a mom like that around here. She could have been born from one of the strays."

"I wondered about that. Is there any way to find out if she has an owner besides putting signs up?"

"We can see if she has a chip, but she looks like she might be too young for that. But head on back. Dr. Amber will take a look."

"I'll do that. Thank you."

I walk back and besides a big Dalmatian sitting next to a teenage girl, no one else is waiting. There's a receptionist sitting on a stool behind a counter that's only big enough to hold a laptop and phone. She grins when she sees the kitten.

"Aww, what a cute kitten. How old is she?" she asks.

"I have no idea. She was outside my house today and I brought her in hoping to find out if she belongs to anyone."

"Okay, let's get your name."

I fill out the forms and then sit down, the kitten nestling into my arms and falling asleep.

The Dalmatian and its owner go back and I wait about three minutes before I'm ushered to an examination room in the back.

Dr. Amber walks in a few minutes later and is unlike any vet I've ever seen. She looks like Cher getting ready to do a concert, with the examination table as an odd prop. She lights up when she sees my kitten.

"Hello, I'm Dr. Amber."

"I'm Tru. Nice to meet you."

"You too. There's just nothing like a kitten, is there?" she says.

"No. It was instalove," I say, nuzzling the kitten to my face. "I've never had a cat and I've also never seen one this small."

She reaches out and I hand the little bundle over to her. The kitten lets out a plaintive meow.

"It's okay, little princess," I say.

"Tell me about this little thing," Dr. Amber says.

"I found her by my back door and looked all over for the mom or other kittens, but didn't see any others."

"What a shame. It happens sometimes. Most likely she was abandoned by a stray mom or was left by an owner, but if that were the case, there would probably be more. She's tiny. She looks about six weeks…maybe seven."

Dr. Amber turns her around and lays her gently on the table, examining her paws and her ears and everything about her, as the kitten mews pitifully. Dr. Amber whispers consoling things as she continues checking her out.

"Ah." Dr. Amber laughs. "Our little princess is a little prince."

"Really? I looked but didn't…I couldn't tell." I laugh.

"Sometimes it's hard to be sure with cats."

She checks him out and then looks up at me with a smile. "Okay, here's what I'd like to try. Since we're not sure how long he's been away from his mother, you can see how he does with food. I have some I'll recommend, but you can also supplement with formula for the next couple of days if he doesn't take to the food right away. Then, if you can bring him back to see me, we'll make sure he's growing at a healthy rate. He looks pretty healthy, all in all, but I'd like to keep an eye on this little guy. Are you up for that?" she asks.

"I am. I'm close enough to work that I can go back and forth to check on him when I need to."

"Great. I'll write down the best food and then—you've never had a cat, right?"

I shake my head.

"You'll need a litter box and kitty litter. Fred will help you find everything and Jenny will make an appointment for you to come back in a couple of weeks."

"Okay, thanks for all your help."

I go back out into the little area where Jenny is stationed and make an appointment, and then I go find Fred.

"Are you all set?" he asks.

"I just need to find a litter box, kitty litter, food, and a little bit of formula." I hand him the slip that Dr. Amber gave me. "If there's anything else you think I need…maybe a cute bed?"

"It's up to you. Kittens can sleep anywhere and they make a game of just about anything." He laughs. He reaches out to pet the kitten. "Have you got a name picked out yet?"

"No, not yet. I thought it was a girl, but it's a boy, so I'm back to the drawing board."

"You're not the first one that's happened to," he says.

I see a cute fuzzy bed and pick it up and a couple of cat toys that make me smile. One is a hamburger with a pickle hanging on a string.

"I better get out of here; otherwise I'm gonna buy every cute thing in this store. Next thing we know, he'll be wearing a fur coat and boots."

"I don't think he'd put up with that," he says, chuckling. "All right, let's get you out of here."

The kitten has slept peacefully the whole time. I have no idea what to expect with a cat, but here we go. We head home and I give the little guy a bit of formula. He guzzles it down and then eats a few bites of food. When I crawl into bed that night, I put him into his bed next to mine, but he starts meowing...loudly. Eventually, I bring him into bed with me, and he cuddles right up, falling sound asleep.

By the time I start drifting off, I think about how long ago it feels since I ran into Henley at the grocery store this morning. That feels like another lifetime ago.

I'm frustrated to be thinking about him and his too-handsome face, but it's not the first time he's crossed my mind today. In a small town like this, and having his daughter in my class, it won't be the last time either.

CHAPTER FIVE

NOWHERE TO HIDE

HENLEY

The next few days go by in a flash. Bree won't be back in town until Sunday, so the girls are with me for the rest of the week. Bree lives just around the corner from me, so I see the girls every day, but one of our agreements when we divorced was that we'd have them consistently in one home so they could stay on a routine. Not that it's bad when parents have to do something different, but for our girls, they've always thrived on consistency. We never wanted them to have to go back and forth from one house to the other all the time, so they've stayed in the home they've lived in most of their lives, and I just make sure I'm still with them as much as possible. It's what works for us. I pick them up from school and have dinner with them most nights, at least during the offseason, and I take them to their after-school activities and games. Cassidy and Audrey are in dance and Gracie is in softball.

Saturdays are usually packed. We've already been to softball practice this morning, and now we're on our way to dance class for the girls' lessons.

"The new sub, Miss Seymour, is so great," Cassidy says.

I turn to her in surprise.

"Really? What do you like about her?" I try to sound interested, but not *too* interested. I'm dying to know everything she has to tell me about Miss Seymour. I wonder if she said anything to Cassidy about our interaction.

"She met me after class yesterday and gave me a chance to read my report to her one-on-one, which was awesome."

"Why didn't you read it in class like everyone else?" I ask.

"I was too nervous."

"Nervous? You? Since when?"

"I hate reading in front of people. You know that," she says.

It's true Cassidy has never loved reading like her mom or Audrey. Now that I think about it, even Gracie likes reading more than Cassidy.

"You're a fine reader. You shouldn't be shy to read in front of your friends. What did Miss Seymour say? Did that finish everything up with your project? Are you good now? Will Mrs. Carboni be happy when she comes back?"

"What's with all the questions, Dad?" She laughs. "Oh,

wait. I haven't told you…" She turns to me, excitement radiating off of her. "Guess what?" she says, her eyes bright. "I don't think Mrs. Carboni is coming back!"

"What happened with Mrs. Carboni?

"I heard that I wasn't the only one she said horrible things to and that she got *fired*."

"No way. She hasn't even been there that long."

"I know. I'm hoping they'll keep Miss Seymour. Mrs. Carboni was *so* boring. The class goes by so fast with Miss Seymour! And I love the way she dresses. She always looks so cool, and she's super nice and pretty."

Damn right, she is, I think to myself.

We park in front of Wiggles & Whimsy and everyone piles out. When we walk into the studio, a class is just ending. I get the girls checked in the way I always do, but I'm caught off guard when I hear a melodic voice saying, "Okay, girls, that's it for today."

I turn and see Tru Seymour in a fucking leotard.

God help me.

She looked exquisite in her suit and heels, but in a leotard and a see-through skirt, she's fucking sinful. She's completely covered, but the effect it has on me, she may as well be naked. She's not wearing glasses today, so her eyes stand out even more. The moment she spots me, her eyes turn cold. She pauses for a second then resumes, telling the girls to have a good week. They thank her for the class and Chelsea Appleton goes up and hugs her leg.

"It was fun," she says in her high, squeaky voice.

Tru smiles down at her and Jacklyn comes over and says hello to me. Jacklyn Toussant is a stunning older woman whom every man over fifty in Silver Hills crushes on, and not just the older men. Penn once said he'd had a sex dream about her and couldn't look her in the eyes when he ran into her at the grocery store.

"Hello, Mr. Ward," Jacklyn says, her husky voice warm as she smiles at me. "I don't suppose I can talk you into joining our class today, can I? We have a lovely new teacher here, Miss Seymour. She could keep you in shape during the offseason."

"I'm sure she could." I laugh. "I think I'll leave it to the girls for now."

"Suit yourself," Jacklyn says.

Tru comes over to the counter and doesn't return my smile.

"Hello, Miss Seymour."

"Mr. Ward," she volleys back.

"You're everywhere I turn. I didn't know you were the new dance teacher as well."

There's a painful silence as she studies me.

"Miss Toussant generously offered me a job here," she says coolly. "So I guess there's yet another place you'll be running into me."

"Looks like it," I say, smiling again.

Disappointment floods through me when she nods and walks away.

"The two of you know each other," Jacklyn says, looking between the two of us with interest.

"We met briefly at Cassidy's school," I tell her. "Didn't get off to the best start," I mutter under my breath.

"We're really lucky to have her," she says.

"Cassidy will be happy to see her. She loves having her as an English teacher."

"Excellent," Jacklyn says, clapping her hands twice.

"I'll head out for a little bit and be back shortly." I look back, but Tru is already busy with the girls.

I'm at a loss about what to do when I leave the studio…
and then I see Serendipity Cafe and stop in my tracks.
Serendipity has not only some of the best sandwiches I've
ever tasted, but their pastries are out of this world. I nearly
talk myself out of it multiple times but finally go in. I get
coffee and sit at the table near the window as I check my
email and text the guys about random stuff, making sure not
to breathe Tru's name. Right before class is over, I go to the
counter and smile at Wyndham, the owner of the cafe.

"Do you need another coffee?" she asks.

"No, thank you. What I need are those." I point to the
batch of cinnamon rolls Greer is pulling out of the oven. "I'll
take two boxes."

"Perfect." Wyndham smiles. "Greer, did you hear that?"
she calls.

Greer sets the rolls down and turns toward me. "Hey,
Henley. How are you? Long time, no see."

Greer's hair is purple and Wyndham's hair is pink. The
two look like they stepped out of a magical forest together.

"I know. Unfortunately I can't come in here too often. I
wouldn't be able to do my job if I did."

Greer winks at me as she starts putting cinnamon rolls in
the box and fills it up before grabbing another and doing the
same.

"We know." Wyndam sighs. "We'll sacrifice seeing you
often if you just keep winning those games."

"What she said," Greer adds.

"How are the wedding plans coming?" I ask.

"Slowly but surely, it's coming together. You know us, we
want to make everything so special, so it's taking forever,"
Wyndham says. "Last weekend, we made a firepit out of the
river rock from our backyard."

I shake my head. "It's going to be fabulous, you guys. Whatever you do will be."

"That's what Bree says too." Wyndham shrugs. "But I think she's secretly tired of all the projects."

"She didn't know what she was signing up for when she agreed to be our wedding planner." Greer laughs.

"She can handle it." I laugh too. "Let me know if you need help with anything. I have time right now, you know."

Wyndham nods mischievously. "I'll put you to work."

"I'm getting out of here," I tease.

When I walk out, I stick a box of cinnamon rolls in my truck and take the other box inside. I nearly back out but pause when Tru walks to the counter. Jacklyn is on the other side of the room, and the girls are putting their things in their bags.

I hold the box out to Tru without saying anything. She looks up at me reluctantly.

"What's this?" she asks.

"Take a look," I tell her.

She opens it and gasps softly when she sees the cinnamon rolls.

"They look spectacular," she whispers.

"Wait until you taste them," I say.

"They're for me?" Her mouth parts in surprise.

I nod. "Think of it as one more apology for how I acted the other day."

Her cheeks flush and she looks down at the cinnamon rolls again.

"Thank you," she says. She turns and puts them in a little cubby where I see her purse and sweater. "I'll be getting into those the first chance I get," she says, and there's not a smile on her face, but there *is* a softening in her expression toward me.

I'll take it.

CHAPTER SIX

BREAKFAST FOR DINNER = BRINNER

TRU

Well, this form of an apology is one I will never turn down.

After I'm home from dance class, I open the box of cinnamon rolls from Henley and inhale the sugary goodness. When I sink my mouth around the buttery, cinnamon deliciousness, I close my eyes and can't even believe how good it tastes. No one has ever given me cinnamon rolls before and I appreciate that he remembered me buying them the day we met.

It's too soon to let my guard down, but I sure don't mind the way he's going about trying to make things right.

Jacklyn raved about Henley after he left, and she also mentioned that he's divorced. I couldn't tell if she was saying it for my benefit or if she's crushing on him herself, honestly, but knowing he's single makes me feel a lot better about the flirtation between us that first time we met. I'm not interested in him now...but is he raising three daughters alone? What's the story there?

When I get out of the shower later, I have another cinnamon roll for dinner. The things are massive, so it will be all I'm eating tonight, but I savor every bite. I watch a movie and wonder if I should do more to show my appreciation, but I did thank him already, so I don't know that I have to make any more of an effort.

It wouldn't be that hard to find him around here.

Nope. I'm not going out of my way. If I'm supposed to see him, I will. I've already run into him three times without trying, and God knows I need to keep my distance from a man like him. His dreaminess could find a way to soften my heart a little too easily.

Sunday afternoon, I get a call from Mr. Hanson, the principal at school, asking if I can come in early Monday morning, and if I'm free to work there all week. I'm hopeful that they're going to ask me to stay, but I try not to get too far ahead of myself.

When I walk into the front office on Monday morning, Mr. Hanson is chatting with Mrs. Davenport and he smiles and says hello. He's an attractive man of an indeterminate age, possibly because every time I've seen him, he's wearing a cardigan.

I make an effort to not be a Petty Patty and smile too

smugly at Mrs. Davenport over the fact that I was called back in to work here.

But it's hard.

"Right on time," Mr. Hanson says. "Come on back."

He ushers me into his office and holds his hand out for me to have a seat.

"I've heard great things about you from the kids," he says. "It sounds like you were a hit with the English students."

"Well, that's great to hear. Thank you."

"Thank *you*. I'll cut to the chase. I would like you to consider taking this job on a more permanent basis. Would you be interested in that?"

There's no hiding the huge smile that takes over my face. "Yes, I was hoping for a full-time job, and I'm loving teaching English here so far."

"Excellent."

He goes over a few details about the job and the school, and he mentions my salary. It's nothing spectacular, but I'm so happy to have a full-time job in Silver Hills. This, combined with the extra money from the dance studio, and I should be able to get by.

We discuss how I will get up to speed on everything since Mrs. Carboni will not be coming back. I'll have my hands full getting caught up, but I could not be happier about this job. Before we're done, I mention my work with Dr. Mathison in college and my thoughts on Cassidy, just to be sure I'm not stepping on any toes if I pursue a few tests with her.

"This is desperately needed here," he says. "We're short-staffed, and if you're willing to put in the extra time, I welcome it. I'd appreciate if you keep me in the loop."

I nod, my excitement building. "I will."

Once I've signed more paperwork, it's official.

"We'll make an announcement over the next week that you're our new English teacher, but the job is yours now. Welcome aboard." Mr. Hanson stretches out his hand and I shake it.

I get to the classroom, *my* classroom, and look around the room with new eyes. Sometime over the weekend, Mrs. Carboni must have come to collect her personal belongings because there are things missing from the walls and desk. I make note of what we might need and what could make the room cuter, and the list grows throughout the day.

Between classes, I look at the students' projects again and grade a few that were still left hanging. When I get to Cassidy Ward's paper and remember her project still hasn't been graded, I think about the interaction with Cassidy and then Henley.

Something still doesn't sit well with me about the whole thing.

There's a section from the book *Wonder* that I love and the kids read it aloud before we discuss it. During Cassidy's class, I ask her to start the passage. After she read for me one-on-one, I'm hoping she'll be more comfortable reading in front of the class, but instead, she freezes and stares at me in horror. Her cheeks get two bright red splotches on either side and her eyes fill with tears. Brandon, who is often talking during class to Luke, the guy next to him, says something that I don't hear, and Cassidy's cheeks bloom even redder.

"It's okay, Cassidy, take your time."

She starts reading and stutters through the first sentence, stopping when she hears laughter behind her. I look around at the classroom and frown.

"Don't be rude, please. Everyone listen carefully. We'll be discussing this section afterward, and when it's your turn, you wouldn't appreciate it if someone was laughing and being a distraction in the background. We treat each other with respect, got it? Go ahead, Cassidy."

She gets through the next few lines, but it's painful to hear and I regret ever asking her to read. I interrupt when she pauses before starting the next paragraph and say, "Elise, can you continue where Cassidy left off?"

I make sure to only have everyone else read one paragraph as well, so it doesn't seem like I stopped Cassidy due to her poor reading. But it bothers me long after we've moved on, and before the bell rings, I ask Cassidy to come see me before class is over. She walks up to my desk reluctantly and I try to give her a reassuring smile.

"Do you have a few minutes to talk after class?" I ask.

"Um, sure," she says.

Once everyone has left the class and it's just Cassidy and me, I try to put her at ease.

"I just wanted to ask a couple questions, if that's okay."

She nods and stands there waiting.

"I was looking over your project again, and I wanted to let you know that you did an excellent job...which your grade will reflect." I smile and she returns it with a wobbly one. "You seem really uncomfortable with reading in the class. Can I ask why?"

"I'm just not a very good reader." She looks down at my desk. "It makes me nervous to read in front of everyone."

"I can understand that. Is that all it is?" I ask and her mouth parts, but she doesn't say anything for a second, and her cheeks burn brighter.

I wait, but when she still doesn't say anything, I lean forward. "I didn't hear what Brandon said, but I want you to know, I'll be speaking with him also. I just wanted to make sure you were okay first."

"Oh. Thank you," she finally says. "I'm okay."

"When you read for me the other day, it came easier, but it still seemed like you were hesitant at times."

She looks down again and her voice comes out softer when she speaks. "I feel like it's so easy for everyone else. For me, it's just...hard."

"How so?"

She makes a face. "I don't know. Even my six-year-old sister reads better than I do."

"Do you read often at home?"

"No. I've never liked to read, so I hardly ever do." She crinkles her nose. "Sorry. I can tell that you love it and I wish I did." Her shoulder lifts with a slight shrug.

I grin at her. "I do love to read, but that doesn't mean you have to. I'm curious though—when you say it's *hard*, can you tell me why that is?"

"It's...I don't know how to explain it. When I have to read, it's like I can't focus on the words and they, um, I don't know...they sort of jump around..." She fidgets with her notebook and looks toward the door. "That probably sounds crazy. I've never said that out loud." She laughs softly, but her eyes meet mine and I can see the vulnerability there.

"That doesn't sound crazy at all, Cassidy. Thank you for sharing that with me. I'd like to see what we can do to make reading more fun for you. How does that sound?"

"I'd like that." She nods.

"I'll reach out to your parents to talk about a few things... a few ideas I have about reading, and then we'll go from there. Sound good?"

"Yes." She nods again and smiles shyly.

I tap my desk and stand up. "Okay, I'll let you get to lunch. I heard there's spaghetti today. Should I pass or go for it?"

"Go for it. It's better than the chicken nuggets." Her nose turns up and she shakes her head. "Make sure to avoid those."

I laugh. "Thanks for the tip. I usually bring my lunch, but I didn't have time today. Sounds like I picked the right day for it."

She walks to the door and lifts her hand in a small wave before she leaves.

I let out a long exhale when I'm alone. The last thing I want to do is reach out to Henley Ward and his ex-wife, but my concern for Cassidy overrides everything else. I get their numbers from Mrs. Davenport and leave messages on both of their voicemails, asking if they could meet today after school or any other afternoon this week. During my next break, I listen to their messages confirming that they can meet today.

As a substitute teacher, I had very little parent interaction, so I'm apprehensive about what their reaction will be when I tell them I want Cassidy assessed for dyslexia. Since I'm new here, I wouldn't blame them for not wanting to hear what I have to say, but the hope in Cassidy's eyes at the offer of help is motivation enough.

CHAPTER SEVEN

LABELS

HENLEY

I stare at the phone for a few seconds after leaving Tru a voice message. She mentioned talking about Cassidy, so my interest is piqued.

"Everything okay?" Bowie asks.

We're just getting started at the gym and I'd hoped to steer the conversation away from Tru, but I don't know how long that'll last. Fuck it, I need their perspective whether I want it or not.

"Bree and I are meeting Tru this afternoon after school. I don't know what it's about..." I glance around to see all four of the guys staring at me, waiting for me to say more.

"Is Cassidy okay at school?" Bowie, God bless him—he's always trying to help us stay focused on what's important.

"I hope so. I guess we'll find out." I spot Rhodes while he lifts and once he's done with his repetitions, he sits up.

"I wish you'd sent the flowers," he says, grinning up at me.

I look everywhere but him when I say, "I gave her cinnamon rolls from Serendipity...oh, and she might be Cassidy's teacher permanently."

"What?" Rhodes sputters, standing up. "Why didn't you start with that? The cinnamon rolls..." he clarifies.

"It was no big deal." I shrug. "She was one of the dance teachers in the girls' class on Saturday and it's right by Serendipity."

"What? You did this on Saturday and we're just now hearing about it?" Penn asks. "And she's the girls' dance teacher now? Bro, you've gotta get these things off your chest."

"I really don't." I laugh.

"You could almost call this serendipitous," Rhodes teases, pulling out a British accent. He does it well—he's always lived in the States, but his dad is from London, England, and his mom is from Cape Town, South Africa, so he can go between their accents like it's nothing.

"Did it work? The cinnamon rolls?" Weston asks, grinning. "Did she soften at all?"

"Minimally." I lift a shoulder and sit on the bench, waiting until Rhodes gets in place to lie back and lift.

"Define minimally," Rhodes says, looking over me.

"Can't. I'm busy."

They all groan and it gives me too much joy to irritate them.

"Well, what are you taking her today?" Penn asks.

I pause before lifting to ask, "Do I have to take her something every time I see her?"

"It doesn't hurt to grovel a little bit." Weston flings a towel over his shoulder and smirks.

"Nah. I'm not taking anything today. Bree will be there and—"

"Bree's moved on. You should too," Rhodes says.

"I have moved on. It's not about that at all. It would be weird if I'm taking Cassidy's teacher gifts…"

When I glance up, they're all looking at me with varying levels of concern.

"What?" I frown.

"You *are* over Bree, right?" Bowie asks.

"I'm absolutely over her," I say. "That doesn't mean I'm not hesitant about relationships, but Bree and I—we're better as friends. I like where we are now."

"Well, don't let her sabotage your chances with Tru, even if it's unintentional," Rhodes says.

"She wouldn't do that. She's dating and happy, and even if she wasn't, she wouldn't want to mess things up for me."

Bree might have thrown my world upside down when she said she wanted a divorce, but I'd known she didn't love the football life. We dated when we were in high school and college, and neither one of us had any idea my career would explode the way it did after I signed professionally. She's a perfectionist who's always had her life planned out, and she admitted later that she'd thought my love for football wouldn't go very far. Me becoming famous and being gone a lot didn't fit into her plans at all.

The more excited I was with the way my career was

going, the more miserable and drained Bree became. We were both tempted to stay together because of the girls, but Bree said she wanted to give the girls her best self and she couldn't do that when she just wasn't happy.

She was completely right, of course. It wouldn't have been healthy to raise the girls in our dysfunction.

Now that I've had a few years to process our divorce, the root of what we couldn't overcome was that we'd been growing apart for years and felt more like roommates who were never on the same page.

Understanding her reasons doesn't mean I haven't felt like a failure though. My parents have been married for forty years and are still going strong. I'd planned on following in their footsteps, whether Bree and I had that spark or not.

"I guess I assume the worst of exes since Carrie is ready to stomp me with her five-inch heels at all times." Rhodes makes a face as he wipes his face with a towel. "I know Bree's not like my ex-girlfriend, but Carrie has put me on high alert."

Coach Evans walks in and pauses when he sees us. "I think you're the only players who aren't on vacation right now. Can't get enough of this place, huh?"

"Could say the same for you too, Coach," I tease. "You know that's why we're your best players, right?"

"Damn straight, I know it. It's the example the four of you set," he says, nodding at Bowie, Weston, Rhodes, and me. "Because *this* guy would likely be on a nude beach chasing tail and drinking endless tequila right about now if it weren't for you guys." He points at Penn, who looks stung initially but then laughs like he's in on the joke.

I'm not sure why Evans is so hard on Penn, but he has been from day one. Penn likes to have fun outside of work, but whether it's the offseason or not, he's as disciplined as the rest of us.

"Penn's the one who got us here today," Rhodes says.

"It's true. He can outlift all of us and knows he's gotta keep us old guys on track," Bowie says.

"Who you callin' old?" Weston says.

Bowie shrugs and grins.

"Well, make sure you fit in some downtime in there somewhere. I want you ready to win another Super Bowl when the time comes," Coach Evans says. He slaps my shoulder and squeezes before walking away.

"I can't win with that guy, man," Penn says. "You'd think by now he'd let up a little bit. He makes it sound like I'm a pervy alcoholic."

"Agreed, it's gone on longer than normal. But I don't think he means too much by it," Bowie says. "I think it's mostly habit by now for him to give you a hard time."

"If you say so," Penn mutters.

The rest of the workout, I zone out and try not to think about anything but my movements, but it's hard to get this meeting out of my mind. Once I'm done, I shower and put on jeans and a nicer shirt than I'd normally wear to a teacher conference.

"Looking good." Rhodes nods, as I walk past him. "Let us know how it goes."

There are a few kids still hanging out when I pull into the parking lot, but it's mostly empty. Bree wanted to pick up the girls today since she's been gone for the past few days, and there's a text from her saying she's dropped them off at home and will be here in a few minutes.

I try not to think about how empty my house is without the girls there. Bree came and got them last night when she got back in town and the silence was deafening after they left. It was nice having them to myself for a while.

When I walk down the hall, it's quiet. I pause outside the classroom door and knock twice.

"Come in," I hear her call.

I step inside and Tru is seated at her desk. Once again, I'm rattled by how pretty she is…and how her eyes don't waver from mine. Without her glasses, her eyes are a punch in the chest. Her plush lips are the color of red wine and even more distracting than her eyes.

"Mr. Ward," she says, coolly.

"Miss Seymour." I smile. "You can call me Henley. You know, we've already established that."

"It's not necessary," she says. "Mr. Ward works just fine. Have a seat." She motions for me to sit across from her.

I want to ask her if she liked the cinnamon rolls, but I don't.

"Bree should be here any minute." I shift in my seat, taking in the way the sunlight makes her hair so shiny. Her hair is up again and I wonder what it looks like when she takes it down at the end of the day.

"Excellent, we can wait to get started when she arrives." Tru puts a few files aside and I can see one with Cassidy's name on top.

"How have you been?" I ask.

She pauses and looks at me with a close-mouthed smile. Her guard is still up, but she's a nice person, so she's extra polite. I hate it. I want to see the uninhibited woman I met.

"I'm doing well. I'm getting settled."

"I'm assuming you're new to town since I'm only just now

seeing you everywhere I turn." I grin and she looks down at her desk.

"Yes, I'm new to town, and I am loving Silver Hills so far." Her cheeks deepen in color and she clears her throat. "The cinnamon rolls were—"

Bree knocks a few seconds later and comes in looking rushed and breathless. I can tell from her expression that she's stressed. She prefers to be everywhere five minutes early, rather than coming in hot.

"I'm so sorry to be late," she says.

"You're right on time," Tru says, her smile wide. "I'm Tru Seymour."

I feel cheated that I didn't get that smile.

"I'm Bree Ward. Nice to meet you." They shake hands and Bree sits down next to me. "Hey, Hen." She takes a deep breath, but her posture doesn't falter. Ever since she started her wedding planner business, I can practically see her wheels turning.

"Hey." I smile back at her and we turn to face Tru.

"Thanks so much for agreeing to meet with me on such short notice," Tru says. "Word hasn't officially gotten out yet, but I've taken the full-time position here as an English teacher and I'll be working hard to catch up since I'm coming on late in the school year."

"That's great. Congratulations," I say.

She's caught off guard by my comment and nods slightly. "Thank you. I'm excited to be here." Her lips lift in the corners and she looks down at her folder. "I want to start by saying I'm enjoying having Cassidy in my class. She's kind and she's smart and I look forward to getting to know her better as the year progresses."

Her lips press together and it's difficult to appear like I'm not watching every move she makes and hanging on her every word.

"I hoped I might get some perspective from you both about Cassidy's aversion to reading." She looks up at Bree and then me, and it's quiet for a moment.

"Her aversion to reading…" Bree starts.

"Maybe I should word it a different way. Cassidy hasn't wanted to read aloud in class and when she did, it was challenging for her. Later, when I asked her about it, she said it's hard for her…that she's not a good reader and the kids tease her about it."

I instantly feel sick. "The kids tease her about it? It's true she's never loved to read, but…I wouldn't think of her as a bad reader." I look at Bree, whose expression is concerned.

Tru presses ahead. "Right. I'd rather not term it as her being a bad reader either, but it does concern me that she says it's hard. In college, one of my mentors specialized in dyslexia, and I worked closely with her. Cassidy's project was excellent, but some of the homework she's turned in since then, the spelling isn't as clean, and the way she read in class and talked about it…I just wonder if she might need a little extra help."

I feel like I've been dealt a blow. This news feels much worse than getting hit on the field, knowing my girl has been going through this for so long…not just the struggles with reading, but she's being teased about it? I shift in my seat, remembering all the spelling corrections I suggested while looking over her project.

"Are you saying she's dyslexic?" Bree asks, leaning forward. "But she knows how to read."

"No, not yet, but I'd like to do some tests to be sure. Having dyslexia doesn't mean you can't read. Whether it's the case for her or not, reading appears to be a struggle. It

doesn't come easily for her, and I'd like to help with that."
Tru's voice is patient but firm.

"It just seems like someone would've noticed by now if she was dyslexic. *We* would've noticed," Bree says. She looks at me and her eyes are watery. "We'd be horrible parents if we missed that."

I reach out and pat Bree's hand briefly and she lets out a shaky exhale.

"We've known she wasn't a reader like Audrey...or Gracie." I look at Tru, feeling helpless. "But I assumed she just didn't enjoy it, not that she struggled with it." I lean forward and my head drops. "God, how could we have missed this? We've talked about how long it takes her to finish doing her homework..." I look over at Bree and she looks devastated. "It's been more of an issue in middle school. It never occurred to me that it could be this."

"No one has ever brought this up with us before," Bree says. "It doesn't make sense."

"Please don't take this as a reflection of your parenting," Tru says. "Kids can learn to mask these things and it does get missed more often than you'd think, especially because she *can* read. If she is dyslexic, she's just having to work so much harder all the time and that can be really taxing."

"What would we do to be sure?" I ask.

"I can do a few tests with her, and once we know for sure, I could work with her one-on-one, or we could see what other options are out there if you'd rather pursue that," she says.

"I just—" Bree looks at me helplessly, and when she doesn't keep going, I look at Tru.

"I'm really grateful you've brought this to our attention. As you can see, we're thrown by this news. It makes me want to reexamine everything." I rub the scruff on my jaw. "I'd like to get started on this as soon as we can."

"She's so busy as it is," Bree says, shaking her head. "Does she have time for one more thing? Can't we do something at home that will help her?"

"I think this is something we have to make time for," I tell Bree. "And apparently we've missed the signs. We need help." I give her a pointed look and she sags against the chair, nodding.

Bree loves our girls with her whole heart, but she hates to admit she needs help. With anything.

"If you're willing, I'll meet with Cassidy tomorrow and start trying to get to the bottom of this." Tru pushes back from the desk.

"That sounds good. What do you need from us?" I ask.

"You could mention to her tonight that we spoke. I told her I'd like to help make reading more fun for her. Whatever you're comfortable with is fine with me," she says. "We don't need to put a label on anything yet. We just want to make this a more enjoyable process for her. Let's see what the tests show and we can go from there."

She pauses and I nod, tapping the desk.

"I really appreciate your time," I tell her.

"It's my pleasure. Thank you both for fitting me into your busy schedules." She stands and we follow suit, saying our goodbyes and walking out in a daze.

I'd wanted to see Tru again, but this isn't anything close to how I'd hoped our next time would be.

CHAPTER EIGHT

UNICORNS AND CELEBRITIES

TRU

My meeting with the Wards went better than I anticipated. I could tell they were shaken by the conversation. I was surprised that Henley was the one who went to bat for Cassidy. Bree seemed apprehensive about the whole thing, but that's understandable. I couldn't tell if she didn't believe me or just didn't like what she was hearing. It clearly threw them, realizing their daughter was having this much trouble reading.

Bree Ward is gorgeous. She's tall, with long blonde hair, sun-kissed cheeks, and hazel eyes. She looks like the girl next door, only a little more glammed up. I can't help but wonder why the two of them aren't together anymore, but it seems like they're on good terms.

I clear out of the classroom and head home, excited to see the kitten. I checked on him earlier in the day, and he was sleeping, but it was still hard to leave him behind. He's so sweet and cuddly. When I walk in now, he's still sleeping, but I pet him and he opens his eyes and moves toward me.

"Hi, little guy. How did your day go? We've got to come up with a name for you. I still can't believe you're a little prince. What shall we call you?" Only funny names come to mind like Ralph or Steve. "Hmm. Maybe Earl." I giggle at the thought. "Earl of Silver Hills. I like it. Funny, but also a big name to live up to. I think you can handle it."

He stretches and curls into my lap. I carry him into the kitchen and get some formula ready. He drinks it, and then I put him in the litter box, and he takes care of business. I smile like a proud mother, and then snap a picture of him and send it to my mom.

> Your new grandkitten.

She texts back within seconds.

MOM

> You're kidding. Oh my goodness, that is the cutest kitten. He's tiny!

> How did you know he was a he right away? I assumed she because—LOOK HOW ADORABLE HE IS.

MOM

Boys can be adorable too.

If you say so. In this case, it applies.

MOM

I'm sorry. Are you twelve or twenty-four? I feel like I'm being transported back in time.

LOL I guess I'm channeling middle school. Ooo, I have news for you! But first…his name is Earl. What do you think?

MOM

Well, I was thinking you'd pick something a little cuter for that sweet face, but…if you say so. <Crying laughing emoji>

The Earls of the world would be so offended by this conversation.

MOM

Well, they can hardly be offended if you're bequeathing such a cutie with that name. What other news besides a kitten? That's a big deal. You've never owned a pet…well, except for that mouse you tried to bring into the house when we lived in Minnesota.

It was cold. <Sad emoji> But yes, you're right. It's a big deal. He showed up at my house and it felt like a sign that I'm in the right place. And then, even better…I got a full-time job at Silver Hills Middle School as an eighth-grade teacher.

MOM

Trudi Eloise Seymour! I knew you'd get a job there! This is so exciting! I'd call you right now, but Dad has the morning off and is still asleep, but I AM ELATED!

> I can tell by all those exclamation points. <Huge grin emoji>

I set my phone down, sadness creeping in through my excitement because my mom is on the other side of the world, tiptoeing around her life. And I'm here, attempting to create a new one.

I look down at Earl and pet his soft head. "I need more friends. Not that you don't count. You will be the best friend I've ever had, I can already tell. But I need some human ones too."

Moving a lot has taught me to make friends quickly, but I haven't learned to hold on to many. I have a couple of friends that I keep in touch with occasionally. It just sucks that we all live far apart. I met Maria in Guatemala. She's three years older than me and took me under her wing when I lived there. We started out writing letters when I moved and then switched to email, and we've kept that up. And Krystal, my roommate during freshmen year, is in New York, so we've seen each other a couple of times since then, but not much.

Even in college, I changed schools several times, moving when my parents did. I didn't want my mom to be stuck with my dad and still held onto the hope that she'd realize she was worth more than the way he treated her, the way he treated us.

My dad never lifted his hand to hurt me. That would have taken too much effort. Instead, he pretended I didn't exist... until some invisible switch would go off, one I invariably wouldn't see coming, and then he flung his words, lazily slinging them like darts to see what would sting the worst.

You look like a cow in that dress.

You'll never get a boyfriend with that face.

Why are you so stupid?

And the list goes on and on.

For years, I tiptoed around him like Mom did, but when I got my driver's license at sixteen and had a taste of freedom, I got louder. I defended Mom when he berated her. I rolled my eyes when he insulted me. Once, I laughed when he said no man would ever want me.

"Fine by me," I said.

It shocked him so much, he was stunned silent.

He didn't mean the things he said was my mom's argument...and it still is. At this point, I don't really care if he means the things he says or not. I had to get away from him before I started believing it.

"Ugh," I tell Earl. "I don't want to go down this dark spiral. How about we go for a little walk? It feels like spring out there. You can ride in my sweatshirt."

Earl blinks up at me and I decide that's answer enough. I grab my zip-up hoodie draped over the chair and put it on. My tennies are by the door and I tuck Earl in my hoodie where he can still see out if he wants.

I end up walking longer than I expected to and end up at Luminary Coffeehouse. Peeking in the window, I see a neon sign that says The Celestial Donut hanging behind the counter and that convinces me to go inside. I love a good cinnamon roll *and* a good donut.

I walk inside, already loving the vibe. I look down to make sure Earl is hidden, and he is. The ceiling is detailed wood painted in black and the walls are white with sunny-yellow touches that cheer everything up. Local artwork is displayed on the walls and it ranges from wildlife and fairies coming out of the forest to monsters that look friendly enough to sit down next to. I love the place already.

A cute older lady is behind the counter—Clara, her name tag says—and she grins when she sees me.

"Welcome to Luminary. What can I get for you?" She makes me feel at ease instantly.

"Well, The Celestial Donut sign caught my eye from the window. I had to find out what that's about. What else is here?"

"Oh, we just added The Celestial Donut to our menu. It's a passion of mine...beyond coffee, which is another great love of my life." She laughs. "There's any kind of coffee imaginable, and if it's not on there, tell me what you want and I'll try to make it." She points to the chalkboard where the drinks are displayed in flourished handwriting and the names are fun with whimsical names that fit the place.

"I'm enchanted," I tell her.

She beams. "Take your time if you need to think about it, but I'm here if you need me. It's slow this evening."

Just then I hear laughter and I turn to see a stunning woman with long dark hair and a gorgeous man next to her. They're laughing at something their little boy has said. I overhear the women sitting at the table behind me gasp.

"Oh my God, he has the best laugh. I can't believe Weston Shaw actually comes here."

I turn and look at the three women. They're staring at the couple I couldn't tear my eyes from, completely starstruck.

"I told you," the woman in the middle says. "That's why we're here. You didn't believe me, but I heard they *all* come here. Well, our favorites anyway. Henley, Rhodes, Bowie... PENN. Oh my God, can you imagine seeing Penn and Henley in real life?"

Of course, my ears perk up when I hear Henley's name. That's not a common name around here, right? It's gotta be my Henley. I mean, the one I've met. He's obviously not mine.

"I'm more of a Bowie and Rhodes' girl myself, but damn, they're all hot," the third woman says.

"Weston and Henley all the way," the first woman says. "You know what? All of them. I don't know what I'd do if I had to choose."

They all laugh. What are they talking about?

When I turn back to Clara, I must look confused because she laughs.

"Are you a Mustangs fan too?" she asks.

"Mustangs?"

Her eyes widen. "Colorado's football team? Winners of the past three Super Bowls?"

"Oh, *football*..." I laugh awkwardly. "I could only imagine wild horses galloping by." I shake my head like *silly me*.

"That *is* their logo," she says, still laughing.

I crinkle my nose. "I'm afraid I'm not up on the sports. I usually have my nose in a book or I'm outside...with my nose in a book." I wave my hand and laugh with her this time. I lean in. "So, is that guy over there on the team or something?" I whisper.

"He's the quarterback," she whispers back.

My mouth falls into an O.

Wait. Does that mean Henley is—

Earl chooses that moment to make his presence known. His head pops out of my sweatshirt and Clara yelps. I rush to apologize for bringing a pet inside without asking permission but she's gushing about how adorable he is.

"I wasn't planning to do anything but walk...but the

donuts." I point to the sign, still feeling bad. "Hopefully no one is allergic."

"True," Clara says, looking around. She winks at me. "I think we're okay."

"Thank you. In that case, I'll take that unicorn donut right there. I can't resist. I got a job today. Actually two jobs this week! Feels like I should celebrate."

"Congratulations. That's amazing! Where are you working?"

"Wiggles & Whimsy and Silver Hills Middle School."

Her eyes widen. "That's wonderful! That means you're a Silver Hills resident, not just passing through. Welcome to our town. I hope you'll love it here."

I don't think I've ever smiled so wide. "Thank you, Clara. I think I *already* love it here."

"I'm sorry to interrupt. Can I sneak past you for some napkins?"

I turn and the pretty woman who was with the quarter-back is smiling at me.

"Oh, sure." I take a step back and she grabs a handful of napkins.

"Sadie, you should meet our new resident," Clara says. She holds out her hand and pauses. "Well, I don't even know your name yet..." She laughs.

"I'm Tru." I smile and then look at Sadie, who's looking at me with interest.

She reaches out and shakes my hand. "Tru," she says, her eyes lighting up with her smile. "It is really great to meet you. I'm Sadie." She nods as she looks at me, and it's almost like she wants to say more, but she just stands there smiling. "Weston," she calls, glancing over her shoulder. "Come meet my new friend, *Tru*."

Weston's eyebrows lift and he picks up the little boy and

hurries over. I don't know what to think about this star treatment, but they seem really nice.

"Hi, Tru," Weston says, smiling wide. "I'm Weston, and
this is Caleb." My knees get slightly weak because he's
almost as hot as Henley, and I just haven't been around many
men that are this good-looking in such close succession.
"Welcome to Silver Hills."

"Thanks so much," I say. "Hi, Caleb. You are adorable."

He gives me a toothy grin and leans his head on his dad's
cheek.

"Eep," Sadie gasps. "You have a kitten in your sweatshirt.
That is the cutest thing I've ever seen. Okay, it's official. Can
we be friends?" She laughs. "I mean, if that's okay with you."

I laugh, too happy and surprised to do anything but stut-
ter, "Y-yes, please."

"Caleb, look at the kitty," Sadie says.

When he realizes there's a tiny kitten in my shirt, he
starts bouncing with excitement. I unzip my sweatshirt a little
bit so he can pet Earl, and Earl's eyes drift shut in
contentment.

"He likes to sleep," I tell them. "Maybe that's normal for
kittens? This is my—"

"You should come to our house for a barbecue," Sadie
blurts out. She presses her fingers over her lips. "I promise
I'm not a complete weirdo. Only slightly." She holds up her
fingers to show how slight. "But say yes. It'll be so fun."

"I'd...yes, I'd love to."

"Amazing." She pulls her phone out of her pocket and
hands it to me to put my number in. Once I do, she looks at
her phone and then smiles at Weston. "Tru Seymour," she
says, nodding. "I like that name."

"Great name," Weston agrees.

I can't help but feel like I'm missing something, but

again…I have so few friends, what do I know about these things? I'm stunted in this area.

"I don't even know what to do with all this niceness," I finally say, laughing.

"Friday night, seven. I'll text our address. We'll introduce you to some of our friends, and you can bring the kitten if you'd like," Sadie says.

"Okay. I'll be there. Can't wait." Does that sound too eager? I think it does, but they seem even more eager than me if that's possible.

Weston tugs Sadie into his side, making me swoon even harder, and Sadie remembers the napkins. She waves them, reaching up to wipe a bit of chocolate off of Caleb's cheek.

"Here's that unicorn donut. You sure you don't want something to drink with that?" Clara asks.

"I'll come in another time for that Lunar Latte. I'm obsessed with Lavender Lattes, but I've gotta pace myself." I hold up the unicorn donut and laugh.

"I'll be here." Clara leans against the counter, smiling. She looks at Caleb wistfully. "I swear he's bigger every time I see him."

"I know. It's crazy how fast he's growing." Sadie gives me an apologetic look. "I wish we could chat longer, but we've got to get him to bed. He seems angelic right now, but lately when he doesn't get to bed on time, he wakes up extra early and is a *handful*."

"Oh no," I say. "It's hard to imagine him being anything but angelic, but I trust you." I wave at Caleb. "Have a good night. It was wonderful meeting all of you."

"See you Friday," Sadie says.

I nod, unable to contain my excited smile.

Weston, Sadie, and Caleb walk out the door and I take a

deep breath. Wow. Such nice people in Silver Hills. I'm so glad I decided to explore tonight.

The three women look at me like I must be a celebrity. One is lowering her phone. I'm pretty sure she went snap-happy with Weston so close.

I glance back at Clara. "You've made my night. I'll be back...probably more often than you want."

She laughs. "Not possible."

Later, I get in bed and google the heck out of Henley Ward. I cannot *believe* he's been on countless magazine covers and is a *huge* football player and I didn't even know who he was. He's been on Jimmy Fallon, for crying out loud. *I flirted with that man.* I told that man *off*.

I make a face in the dark, cringing, but in the next second I'm laughing about it. I'd do it again. Hell, yes, I would.

I'm still smiling when I fall asleep.

CHAPTER NINE

TABLE TALK

HENLEY

The mood is somber when I get to Bree's house. Gracie opens the door for me, her eyes wide.

"Mommy's crying," she whispers.

I lift two bags of takeout from Starlight Cafe. "Hopefully this will help."

She perks right up. "Did you get pie too?"

"Would I leave Starlight without pie?"

"I hope you got the chocolate because that's my favorite," she says.

"Peanut, when have I ever left you hanging?"

She grins and wraps her arms around my waist, squeezing tight.

Audrey jogs down the stairs, also looking shaken.

"What's up, buttercup?" I'm waiting for the day when one of them rolls their eyes at me for still calling them the nicknames I always have, but so far, that hasn't happened.

When she gets to the bottom stair, she leans her forehead on my shoulder and also peeks in the bags. "Yay," she cheers quietly. And then, "What's going on with Mom and Cassidy?"

"Where are they?" I pause to listen and it sounds like they're in the kitchen. "I'll just let them know dinner's here. Give me two minutes."

Every Monday night that I'm not playing football or traveling, I bring dinner and help with homework. Bree eats with us sometimes or catches up on work. It was awkward the first year after we divorced, but now we're a few years in and we've settled into our new normal. It took some work, but I'm proud of us for being adults and putting the girls first.

When I get near the kitchen, I hear Bree saying, "Why didn't you tell us?"

I knock on the doorframe and they turn to look at me, both with red-rimmed eyes and blotchy faces. I set the bags on the island and reach out for Cassidy. She moves into my arms and cries.

"It's okay, bunny. We're going to figure this out, okay?"

"I feel so stupid." The wobble in her voice breaks my heart and I smooth back her hair and tilt her chin to look up at me.

"You are not stupid, Cassidy. Listen to me with everything you've got, okay? Just because some things might be harder to figure out, it doesn't take away from the fact that you are so smart. I'm blown away by the way your mind works, the funny things you say, the brilliant way you look at the world. We're going to get help. Miss Seymour would like to do some tests and it sounds like she's got experience with this. Between us and Miss Seymour, I think it can get better. And if the three of us can't figure it out, we'll find someone else who can help too. How does that sound?"

She nods and sniffles. Bree passes a tissue and Cassidy wipes her nose. "Okay." There are a few more tears, but she wipes them away and takes a deep breath. "Okay." This time it sounds more resolute, and I smile.

"That's my girl. I've got some burgers and pie with your names on it. Should we eat it or—" I take the huge slice of strawberry pie, her favorite, out of the bag and lift my eyebrows.

She snatches it out of my hand and grins. "We should definitely eat it."

Bree shoots me a grateful look and I start unloading the bags.

"Girls, come eat," I call, and Audrey and Gracie are there so fast it's obvious they were eavesdropping.

We take a time-out from all the serious talk and sit down at the table to eat. The conversation is light. Despite Cassidy still looking sad, I try my best to pull her out of it and so does Bree.

While the girls clean up, I refill my water bottle and chat with Bree.

"I haven't seen Alex in a while. How's he doing?" I ask.

"He's good. We had a good trip this weekend," Bree says. She smirks.

"He's wishing he could do a workout with you and the guys. Get in shape a little more."

I laugh. "He's welcome anytime, but he seems in shape to me."

"Yeah. He's all talk, but he does sit behind a desk too long every day, so he could stand to get a workout in more often."

Bree's been dating Alex for the past four months or so. I like the guy. He's a financial advisor and way more type-A than I'll ever be, which fits Bree a lot better. He's nice, but more importantly, he's good to the girls. And he doesn't seem to mind that I'm around a lot, which is the way it's got to be.

I look over the worksheet Gracie is working on, and Audrey and Cassidy come back to the table with their backpacks in tow. When Audrey's done, she goes upstairs to get her shower and Gracie watches a show. I sit down with Cassidy and look over her work. She's frustrated and puts her head on the table.

"Can you tell me a little more about what happens when you read?" I ask.

"I don't even know how to explain it. It's like the words just jumble together or jump around. I don't know." Her eyes fill with tears again in frustration.

"Would you like to do the tests Miss Seymour suggested?"

"Yes." Her voice is soft. "I'm tired, Dad. Do you think I can go to bed early tonight? I'm done with everything that's due tomorrow."

"Of course. Get to bed. We can talk more tomorrow. I think the tests will help us know better the approach to take. That's the impression I got from Miss Seymour anyway. Just please keep talking to us, okay? You know, you can tell your mom and me anything, right? *Anything*, always. It doesn't matter what it is or how hard it seems. We're gonna try our

best to work through it with you and we'll love you uncondi-
tionally. Got it?"

She nods. "Thanks, Dad. I love you too." She hugs me
and I watch as she leaves the kitchen, looking older than I'd
like.

I stop by Bree's office on my way out. "I'm heading out
for the night.""Thanks for dinner, Hen…and for everything. I
don't know why I lost it, but I'll try to work it out on my own
time. I want to be there for her the way she needs me to be. It
just breaks my heart that she has never said anything about
this and that we *missed* it."

"I know. I hate it too." I lean against the doorjamb. "I feel
awful about it. But all I know to do is work our hardest to
help her figure it out now."

"I just don't want to put any labels on her that are unnecessary. You know? It's hard enough to get through middle
school without that."

"No one's trying to put any labels on her."

"I'm not sure. Miss Seymour was quick to jump on the
dyslexia wagon." She lifts a shoulder. "How old is she
anyway, like twenty?" She rolls her eyes.

I'm pretty sure I flinch when she says that. That's not
possible, right? No. What am I thinking? She'd have to be
older than twenty to be a teacher in the first place. My heart
returns to its normal rate.

"The bottom line is that, for whatever reason, she needs
our help reading. I think we should only be grateful that…
Miss Seymour…saw what we were missing. Now we can do
something about it."

She frowns slightly and nods. "Yeah, you're right. And I
am grateful…it's just hard to hear."

I tap on the doorjamb and say goodnight to her and then
the girls.

Why is it so hard to be a parent?

Parenthood seems to come with a built-in guilt mechanism, but holy fuck, the guilt is at an all-time high. I've considered myself a good dad—loving and present when we're together. I try to say yes more than I say no. I try to let them know they're the center of my universe but that it's also important to pursue your passions.

But missing this...it's proof that I'm not doing as well as I thought.

Knowing my daughter has suffered quietly all these years. It's devastating.

"Later, Charlie," I say to the night guard.

"Night, my man," he says.

I miss the old guy. I have Beau and Linc at my place and they're great too, but Charlie was with me from the beginning. When Bree and I divorced and I moved out, I asked Charlie and Dave, the daytime security, to stay here since the girls' safety is my priority.

My house feels empty when I get home. I look at Tru's number that I put in my phone after she left the voicemail. I think about texting her, but we're not friends, and with her being Cassidy's teacher, it would be even weirder. I meant what I said to Bree though—I'm grateful Tru opened our eyes.

CHAPTER TEN

PROFESSIONALLY SPEAKING

TRU

It's been a busy week. After meeting with Mr. Hanson to discuss Cassidy Ward and my thoughts on her reading, I proceed with his approval. There's no doubt in my mind after her tests that she needs this extra help. I'm amazed that she's done so well in spite of it, but I come up with a plan that I think will greatly benefit her.

I email the test results to Henley and Bree, mentioning we can meet anytime to talk about it, and Cassidy and I meet two

afternoons in a row to work together. On Wednesday afternoon, I get a message from Henley asking if we can meet the
next afternoon to discuss everything. Bree emailed, thanking
me for the information, but I don't know if she'll make it to
the meeting or not.

On Thursday, it's possible that I put a little more effort
into my appearance than normal when I get ready for the day.
Well, Mrs. Davenport thinks I put in too much effort every
day, but that's just me. For my first day here, I was dressed in
my most conservative suit, but now that they've hired me,
I've pulled out the vintage dresses. Why not? Life is short. I
like consignment shops and repurposing things, especially
clothes. Today's dress is a '50s Kelly green dress with white
piping and three large buttons at the top. It's fitted and hits
my knee, modest but fun with the white detailing.

When Henley walks in that afternoon, I try to act unaf-
fected by his sexy, hulking frame in my classroom. It's impossible. He affects me and I wish I were a better actress.

"Your hair." His voice is gruff as he stares at me with
wide eyes.

I put a hand self-consciously on my hair. "Is it going
haywire?"

"It goes to your waist…"

"Oh, yes. It does." I chuckle awkwardly. "I don't wear it
down to school very often, but I washed it last night."
Another laugh from me that makes me sound like I'm one of
the students here.

"It's beautiful." He smiles.

"Thank you." I gulp.

"How's your week been?"

"It's been great. How about yours?" I look down at my
desk, feeling uncertain of how to even deal with him.

My heart is thundering out of my chest because of his

compliment and just being near him…and he's the father of one of my students. I'm attracted to him and things between us have been a little wonky from the get-go.

He's just a man, I tell myself. An extremely hot man who makes me want to take a bite out of his biceps, but whatever.

"I've had a good week too." His eyes meet mine, warm and friendly, and I have to glance down at my desk again or he'll be able to see the attraction.

I wasn't afraid to show it that first day, but we're on a whole other playing field now.

"I wanted to talk to you about the plan I have for Cassidy and hear your thoughts on it. Are we waiting for Bree or is it just us?" My face heats when I say *us* and I hope he doesn't notice.

"Just us. Bree will be on board with whatever needs to be done, but she had to work this afternoon. Thank you for meeting with me. I'd like to understand what's going on a little better…a lot better." He clears his throat and looks at me almost shyly. "Cassidy is already encouraged by the things you've worked on together and I just want to thank you for that."

I set Cassidy's folder down as I look at him. He's making this really hard. I preferred being annoyed at him rather than the tidal wave of desire that's flooding through me. And I'm really touched that he's so involved in his daughter's life.

"Oh, it's…I'm so glad to hear that. I was worried I came on too strong when I met with you and Bree the other day."

"Not at all."

I open my laptop and Cassidy's folder and show him what we've been doing, exercises that can help her, and even games that she can play at home that will make learning these techniques more fun.

"This is incredible," he says, after we've talked for almost fifteen minutes. "No wonder she's been happier the past few days. This is fun."

"The best way to learn, in my opinion." I grin. "Another simple trick that will help her: large font. Since each student has an iPad at the school, which I *love*, I put some of these things I've shown you on her iPad, but also, with any book she reads on it, she can increase the size. There are even fonts created for those with dyslexia that show more white space. Cassidy read something for me yesterday using one of those fonts, and her reading was so much faster and more accurate."

"This is impressive, Tru…is it okay if I call you that?"

I smirk. "Yes, Mr. Ward, you may call me Tru."

He sighs, but he's smirking back and it's hot as hell. "But you're still going to call me Mr. Ward?"

I lift a shoulder. "You *are* my student's father. It's the professional thing to do."

He leans forward, and the way his eyes take me in feels so far removed from professional, it's not funny.

"But when we met, we didn't know that I was your student's father and I'm having a hard time forgetting *that* little interaction…"

Damn. I'm having a hard time forgetting it too. Especially with his raspy voice and those eyes drinking me in like he's been in the desert for years and years.

He frowns suddenly. "Do you mind if I ask how old you are?"

I straighten. "I don't see how it's relevant, but I'm twenty-four."

He leans back against his seat, and I can't tell if he's disappointed or relieved. "And that's also why you're calling me Mr. Ward…" He clears his throat. "I apologize if I've been out of line. You're right. And I respect you for keeping this professional."

My head tilts as I study him. What just happened?

"So tell me, Miss Seymour, what can I do to make this process easier for both you and Cassidy?"

One second, I thought he was flirting with me and the next, he's backtracking faster than a woman who doesn't want to get her hair wet in the rain.

"Uh, well…I'm happy to keep going with these afternoons with Cassidy, Monday through Wednesday. I'll be teaching dance on Tuesdays and Thursdays, but I start a little earlier on Thursdays." I give him an apologetic look.

"That's okay. We're grateful for any time you have."

"There's only one complication…" I hesitate to tell him.

"What is it? I'll do whatever I can to help."

"Well, a kitten showed up at my place and now I'm in love." I can't help but smile talking about Earl. "He's tiny and it was too soon for him to be weaned, so I've been running to the house during my lunches and as soon as school is over to check on him. Today, I felt really bad leaving him, but he's not allowed on the school premises. If Cassidy would be okay waiting just an extra ten minutes or so before we get started…"

"We could do that. Or…and this might not work for you, but…you'd be more than welcome to bring your kitten to our house and work with Cassidy there. The girls would love to play with him and maybe it would stave off their requests for pets." He smiles and that crinkle-eyed smile gets me every time. "Bree will be neck-deep in wedding plans during the afternoons for the next couple of months. She's a wedding planner," he adds. "So I'll have the girls at my place for a few hours in the afternoons…"

I swallow, pausing to quiet the rush of adrenaline at the thought of seeing Henley Ward in his element.

"You really wouldn't mind? I'd like to work with her for about an hour on those days. That's a lot of time to have a guest and pet in your home."

His smile widens and my whole body sings like it's on high alert.

"It's no trouble."

I pick up a flyer and fan my face. This man is doing crazy things to my temperature regulation.

"Okay, if you're sure. That would be great. And then on the days I'm not with her, if you could still work with her for ten or twenty minutes each day. You'll see a huge improvement, I promise."

"You've got it," he says. "I'll follow your lead, Miss Seymour."

His tone is slightly teasing, but his eyes are serious and genuine.

I stand and his gaze slides down my body, making me feverish, but then he gives his head a slight shake and his eyes squint, focused on mine. I cannot read this man.

"I hate to cut this short, but I should go check on Earl and then get to dance."

"Earl, huh. Cute." He stands and it's my turn to get a better view of him.

His broad shoulders and tapered waist should've been a clear indicator that he's an athlete. It's obvious hours have been spent honing this body. My mouth goes dry.

"We'll see you on Saturday," he says.

"What?"

"At dance…"

"Oh, right. Yes, Saturday. I'll see you then." I nod and go

for cool, calm, and collected as he smiles and walks to the door.

For a second, I wish I had any job but this one because otherwise, I would be exploring whatever this is with Henley Ward.

He makes me feel things I've never felt.

Two things specifically come to mind.

Number one: No guy has ever made me sweat.

And number two: I've never felt the urge to lick my way up a man's neck until I reach his lips…until right now.

CHAPTER ELEVEN

BURY AND DENY

HENLEY

WESTON

You're still coming tonight, right?

RHODES

Dude, where are you?

BOWIE

<cry/laughing emoji> I was just grabbing my
phone to ask the same thing.

I'm getting in the SUV when I check my phone and laugh at the guys. Weston's already texted a few times this week to make sure I'm coming to the party at his house.

> Wow. Eager much? It's only been a few hours since we saw each other.

PENN

> We miss youuuu.

> Right. Well, I'm leaving Bree's now. I stayed with the girls until Bree got home from work. You'll see this mug in about five minutes.

With the warmer weather we're having, Jupiter Lane is buzzing. I enjoy the crisp transition from winter to spring around here, but this feels like summer's arrived in March. The girls were happy about it earlier—they run cold and I run hot. I pass Pet Galaxy and smile when I think about Earl, the kitten Tru told me about. I haven't told the girls that we'll have a visiting kitten starting Monday. They'll lose their minds.

When I pull up to Weston's front gate, his guards, Joey and Seth, wave me through. I park next to Bowie's new Audi and admire it as I walk past. When I hear laughter outside, I follow it to the backyard. Weston and Sadie's property is gorgeous—a pool overlooking the same lake mine faces. At first I was the only one living on the lake. The house Bree and I moved into after I signed with the Mustangs was more house than I ever thought I'd have, but I got addicted to the view. The lake is gorgeous, with a wooded area framing it, and the mountains standing majestically in the background.

When I got divorced, I moved into a house farther down on the lake, and the guys have found their way over one by one on the same lake, which is great. Silver Hills isn't a big town to begin with, but there aren't many private areas like this.

The first thing I see is a roaring fire in the elegant outdoor fireplace. It's beautiful and warms up the space. Bowie and Rhodes are laughing with Weston's sister Felicity, who lives in the ski town about an hour and a half from here, Landmark Mountain. It's always great to see her. We all got close to Felicity when she lived with Weston for a short time, and when she and Sutton got married, we couldn't help but love him and his son Owen as well.

And then I turn and there stands the last person I expected to see at Weston and Sadie's house. Her eyes meet mine at the same time, like she can hear me thinking about her.

Tru Seymour.

She looks like a dream. She's wearing a pale pink dress, looking like pin-up perfection but right at home in this back-yard. Her hair falls down her back in waves that reach her waist. My eyes have no willpower, zeroing in on her pink lips before sliding down the rest of her body. She takes my breath away.

She's twenty-four, I remind myself.

I have never ever been so attracted to anyone this much younger than me. Age aside, I'm not sure I've ever been this attracted to anyone, *period*. But the age thing is unsettling. I think the biggest age difference I've considered is five years...and that was maybe one or two women. She's twelve freaking years younger than me but looking every bit old enough when she looks me up and down like she's liking what she sees.

I tug my shirt away from my neck, needing a little more air, and walk toward her. I'm intercepted by Weston and Sadie. He's unable to hide his smirk. The text thread with the guys makes a lot more sense now. I level him with a stare.

"How long have you been cooking this up?" I ask.

Sadie giggles. "It just *happened*," she whispers. "We met her the other night at Luminary and *hit it off*!"

Sadie is adorable and has become one of my close friends. I love the woman, so it's impossible to be upset with her on a normal day, but especially when she's so happy and animated about her new friend.

"That doesn't surprise me. I hit it off with her the first time we met as well," I say under my breath.

Weston elbows me. "And now it's time to do it all over again, only in a more romantic environment than the grocery store," he says quietly.

The two of them look like they're about to dance across the room, they're so excited. I scrub my hand over my face.

"I can't believe you guys did this," I say between clenched teeth.

"Come on, it'll be good. When we ran into her, I thought it was just meant to be," Sadie says, eyes bright. "Okay, don't look, but she's behind you," she whispers.

I can't help myself because I'm dying to look at Tru again. I turn and she's right in front of me.

"What a surprise running into you," she says, grinning.

"The surprise is on me. I had no idea you'd be here," I tell her. She looks like she doesn't believe me.

"Yeah, I didn't tell him we met you the other night," Sadie says a little too brightly. "You guys know each other?" It's said so innocently, but it's obvious that she knows better. She couldn't be more obvious if she tried.

"We've met," Tru says. "Several times now. Everywhere I turn, you're there." She laughs.

I smirk and her cheeks turn rosy. I fucking love it.

"Yes, Tru is Cassidy's English teacher *and* Cassidy and Audrey's dance teacher as well."

"Wow," Weston says. "You guys are just running into each other all over the place."

I look at him sharply, but he just grins. Maybe it's good that this is happening. Maybe it'll send Tru running in the other direction when she sees me coming, so I don't have to deal with being so attracted to my daughter's English teacher...*who's twelve years younger than me.*

"It's nice to meet people as soon as you move into a new town," Weston adds. "We wanted to introduce her to some of our friends."

"Even Caleb was won over right away." Sadie grins at Tru, who beams back.

Damn, that smile.

"Where is that guy by the way?" I ask.

Not even a second later, I hear, *"Unca Hen!"*

I turn, laughing, and see Caleb running my way. His grandma Lane is chasing him.

"I'm sorry," she says, laughing and out of breath. "I was trying to keep him inside so you guys could enjoy some adult time, but he saw Henley through the window and was out the door before I could stop him."

The little guy collides into my legs, and I sweep him up high in the air while he cackles. "Hey there, little buddy. How are you doing tonight?"

"Dood," he says.

I chuckle, loving the way he mixes his G's with his D's. Lane and Tru gasp when I toss him in the air, and Caleb laughs so hard. Weston and Sadie are used to it by now, but they all sigh in relief when he's safe in my arms.

"A-dain, a-dain," Caleb cries.

"One more time. I don't want to give your grandma and parents a heart attack." I toss him in the air again and when he comes back down, he burrows his face in my neck and cracks up.

I'm crazy about this little boy.

"How about we go get some ice cream?" Lane asks.

Caleb perks up.

"Ooo, ice cream. That sounds like a great idea," I say.

"Should we go pick out a flavor?" Lane asks.

We all look at Caleb and he nods. I put him down and he clambers off to take his grandma's hand.

"I be back, Unca Hen," he calls before he goes in.

"Okay, buddy. I'll be here."

When I look at Tru again, she's staring at me with an unreadable expression. It's been a while since I've tried to figure a woman out, and even though the guys claim that women fall at my feet over my charm, I call bullshit. Having a divorce behind me proves that I've probably never been great at figuring women out, but damn, I wish I knew what was going on in that pretty head of hers.

"Caleb is crazy about his Unca Hen," Sadie says, laughing.

"That is the cutest thing I have ever seen," Tru says.

Well, that's something. The way my ego puffs at that praise is all kinds of wrong since a child's love for me is not the way to win over a woman, but...hell, I'll take the help where I can get it.

Not because I *want* her, but because I need to have my daughter's teacher thinking I'm a decent man.

You are so full of shit, says the devil on my shoulder.

"Hey, Hen," Penn says, holding out his fist for me to bump. Bowie and Rhodes make their way over and surround us.

They try to act nonchalant, but the nosy bastards are dying of curiosity. I can tell that Weston's already got them up to speed about who Tru is or else one of them would've been flirting with her by now.

"I don't believe I've met you yet," Bowie says, holding his hand out to shake Tru's.

I'm glad it's him. I trust the guy with my life—not that I don't trust the others—but Bowie is more like me. He's been taking his time getting back out in the dating world. He isn't as much of a player as Rhodes and Penn. They're unable to turn off the flirt when they see a pretty woman.

"Bowie Fox," Bowie says.

"Nice to meet you, I'm Tru. Tru Seymour."

"Nice to meet you too," he says politely.

"It's a pleasure to meet you, Tru Seymour. I'm Rhodes Archer." Rhodes shakes her hand and when he smiles, his dimples come out in full force.

Tru looks wowed, as most girls do. I don't blame her. He's a handsome guy. Even my mom gets swoony when she talks about Rhodes Archer.

Tru glances over at me and there's a twinkle in her eye as she says, "So you're the infamous Rhodes. I was at Luminary the other night and heard these girls talk about you." She points at Penn. "And you must be Penn."

Her fingers stretch out to shake Penn's hand. He grins, the smug bastard. He's the one I'm most worried about. Bree says Penn is the hot one and he's way closer to Tru's age.

"You've got that right. It's great to meet you, Tru. So... what did you hear at the coffee shop?" he asks, holding her hand longer than I'd like.

"Well, I'm sorry to say I had no idea who any of you were," she says, cheeks flushing slightly. "And now I only know because those girls couldn't stop talking about all of you. I heard Henley's name and had met him already. I did think he looked like he could barrel through people without losing a breath, but no, no clue."

I'm not sure how to take that, but everyone laughs, including me.

"So Clara informed me that you're football players!"

"You really didn't know who we were?" Rhodes asks, with a mock hurt face.

"No idea." She laughs.

"I love this." Sadie laughs. "Bet that never happens anymore, does it, guys?" She's still laughing as she hooks her arm in Weston's.

Tru looks at me and the smile on her face nearly does me in. Damn. I don't know what to do with this. Why now? Why her?

Time to bury whatever this is I'm feeling *way* down.

CHAPTER TWELVE

FIRESIDE CHATS

TRU

I don't know why it surprised me when Henley showed up at the party, but it was a nice surprise.

He looks so good in his shirt and hoodie, unzipped. Relaxed and oh, so hot. Those broad shoulders make it hard to look away. It doesn't help that every time I make eye contact with him, he's looking at me, his brown eyes assessing and playful.

When I texted Mom that the guy I'd met at the grocery

store and then had a run-in with ended up being a professional football player, she wanted to know more details immediately.

MOM

HENLEY WARD?!

She'd texted in all caps.

MOM

ONLY YOU COULD GET HIT ON BY THE MOST WELL-KNOWN WIDE RECEIVER OF ALL TIME AND NOT KNOW IT.

I don't even know what a wide receiver is.

It'll be a long time before she stops teasing me about meeting someone famous and being clueless.

Everyone I've met tonight has been great. I absolutely love Sadie and Felicity, Weston's sister. I find out that Sadie and Weston are engaged and deep into planning their wedding. I also find out that Sadie is not their adorable little boy's birth mom. I don't know the full story there, but he is clearly obsessed with Sadie, who he calls Mama.

But he worships the ground *Unca Hen* walks on, which I have to say does something to my ovaries.

We sit around the fireplace and make s'mores, the handful who are left. Several other players from the team and their spouses left, and it's just me, Henley, Weston, Sadie, Felicity, and Penn. Bowie had to get home to his daughter and Rhodes had to get home to his son. Couches surround the fire and they're roomy, but these guys are large, so it makes the space feel smaller than it is. Henley is next to me, close enough that his side is touching mine. I'm hyperaware of every move he makes.

It's dark and cozy now, the firelight flickering across each face. We all chat for a while and then conversations shift and I interact more with the girls while the guys talk about something that happened at the gym.

I love the way the guys all talk about their kids and the way they tease each other. They seem like a really close-knit group and I can tell they adore Sadie too.

Henley stretches his leg out, bumping mine, and I tense. I'm glad it's dark out here because I have no doubt that I'm flushed.

"Sorry, I'm not trying to hog the couch." He laughs.

"No worries. It must be hard to know where to put those long legs all the time."

Ugh. Did I just say that?

He chuckles. "Your long legs must deal with some of that too."

My heart feels like it's going to thump out of my skin. Knowing I should stay away from this man while also thinking he's the sexiest thing I've ever seen is doing a number on me.

"Were any of you friends before you were on the team?" I ask.

I shiver and rub my hand over my arm.

"No, we only met once we were all with the Mustangs. Hang on a sec," Henley says, standing up.

I watch, trying to keep my mouth from dropping when he takes off his hoodie. His long-sleeved shirt rides up for a second, giving me a glimpse of his six-pack. I swallow hard and give him a weak smile when he hands me his hoodie. He holds it out for me.

"Here you go," he says.

I refuse to let my feelings trip over themselves just

because a guy is chivalrous, but I've not had much experience with that, so it's taking a concerted effort.

"That's so nice of you. Thank you." I take it and he helps me get my arms in the sleeves.

I inhale deeply and sigh over how good it smells. Just like him. Leather and wood and something sweet.

"Much better." I smile over at him and he grins back.

I melt.

"Good." We stare at each other, a long, weighted look.

Is he feeling this overwhelming pull that I am?

I get chatty.

"But this has been the perfect day. This weather's been crazy, right? It's not normally as warm as it was today, is it? Just cool like this at night," I say it all a little too fast, but he just calmly shakes his head.

"I've never seen it this warm so early in the year," he says.

"I love it," I admit.

He leans in and I catch another wave of how delectable he smells.

"It sure was a surprise to see you here tonight," he says softly.

"You're probably sick of running into me by now."

His eyes dance over my face, and the way the light from the fire highlights his chiseled jaw and those smiling eyes, makes my airwaves fluttery.

"Not even close, Tru," he says. "Do you know how many times I've wished I could go back and redo that meeting in your classroom?" He shakes his head.

I give him a sideways glance, smirking, and he laughs under his breath.

"You did make up for it pretty well with those cinnamon rolls," I have to admit.

"Oh, did that work?" he asks, laughing again. He scrubs his hand over his face. "I wasn't sure if that did the trick or not."

"It did help."

"Well, good," he says. "I was a real jerk."

"Yep."

He makes a face and now I'm the one laughing. My marshmallow is perfectly roasted and I take a big bite, barely holding back my moan. I haven't had one of these in so long.

"So, are you getting settled into teaching at the middle school? Liking Silver Hills, hopefully?"

"I love it," I tell him, honestly. "We moved a lot growing up, so I've been looking for a place that feels like home. And besides Guatemala, even in the short amount of time I've been here, this is the closest I've come to feeling that way."

"Guatemala, wow. That must have been an exciting place to live."

"For me, it was probably because it was the opposite of exciting. It was more the sense of community I felt while I was there. We weren't going nonstop and doing activities all the time, filling it up with busyness like we do here...I don't mean Silver Hills, I mean in the States. Everything felt simpler to me. I made some lifelong friends there that I still keep in touch with...Maria and I still write back and forth."

"I love that," he says. "What took you to Guatemala?"

"My dad's job. He's an engineer."

"Interesting. Were you mostly out of the country?"

"No, but my parents are in Australia now. And I've lived in California, Texas, Illinois, New York...and spent some time in Boulder."

He whistles. "That's all over the place."

"Yeah, I don't know what to say when people ask where I'm from."

He smiles, and it's really such a lovely smile. He leans in and I gasp when his thumb swipes over my bottom lip.

"You have a little bit of marshmallow…"

My tongue flicks out and I accidentally lick his thumb as he's pulling it back. We both stare at each other and he grins.

"You got it," he says.

Then he licks the marshmallow off of his thumb…

And.

I.

Die.

"I'm really glad you're liking it here. Silver Hills is a good place."

"Uh, did you grow up here?" I ask, somewhat shakily.

"No, actually my family is from Minnesota, and my parents still live there now. But I've lived in a few places because of football. This is the place I would have wanted to stay though, even if there'd been another transfer for me to play elsewhere. It's not going to happen now, at least I'm not planning on playing anywhere else…I'm already playing overtime at this age. Most are retired when they hit thirty-six," he adds.

He gives me a pointed look when he says that, like he's letting me know just how old he is. Message received. I swallow hard, wanting to go back to what he said about football.

"That would be hard to stop doing something you love so much…well, I'm assuming you love football since you're still doing it. Maybe you're ready to be done."

He leans forward, his elbows on his knees. "I do love it so much. I never thought it would take me this far, but it's been amazing. But yeah, I will be okay when it's over too. My body is tired and it's cost me…this job has cost me."

"What do you mean?" I ask.

"For one thing, Bree didn't sign up for a professional football husband. And I don't have regrets that things are the way they are now because I know it's how it's supposed to be. We're in a good place. We're friends. It's probably all we ever should have been. But when our marriage fell apart, I didn't quite see it that way."

"I've noticed you two seem close. I wasn't sure if you still hoped to be more or if it really is over," I admit.

He turns and looks back at me. "No. We're much better off as friends, and I'm content with that."

The way he looks at me when he says that...I swallow hard. I know he's feeling something too. My hands are shaky as I lift one to push my hair back.

He's your student's father, I remind myself. *This can't work.*

We stare at each other, the fire twinkling in his eyes, and longing stirs in me.

"Tru, would you like to go—" he starts.

I shoot up. "Oh, I should be getting home. I need to check on my...Earl. I need to check on Earl. And I need to get ready for tomorrow. Dance will come early," I say, laughing awkwardly.

"Oh, right. Yeah, sure. Can I help you?" He reaches out to grab me before I trip into the fire and I mumble *thank you* under my breath. I start to shed the hoodie and he shakes his head. "No, it's okay. You keep it. Stay warm."

"I'll give it back to you the next time I see you. I promise."

"Not a big deal," he says.

The mood is broken and I feel bad because I'm the one who put a halt to how magical things were feeling between us. But what else can I do? I want to get lost in his eyes and possibly jump the guy's bones, but I can't exactly do that, can I?

Sadie looks up and her face falls when she notices that I'm gathering my purse. "Oh, are you leaving?"

"Yeah, I need to get home and check on my kitten. I feel bad for leaving him for long stretches of time."

"You should bring him. Next time you come over, bring him." She gets up and hugs me and Felicity does too.

"I had such a good time. Thank you so much for inviting me." I turn to Felicity. "And I'm so happy I got to meet you too."

"Me too," Felicity says. "Have Sadie bring you to Landmark Mountain sometime. It's a whole other vibe there, but you'll love it."

"That sounds fun."

I say bye to everybody, avoiding eye contact with Henley. If he smiles at me one more time, I'm not sure I'll have the strength to leave. Sadness overrides all the warm fuzzies I've had from such a great night, and I walk away feeling like I'm missing out on a chance.

There's no doubt in my mind that I will regret it later.

Because I already do.

CHAPTER THIRTEEN

BOLT & BARREL

HENLEY

"Well, that went well," Sadie says excitedly, when Tru is out of earshot.

"Yeah, man, it looks like you guys were hitting it off." Weston grins.

Sadie does a little shoulder shimmy and I groan. "Yeah, it went so well that she just *bolted* right when I was about to ask her out."

"Oh no." Sadie's face drops. "But… so you *didn't* ask her out yet?"

"I got out the words, 'Tru, would you like to go' and she found a reason to practically run out of here…"

"No, she was probably just anxious about Earl," Sadie says.

"Yeah, I don't think so. I think she was anxious to get away from *me*."

"Nobody is anxious to get away from you, Henley," Felicity says. "Trust me, no single woman wants to do that."

Weston glances at her. "You better be glad Sutton's not here and that you just clarified with the single woman part."

"Are you kidding? Sutton would agree with me. *Sutton* doesn't want to get away from Henley. He's as obsessed with Henley as Caleb is."

"*No one* is as obsessed with Henley as Caleb is," Sadie says, laughing.

We all laugh. Felicity's husband Sutton is a good guy.

"Too bad hanging with the guys isn't getting me a date." I shrug.

"While you were over there deep in conversation, the guys have been blowing up the phone," Weston says. "Take a look at our thread."

I pull my phone out of my pocket and see the slew of texts that have been going on while we've been sitting here.

"Nope." I start shaking my head.

"What are they saying?" Sadie asks, laughing. She's been around long enough to know their foolishness.

"They want to know if I'm taking Tru home with me tonight, and if for some reason it all goes south, what night next week can we hit the club?"

Weston groans. "You need to ask her out. You didn't get

the words all the way out. She didn't have a chance to turn you down."

I shoot him a look. "She was gonna turn me down."

"She's into you," Felicity says.

"*So* into you," Sadie adds.

"How can you tell?"

"She couldn't take her eyes off of you, and when she looked at you, her eyes were like this." Sadie makes dreamy eyes, her hands up close to her face like she's panting.

I burst out laughing. "You look like a puppy dog. She did not look at me like that."

"You didn't see what we were seeing then," Felicity says. "She's into you, no question. She might think she shouldn't be, for some reason...like the age difference, maybe?" She lifts her eyes to the sky coyly. "I know a little something about that and trying to decide whether I should or shouldn't. If she were here still, I'd tell her *hell, yeah, she should.*" She and Sadie crack up.

There's a big age difference between Sutton and Felicity too.

"Yeah, it could be that and the fact that she's my daughter's teacher."

Weston nods. "The whole forbidden thing." He lifts his shoulder. "Some women like that."

Sadie looks at him and laughs. "Oh, is that right?"

He leans over and kisses her nose. "You know I'm right, Chapman." He waves his phone. "Hell, I'm with the guys too, man. If you're not gonna pursue this with Tru, and I still think you should, then yeah, let's get you out. This is the most I've seen you interested in anyone ever, so I think you should pursue *her*. But if you're saying that's impossible, then let's have a night out."

I stare at the fire, feeling like a moody asshole. The last

thing I want to do is go out clubbing. But I know once the guys get something in their heads, they have a hard time letting it go.

"We'll see," I say, and leave it at that.

The next morning, Tru isn't there when I drop the girls off at dance. I wait around a little bit to see if she's in the back room or something, but when she doesn't come out, I don't hang around. The Pixie Pop-Up Market is going strong today. We've had a few nicer days, so the whole town is out enjoying the market. Tiana is playing her guitar on the corner, her long blonde hair blowing in the breeze. Vendors line each side of the street—raw honey, soap, fresh flowers. There's even a small petting zoo where Charlie Newcastle lets the kids pet his animals.

I go to Serendipity for a little bit, and when I go back to the dance studio to pick up the girls, I see Tru. I smile and wave, and she does the same. But she's busy with the extra kids in there. On my way in, I noticed the sign out front said something about parents leaving their kids there while they shopped.

The girls and I walk around the market for a while and then stop at the petting area so they can spend some time with the animals. A hand squeezes my shoulder, just as I hear, "Here he is."

I turn and Rhodes is grinning next to me, Penn comes up on the other side, and Bowie catches up, stopping in front of us.

"Hey, what are you doing out here?" I ask. This does not seem like their jam.

"We were looking for you. You're not answering your

texts and an opportunity has presented itself," Rhodes says. "Look at us, no kids." He points to the three of them.

"I was trying to avoid you guys." I laugh.

The girls run over and hug them and then go back to the animals.

"As you can see, I've got the girls. I'm surprised Weston's not out here. Sadie usually brings him out as soon as the market opens."

"Were you looking for us?" Sadie asks, popping around in front of me. I laugh, and she goes over by the animals to hug the girls too. Cassidy turns every shade of red when she sees Weston, which used to drive me crazy, because I did not want to see my little girl crushing on *anyone*. But it happens so frequently with Weston now that I've sort of gotten used to it.

Scratch that. I'll never get used to it.

"Did these guys talk you into going out yet?" Weston asks.

"Are we still on that?" I stick my hands in my pockets, going into full grump mode.

"Yes, we are. I heard it didn't go great last night," Rhodes says.

"It went fine. She just doesn't want to go out with me."

"Well, if that's the case, she's crazy," Penn says.

"We can't call everyone crazy just because they don't want to go out with us."

Penn looks wounded by my scowl and I make a face at him to lighten up. The guy's young, but he's been a good friend to me since the time I met him. He grins back, worry lifted just like that.

If everyone were as easy to win over as Penn Hudson...

"You can at least see if you're ready to get back out there," Rhodes says under his breath.

Every few minutes, I've checked to see if any of the girls

are hearing this and fortunately, they're still busy petting all the baby goats.

"All right," I give in, "when I drop the girls off, I'll be free. What time are we going?"

"Well, the fun doesn't start till ten," Penn says.

"Ugh," I groan. "I'm too old for this."

"No, you're not an old man, you're just acting like one right now." Weston laughs.

"Oh, now you say that. Every other chance you get, you guys are telling me how old I am." I snort.

I know I sound like a freaking fossil. But seriously, when was it ever fun to start the night at ten o'clock? I've always been a morning guy myself, and if I hadn't been, having kids would've forced the issue.

"He said *yes*," Penn turns to point at Bowie, "so you've got to go too, Bowie."

"Me? Why? No." Bowie starts backing away.

"Okay, if I have to go, you have to go," I tell Bowie.

"Fine," he says. "You know what? I'll do it. I can use the night out. Becca's at my parents' for a few days, so I don't have an excuse, except I need to catch up on a million house projects. But you can definitely use the night out." He nods at me. "And it doesn't have to be all about finding women."

"Hell, yeah, it does," Rhodes says.

I'm rethinking everything as I drive over to Weston's to meet everyone. After working out and not sleeping much last night, the last thing I want to do is go clubbing. But we drive into Denver and hit one of Rhodes' and Penn's favorite spots. The music is pounding, the bass thumping loud enough to feel it in my chest and balls.

Penn and Rhodes look so excited that I can't help but soften my stance and be glad that I came. We're escorted into the VIP area, waitresses already surrounding us, ready to give us whatever we want. It doesn't take long before we're noticed, phones already snapping our pictures.

Women start coming over to each of us, one by one, or in the case of the women in front of me, the three of them came over together and surrounded me.

"I just love watching you play," the redhead purrs.

Her hand strokes my arm, and I jump back, not expecting it. She just laughs and steps in closer.

"Oh, are you jumpy tonight? I know a way to relax to you," she says.

"So do I," the blonde next to her says, her hand roaming up my chest.

My God, they're like leeches, ready to suction themselves to my body.

I look around for one of the guys to save me, but they're all in conversation. Penn and Rhodes are with two women who can't stop giggling. And Weston and Bowie are talking like they haven't seen each other all day. I try to get Bowie's attention, but he's laughing at something Weston has said, and then they stare out at the people dancing.

Just when I think I can't take another second of these whimpering, purring women—whoever thought that was sexy?—long, dark hair catches my eye. Her hair is down tonight, swishing around her waist, and *fuck me*. She looks so good.

Tru and Sadie walk past us like they don't even know that we're there. I glance at Weston and it seems like he hasn't noticed them. Did they plan this? Just then, I see Sadie turn back and wink at Weston. Those little matchmaking fuckers. Of course, they planned this.

Tru and Sadie go out on the dance floor and start dancing. And holy hell.

I just thought I was interested in getting to know her before, but now, watching her move, watching the carefree way she throws her head back and laughs. The way she moves that body.

It's going to be hard to scrape this image of her out of my head.

She's *beautiful*.

I watch her dance for so long that the women trying to get my attention become antsy, but I can't help myself. Tru takes up every ounce of space in the room for me.

Sadie says something to her when the song slows. They laugh and Sadie points to the VIP section. I brace myself. Does Tru know I'm here? Did she plan this too?

As she's walking toward me, I can tell the moment she spots me. No, she did not realize I was here.

Her eyes glaze over when she sees the redhead put her hand on my arm. And I'd be lying if I said I didn't like the look that crosses her face. A flicker of white-hot *jealousy*.

"Excuse me, ladies," I tell the three women. "I have someone I need to see."

"But—"one of them says, as I'm walking off.

I don't pause for a second. That look on Tru's face was all I needed to see to give me the nudge forward.

"Hey," she says breathlessly. Almost like a purr, but I like everything about the way it sounds when she does it. "How long have you been here?"

"Long enough to see that you were born to dance."

Her lips shift to the side as she tries not to grin. "Maybe a little," she says.

"No, completely. And way more than me." I grin.

Her eyes roam over my lips before they reach my eyes,

and my hand tightens around my glass. I don't think anyone has ever made me nervous before, but my insides are doing jumping jacks right now.

"Can I buy you a drink?" I ask.

"Sure, I'll have a glass of wine."

When the bartender comes over, Tru gets a glass of sauvignon blanc. Her full lips pucker as she takes a sip, her eyes on me.

"I bet you've got some moves, Mr. Football Player," she says.

"Hmm, is that right? For some reason, I recall you saying something like I could barrel through people without—what was it? Without losing a breath?" If she knew how winded she makes me, she'd take back that statement.

She laughs. "Well, you might not be the most graceful man on the dance floor, but hey, how will I ever know if I don't see you dance?" She takes a step back and looks me over and I take the opportunity to do the same to her.

"I'd be willing to give you some pointers," she says.

"Would you now?"

She lifts her eyebrow and one shoulder. "You looked a little busy over here though. I didn't mean to chase anyone away."

"I came to you, remember?"

"Oh, that's right." She grins. She takes a long swig of her wine and sets it at the high-top where Bowie and Weston are standing.

Shocker, their conversation came to a stop the moment Tru and I started talking.

I take a step forward and put my hands on her waist, loving the little hitch in her breath when I do.

"Show me how to dance, Tru."

CHAPTER FOURTEEN

MOVES LIKE HENLEY

TRU

The minute Henley takes my hand, I know I would go with this man anywhere. His large hand engulfs mine and I've never felt so protected, yet so desired, when he walks out on the dance floor confidently and then manages to smoothly flip me around so my back is against his chest. For a second, I wonder if he needs to catch his breath like I do, but the next thing I know, he twists me around until I'm swinging out and then twirling back against his chest. He dips me back and we stare at each other, suspended. When he lifts me up, we share a smile.

Oh, game on.

"So, you *do* have the moves," I say.

"Hmm." He grins, his eyes dancing.

He looks so dangerous right now.

We lose track of time as we move and it's not just a simple sway back and forth. It is steaming hot, sexy *dancing.* Like he was made to do this.

I can't believe this guy plays football. Granted, I've never watched a game in my life, but he makes me want to start.

It's the most fun I've ever had dancing. I've never danced with a man who could keep up with me, so the most enjoyment I've had is dancing with friends in college or by myself in dance studios. *This...*I could get addicted to this.

We dance until it seems like we're the only ones left on the floor, and we still keep going. When the music slows down much later, he pulls me against his chest and rocks me back and forth.

"What do you think?" he asks. "What do I need to work on?"

"Not a single thing," I tell him, and I mean it.

Sadie and Weston walk up then and stop in front of us.

"You guys look great out here," Sadie says. "Oh my goodness, you need to show me how to dance like you. I've always wanted to be able to move like that, but never could."

"You move just fine, Chapman," Weston says, pulling her against his chest.

"I agree. You were great out here," I tell her.

"Not like you guys were," she sings. "Hey, girl, I think I'm gonna head out in a little bit. Are you ready pretty soon?"

Henley clears his throat. "I can take her." He looks at me. "I can take you home if you'd like."

I smile. "That'd be great. Is that okay, Sadie?"

"Sure!" She grins happily.

"What do you think, shall we dance a little longer? Or are you ready to go?" Henley asks after we've said bye to everyone.

"I've loved this so much, but I am exhausted," I admit. "I'm not used to staying up this late."

He laughs. "Neither am I. The guys talked me into coming out tonight against my protests. But damn, am I glad I did."

"So am I." I smile at him and we make our way toward the exit.

He holds his hand out and I take it, my stomach doing its own little dance.

"I guess I'm glad now that we came in my truck." He laughs. "Those guys are something else. I guess they all piled into Sadie's compact SUV."

I crack up, imagining it. "That thing isn't big enough for all of them."

"They *are* a bunch of circus clowns, so I guess it works." We both crack up at that. "Maybe they took an Uber, who knows? Penn probably went home with that brunette he was dancing with, so that would be one less brute."

The drive to my house goes surprisingly fast. It's about half an hour to get there. We talk about Cassidy and the steps she's been implementing at school. And we talk about what his schedule is like when football starts back up. It sounds like a whole other life than the one he has right now. I'm reminded of what he said about Bree not expecting to be married to a professional football player.

"Did you not play football when you were dating Bree?"

"I did. But so many don't make it. Her dad played...got picked up by a team, but never made it off the bench. I think she just thought it was a passing dream, that I wouldn't get very far and it wouldn't last long. And then she'd have a nine-to-five husband. And well...it didn't go that way."

"I'm surprised she wasn't so excited for you. It seems like a really big deal. I mean, *understatement of the century.*" I laugh awkwardly and he joins in. His laugh is big and gravelly, just like him. "Clearly, I know nothing about sports, but...the Super Bowl? That's kind of huge, right?"

He laughs again and wow, I really like making him laugh.

"You're kind of adorable," he says. "In a complete and utterly fucking perfect way."

Oh, I can't even breathe for a few seconds. I just stare at him and he glances over at me like he didn't just shake my world upside down. He smiles and looks back at the road.

I swallow hard and thank him in a raspy voice. I don't even know what to do with myself. I'm floored by this man. When we pull up to my house and he idles in the driveway, I want to invite him in. It feels too soon, but I feel more than ready. The Cassidy thing is hanging over my head, but God have mercy, I want him so much.

He turns to look at me. "I'm going to walk you to your door," he says, his voice like velvet. "I'd really like to kiss you too, but I'd understand if you're not comfortable with that."

That feeling of fire licking up my body? That's what Henley's words do to me. I nod and realize when he gets out of the car and walks around to my side, that I didn't really make it clear what I wanted. He holds his hand out and I take it, climbing out. We walk slowly to the front door, and when we reach it, I turn to face him.

"I'd really love for you to kiss me," I whisper.

His lips are on mine before I've even gotten the words all the way out. Warm, full, soft lips that send me floating in the clouds. Firm and dominant yet yielding. My mouth opens to his and I let him inside. A little groan escapes my mouth when I taste the cinnamon from the gum he'd been chewing. My body feels swept away and yet anchored with the way he holds me. I'm greedy. My hands try their best to reach every-thing they can, his chest, his neck, his back, his hair. *All so good.* I tug on his hair and he breaks away, both of us breathless.

"Tru," he whispers, "that was—"

"Incredible," I finish.

"I'm trying to think of an even better word, but yeah, speechless." He leans his head against mine. "Thank you for an amazing night," he says. He gives me one more quick kiss and then backs up, still watching me.

Our eyes are hungry, but we grin at each other like fools.

Finally, I turn to unlock my door. When I step inside and turn, he still stands there, smiling at me. He puts his hand over his heart.

"You've given me a lot to think about tonight," he says.

I smile and go inside, collapsing against the back of the door. A feeling of utter elation in my bones.

When Monday rolls around, I have no idea what to expect from Henley Ward. I've been both relieved and disappointed that he hasn't reached out to me since Saturday night. But the overwhelming feeling leans toward disappointment. He has my number. I thought I might get a text or something to clarify what to expect when I get to his house this afternoon. We'd already set up a time for today, so there was no need for him to reach out over the weekend really, except maybe to talk about *the kiss we shared*.

I've had an impossible time getting my mind off of that kiss.

It basically rendered me useless yesterday.

I did laundry and cuddled with Earl, watching sappy movies and imagining Henley as the hero in every single one of them. He's much better looking than all of them put together, so it wasn't hard to do.

When I pull up to the gate, a guard waves me through, giving me a friendly smile. I gasp when I see the beautiful chalet at the end of the driveway, the lake shimmering in the background. The mountains surrounding Silver Hills are one of my favorite things about the town, but this lake, it's spectacular as well. Henley lives on the same lake as Weston and Sadie, but it was too dark to really enjoy it when I was at their place. This afternoon, the sun highlights the water and when I park the car and get out, I stand there for a moment, just taking it in.

"It's a nice view, isn't it?" Henley says.

I turn around and he's standing a few feet away. He's in jeans and a white T-shirt, bare feet. I've never seen anything sexier.

"It's stunning," I say, looking back at the water.

"I've thought about you so much since Saturday," he says softly.

I turn to him, surprised that he's going there. "You have?"

"Oh yeah, I have." He nods, his smile luring me in like he's telling me a secret.

"I've thought about you too," I admit.

"What have you—" he starts, but a little voice interrupts.

"Hi, Miss Seymour," a little voice calls.

I turn to see the smallest Ward daughter. She looks so much like Henley, I can't get over it.

"Hi, you must be Gracie," I say.

"Yep," she says. "I've seen you at dance before, but we've never met."

I nod. "I've seen you too." I smile and she smiles back.

"Cassidy said you're a really nice teacher and Audrey said you dance really good," she says.

"Well, I'll have to thank your sisters for saying that. I'm enjoying teaching both of them. Will there ever be a time when I see you at dance class besides coming in to get your sisters?"

"No, probably not." She sighs dramatically. "I'm more of a softball kind of girl." She adjusts her hat. It's white with a teal horse and says, Colorado Mustangs.

"I like your hat."

"Thanks. It's my dad's team. Sometimes I get cool things from the team, right, Dad?"

"Yep, it's one of the perks, peanut." Henley grins and tugs on her braid.

"Well, it's pretty great. That horse is cute," I say.

Henley snorts. "Yep, exactly what the league was going for," he says softly.

I cut my eyes over and he sobers, trying to not laugh.

"Very cute," he says in a serious voice.

Gracie giggles.

I laugh and we walk inside.

"Wow, this place. I've never seen anything like it."

"Uncle Bowie says this is really his house. Why does he say that again, Daddy?"

"Because it has authentic Austrian murals and hand-painted elements all over the place, and Uncle Bowie grew up in Austria," he says.

"I didn't know that." I study the mural in the living room and the huge arch-shaped window with the lake on the other side.

"He's been in the States since he was twelve but still has extended family in Austria," Henley says.

"That's so cool. I bet he did want to switch houses when he saw this."

It's so pretty and cozy while still being massive.

"He prefers a more modern look, but when he's homesick, he comes over." Henley laughs.

"It's beautiful, Henley. Really beautiful."

"I have Sadie to thank for a lot of this. She's been so helpful, making it feel this—"

"Cozy?" I fill in.

He smiles. "If that's how you see it, I'm glad. It's a big house, but I didn't want it to feel cold or like we have to be careful where we put our feet."

Instead of the black leather I've come to expect from a bachelor, it's so refreshing to see neutrals with pops of muted color here and there. The woodwork and windows are such masterpieces, it would take away from the architecture to have anything distracting from it.

We walk into the living room and Audrey waves from the couch.

"Hi, Audrey. Good to see you today. How's your week going so far?"

"Not bad, I'm almost done with my homework already."

"Wow, good job." I smile at her and she returns it shyly.

She's so pretty. I think she looks like a perfect combination of both Henley and Bree, and Cassidy looks most like Henley.

"Cassidy's in the kitchen. She was trying to get done before you got here, but she hadn't finished all the dishes yet."

"I had a little snack ready after school," Henley says. "There's still some left...would you like some pepperoni bites?"

"I'll never turn down pepperoni bites."

"Me either!" Gracie says.

"Come on back, let's get some food in you," Henley says.

Gracie and Audrey both follow us into the kitchen and look at me in alarm when I gasp.

I put my hand on my throat and laugh. "I'm sorry. It's just…this kitchen! Some of the cabinets have turrets? *What?*"

They all look at me with wide eyes and smiles.

"Hi, Cassidy. Sorry, I'm gonna need a minute before I can function like a normal human being." I overexaggerate my deep inhale and they all laugh.

"We love this kitchen too," Cassidy says.

"*And* there's a spiral staircase," Gracie yells.

Henley's eyes widen with her volume.

"We're excited you're here," he says. "Girls, Miss Seymour is here to help Cassidy work, so we'll need to give them some privacy. But she needs to eat first, right?" He grins at me. "Right?"

"I do," I say, smiling back. "I'll eat quick and then we can get to work," I tell Cassidy.

She nods and smiles sweetly, turning to hand me the plate of pepperoni bites.

"Thank you. I'm getting the royal treatment here." I take a bite and hum. "Delicious. Oh, this is so much better than the sad sandwich I ate for lunch."

"She likes pepperoni bites. Noted," Henley says.

I swallow hard. Oh, this is bad. This is very bad.

My face is an open book.

How am I supposed to hide my staggering crush on this man in front of his girls?

Fortunately, Earl chooses that time to make his presence known. He pops out of my hood and lets out a long, plaintive meow. The looks on their faces…priceless.

"THERE IS A KITTEN ON YOUR BACK!" Gracie yells.

"Oh, did I forget to mention I'd be bringing a guest?" I'm still laughing as they crowd around me, petting Earl.

"I knew, and he still managed to catch me off guard," Henley says, chuckling. "Oh, he is…the perfect little sidepiece for you."

"*Dad!* Gross!" Cassidy is mortified. "Sorry, Miss Seymour, my dad can't possibly know what sidepiece means."

"And you do?" Henley lifts his eyebrows and smirks.

I press my lips together as I try not to laugh. And fail.

"Remind me to cut off all reality TV for you," Henley tells Cassidy.

"*Dad*," she groans and looks at me apologetically.

Distraction always works in the classroom, so I try it now, taking Earl out of my hood. Another round of gasps and adoration makes me laugh.

"That kitten is the cutest thing ever," Henley says. And under his breath, I think I hear him say, "I'm so screwed."

CHAPTER FIFTEEN

ROUND AND ROUND

HENLEY

Once Tru has eaten and Audrey and Gracie have gone into
the living room to play with Earl, Tru looks at me and
Cassidy.

"For this initial session, I'd like to have both of you here,
if that's okay with you," she says to Cassidy.

Cassidy nods. "Okay."

"I'd like your dad to see what we'll be working on, and
that way, when I'm not around, he can help you with anything

you might have questions about, and you can also show your mom when you're with her."

"That sounds good to me," I add.

"Okay, great, let's get started."

And for the next hour, I go through the full gamut of emotions as I watch Tru work with my daughter. It's alarming to see the things Cassidy is struggling with firsthand. Since she first started reading, I've heard her countless times, but it's been a while now. She's read stories she likes to the girls, but now I'm wondering if those were stories she mostly knew by heart. As Tru goes through exercises, it's difficult to see how frustrating and painful this is for my little girl. She stumbles often to get the right word and is on the verge of tears. It's hard not to get weighed down by that. But Tru is patient and thorough as she tells Cassidy fun ways to help her remember difficult words.

When Cassidy gets upset with herself, Tru reassures her that this will take time and that she's here for the long haul.

"We're going to be working on this until you feel more comfortable reading," Tru says emphatically.

Cassidy looks at her with something close to worship.

It's amazing to watch when Cassidy begins to grasp certain information with more understanding. It's not a miraculous transformation in so little time, but it's a step toward figuring out how to solve the problem when she can't remember what a word is.

I couldn't be more grateful that Tru saw what Cassidy needed when she did, so we can know the steps to move forward now.

Of course, I beat myself up about it. I feel like the worst parent in the world. Because now that I'm seeing it, I don't know how I ever missed it...the way I tried to rationalize what I did see.

It's devastating to realize that Cassidy has been doing this alone.

But even by the time the session is over, I can tell she's exhausted, but there's a spark of hope in her eyes that was missing before.

Tru starts gathering her things.

And I try to come up with reasons to make her stay.

"I can't get over this kitchen," she says. "The cream cabinets with the little roofs on top. I've never seen anything like it. They are so pretty. And the woodwork in this house, it's so beautiful."

"I've never been to Austria, but Bowie says this place is like stepping into his grandmother's house…only with major updates." I laugh. "Would you like to see the rest of the house?"

"I'd love to," she says.

Cassidy goes to find the girls and Earl, and I take Tru around the first floor of the house. She stops at each window, going on about the view of the lake. The sun is starting to set, so it's an exceptionally beautiful night. We step outside and she sighs when she sees the hot tub and pool.

"This the life," she says, grinning. "Do you ever put this to use?"

"Oh yeah, we're in the pool all summer. And I'm in the hot tub after just about every game."

"It's so great out here," she says.

We go back inside and up the stairs. I take her around to the guest room that has a spiral staircase leading up to the attic room.

"Wow. The girls must love being here."

"They do. Although they've got a pretty nice setup at their house as well."

"How long have you lived in this house?"

"About three years."

"Hmm." She looks over at me shyly when we get to my bedroom, and we move in front of the window. "I'm very impressed, Mr. Ward. This doesn't look like a bachelor pad at all."

I chuckle and the longer we stare at each other, the more I want to kiss her. Electricity ripples between us, but I'm trying to gauge her mood. She seems comfortable and open, but I still feel some hesitation on her part...like she's trying to be careful around me. I don't want to scare her off, but I'd really love to get to know her better.

"You were incredible with Cassidy," I say, leaning my back against the window and facing her.

"She's the incredible one. I'm so impressed by her determination. The fact that she's come as far as she has while struggling with this."

"It's going to take time for me to forgive myself," I admit.

She frowns. "You can't blame yourself. You're an attentive father. Anyone can see that. And as someone who doesn't have a father like that, I'm telling you...you're doing a good job."

"Thank you," I say quietly. "What are your parents like? You said they're in Australia?"

"If you met my dad today, you would be charmed and impressed. He's well-spoken and smart, funny and charismatic. At home, not so much. He just knows how to turn it on when he needs to and when he's around me and my mom, he doesn't feel that need..."

I frown. "But home is where he should be showing that amazing side of himself the most."

"That's what a good dad thinks," she says. "He shows his true self when he's home. The other is all show, all an act to get support behind whatever project he wants funding for at the time. It's nauseating, actually. Sorry, I don't want to just talk bad about my dad. I don't know why I'm telling you all this. You're just easy to talk to. My dad and I are not close at all, as you can tell. But I love my mom. She's wonderful. She's everything he's not. And I wish she knew she was worth so much better than the way he treats her."

"He's not violent, is he?"

"Not physically. He is verbally abusive, though. And that does a number on her, even though she won't admit it. She's said it's not like he hits her or anything, which makes me wonder whether she would leave if he did. Since he never has, she thinks it's not that bad to endure insults."

God, I hate this. I've never understood men who need to reduce everyone around them to feel better about themselves.

I clear my throat and hold my tongue about the rage I'm feeling about her dad.

"That must be really hard to watch her go through that," I say instead.

Her eyes soften when she looks at me. "It is. Not a day goes by that I don't wish that she'd leave. I'd do whatever I could to help her start over."

"How soon can she visit?"

She laughs. "Do you have a plan in mind?"

I grin. Her laugh is impossible to resist. "We could show her how great Silver Hills is, introduce her to Clara and Lane, and the guys and Sadie…"

"And you and the girls…" she says, smiling.

"Me and the girls," I echo.

"I'll have to work on that. I think she'd love it here, I really do. She'd definitely like your house."

I pretend to be hurt, clutching my heart. "Just my house?"

She laughs. "And your pepperoni bites."

"I'm wounded. Wait until you taste my lemon chicken or

my burgers or…shrimp fettuccini." I keep throwing out food to see which makes her perk up the most. "My pizza?"

"Wow. You can make all that? I'm impressed."

I reach out and take her pinky in mine. She looks away, her lips quirking up higher.

"What were you going to say earlier? When you said you'd been thinking about the kiss too…" I say.

Her cheeks tinge with pink. She glances at me, eyes wide, and it makes my stomach freefall into the ground.

"Yeah. Definitely been thinking about it," she whispers.

I move in front of her, one hand on the window frame near her head and the other on her waist. She stares up at me, and I drown in her green eyes.

"You can't possibly have been thinking about it as much as I have," I tell her.

She smirks. "I assure you, probably more." She bites her lip. "But I'm not sure we should ever do it again."

I run my thumb over her lower lip. "Oh, we should definitely do it again." I lean in and kiss her and it is even better than I remembered. She kisses me back, lifting to her tiptoes to get closer and the eagerness in her sets a fiery need inside of me. Things quickly going from zero to one thousand.

"Dad!" Gracie yells from downstairs, but Tru jumps and sidesteps me like one of the kids is seconds from running into the room. "Never mind," Gracie yells again.

Tru laughs shakily. "Sorry. That was a dramatic reaction for…just…yeah…ugh, you've got me all tongue-tied." She laughs again and I do too, even though when her expression sobers, I can tell I'm not going to like what she's about to say.

"It just makes me nervous to get involved with…a parent," she says. "I don't want to do anything to jeopardize my job…or Cassidy's education."

"We wouldn't let it. Would we? Or maybe…it's the age difference too?" I ask.

She bites her lip. "It doesn't bother me if it doesn't bother you."

"It concerned me when I first found out, but more because I thought I *should* be bothered…and that it would bother you."

We laugh at the way this conversation is going round and round.

"What if…we keep getting to know each other," I say.

She drops her hand from my chest and I lift it back up to my lips, kissing her knuckles softly. Her mouth parts.

"This is just for us. Whatever happens," I say. "And we won't let anything stand in the way of your job or Cassidy's education."

"In theory, that sounds—"

"Dad—" Gracie rounds the corner and now Tru does bolt to the side and away from me.

I scrub my hand down my face. "What's up, peanut?"

"Can we get a kitten?"

I give Tru a long-suffering look. "I knew this would happen. Now I'll never hear the end of it. The request for a pet is already happening on the daily."

Tru giggles and lifts a shoulder. "They are awfully fun."

"So, can we get one, *please*?" Gracie presses her hands together. "Audrey and Cassidy want one too."

I snort. "You think this is news to me?"

I tug on one of her braids. "Your mom would have to be agreeable to it, since the cat would be at her house."

Gracie pokes out her lower lip. "She's already said no. Why can't we have one at your house since we're here lots too?"

"Because then I'll have to take care of it, and I'm gone a lot, remember?"

She sighs pitifully, shoulders drooping. "We would help."

"It's almost time for me to take you home. Let's not spend it being sad, okay?" I rub her shoulder and tuck her chin up so she meets my eyes. "Wanna help me with dinner?"

"Pepperoni bites wasn't dinner?" Tru says. Her eyes widen when we turn to look at her. "Sorry, forget I'm here."

I chuckle. "Wanna stay and eat with us? We're having steak kabobs, veggies, and salad…I just need to get the grill started."

"Uh—" Tru hesitates.

"Stay!" Gracie claps her hands. "Say yes! Audrey's making cookies right now!"

"Oh, there will be cookies?" Tru takes Gracie's outstretched hand and lets her lead her out of the room. She looks at me over her shoulder, her eyes questioning if I'm okay with this.

I try to give her an understated, sexy grin instead of the cheese I'm feeling inside.

I am more than okay with this.

CHAPTER SIXTEEN

DETERMINATION AND PERSUASION

TRU

Dinner with Henley and the girls is an experience. It's a spirited affair, to say the least. There's nonstop chatter, which is one thing my dad never tolerated at the table. If anyone was talking, it was the adults, and usually him. But Henley gives the girls free reign over whatever topic they want to discuss. They're respectful too. They don't speak over each other, but they keep things going as they joke and laugh about school and dance and Earl, which turns into pleading with Henley for a kitten.

I love sitting back and watching them interact with each other. I'm in awe of the way Henley treats them, and it's adorable how well his daughters get along. Every now and then Cassidy will roll her eyes at what one of the others says, but she makes up for it by saying something sweet to them afterward to let them know she's being playful.

Henley keeps trying to draw me into the conversation, and I'm talking, but I'd rather watch them. They're just so dang entertaining. But they refuse to let me off the hook.

"Do you have a boyfriend, Miss Seymour?" Gracie asks.

"Gracie, don't ask her that," Cassidy says. "Sorry, Miss Seymour. Gracie is so nosy."

"It's okay." I laugh. "No, I do not have a boyfriend." I keep my eyes trained on Gracie's when I say it, even though I feel Henley's eyes on me. I can see his grin out of the corner of my eye.

"But you're so pretty," she says.

"Thank you." I smile at her and she smiles back.

"Mommy's got a boyfriend. I don't like him very much, but he is nice. I mean, I do like him…just not like Dad."

Henley looks at her with concern. "Why are you saying that? I know for a fact that you like Alex very much. He's a great guy."

"He's okay, but he's not like you," she says.

"Well, he's not trying to be like me. He's trying to be himself, and you shouldn't compare him to me, peanut," he tells her.

"You like him," Audrey says to Gracie. "You just try to act like you don't when you're around Dad."

"I do not," Gracie says, sticking out her lip. She reaches

out and puts her hand on Henley's arm. "You're way better, Daddy."

Henley frowns. "Gracie, I want you to like whoever your mom dates if he's a good guy and treats all of you well. Is there a reason you're saying all of this? Anything I should know about Alex?" He looks around at all three girls.

Audrey and Cassidy shake their heads.

"We like him," Cassidy says, shrugging.

"But don't you think you'll be with Mom again one day?" Gracie asks.

Henley lets out a long, rugged breath. "Okay. How about we talk about this later? I didn't know you were thinking this way."

We're all staring at him and he gives me an apologetic smile.

"This has been so good," I say. "Thank you so much for dinner. I should probably be getting home."

"Do you have to go so soon?" Henley asks.

"Yeah, I need to." I can't get out of here fast enough after that little conversation. "I'll help clean up though."

"That's not necessary. We're going to clean up and then I'll take the girls home," Henley says.

I pick up my plate and take it to the sink and the girls follow. When they go back to take the rest of the things off the table, Henley leans in.

"Stick around and we can have a glass of wine after I get back from dropping off the girls?"

"I should really get going," I tell him.

"I'm really sorry about that in there." He nods toward the dining area, his voice low.

"Don't be. It just lets me know there's more to all of this that I haven't even thought about. It's a good reminder to pump the brakes," I whisper.

He curses under his breath. "I didn't see that coming. I didn't know any of them were thinking that way. I don't think Cassidy and Audrey are, but maybe we need to talk about it."

The girls walk back into the kitchen and we continue putting things away. I wash a few pans, even though Henley insists that I shouldn't worry about cleaning up, and the girls load the dishwasher.

"My mom taught me to have good manners when I go to someone's house, no matter what." I grin at Audrey who's standing closest, and she giggles.

"Sounds like my mom," she says.

When we're done, I gather my things and thank them again, and I head home with Earl in tow. I missed a call from Mom when I was driving, so I call her back after I've gotten Earl settled. We've texted pretty much every day, but have been playing phone tag since Henley and I kissed.

"Hey," she says when she answers. "How's your week going?"

"It's going really well. How's yours?"

"Boring, compared to yours." She laughs. "How's it going with Henley Freaking Ward?"

"Well, a lot has happened since we talked…"

"So help me, if you've had sex with the man and didn't let me know," she says.

"Mom! No, we didn't have sex," I say, laughing. "But, I don't know. I don't think it can go anywhere. I just got back from his house after having dinner with him and his three daughters, and I can't—"

"Why? Because he's older? I've studied him in every picture I could find since you told me you met him, and he is so hot."

"My mom is not supposed to say things like this." I laugh

and she does too. "It's not as much about the age difference as it is that he's the father of my student."

"Forbidden romance with your student's dad, I love it," she says with a dreamy voice.

"You've been reading too many romance novels," I tell her.

"Guilty," she sings. "And proud of it. Romance novels get a bad rap and it's really unfair. They're the best way to learn how to live an awesome life." She laughs.

"Look, you'll get no argument from me there, but I still don't know what to do. We danced the other night. The man can move, Mom. I mean, really move."

"Well, for you to say that, dancing queen, he must really be something. And it doesn't surprise me one bit. Maybe that's the benefit of dating an older man."

"We're not dating," I argue. "But we did kiss."

She squeals and I pull the phone away from my ear.

"You're just now telling me this? How was it?"

"It was perfect. Everything about him is perfect. Beyond our misunderstanding in the beginning, he's been a dream. His friends are great too."

"So what's the problem?" she asks. "I don't think him being your student's dad is enough of a reason."

"It is though. I'm helping his daughter with some extra tutoring. It's going to take time, and if things are complicated between me and him, it'll make that whole situation so awkward. Plus, I think his kids want him to be with their mom, his ex-wife. And that just sounds like a heartache waiting to happen. Not to mention, I'm just getting settled here. Running into someone after a fling has gone south in this small town—that's the last thing I need to worry about."

We talk for at least half an hour with her trying to convince me to go out with Henley. When I get off, I take a long bath and crawl into bed early. My phone dings and I check it, surprised to see a text from Henley.

HENLEY

I really enjoyed having you here today.

> Thank you for dinner. Your girls are wonderful.

HENLEY

Thank you. They think you're pretty great too. And so do I. I want to continue the conversation about getting to know each other better.

> I don't know if that's a good idea. There are just so many red flags.

HENLEY

Name one thing you don't like about me.

I laugh and it sounds loud in my bedroom.

> There's nothing I've seen yet that I don't like.

My cheeks burn with my admission.

HENLEY

<Grinning emoji> Then I see nothing wrong with this.

> You don't have any reservations?

HENLEY

I do have concerns about the girls...Cassidy in particular. But honestly, Tru? When I'm around you, all concerns seem to go out the window.

> Have you always been so determined?

HENLEY

> Only when it comes to making sure my girls
> are happy. And football. But the more I get
> to know you, the more I want to know...

> What do you want to know?

HENLEY

> Everything. How about I come up with a list
> of things and we'll go over them the next
> time we're together?

> You're very persuasive, Mr. Football Player.

HENLEY

> I can be very single-minded when I want
> something.

I place the phone on the nightstand, hands trembling as I stare at the ceiling. That was hot as hell.

I'm not sure I have the willpower to withstand Henley Ward's charm.

CHAPTER SEVENTEEN

HARD TRUTHS

HENLEY

I drive to the gym, thinking about my conversation with the girls last night.

I asked them if they all felt like Gracie and were holding out hope for their mom and me to get back together. Audrey and Cassidy didn't say anything right away, but when Audrey spoke up, she said, "Maybe a little."

And Cassidy said, "You guys just seem so close still. I guess I've thought it could happen."

I glanced at Audrey and Gracie in the backseat, meeting Audrey's eyes in the rearview mirror, and then at Cassidy next to me, feeling absolutely floored.

"I had no idea the three of you felt this way. I'm sorry, girls. I feel like your mom and I should have made it clearer that we're not getting back together."

"But why not?" Gracie asked.

"We were better off as friends," I said. "Your mom doesn't think of me romantically anymore and I don't think of her like that either."

"Did you never really feel that way?" Cassidy asked.

I paused before I answered because, when I stopped and thought about it, of course I loved Bree. But I couldn't say I ever felt all the things I should have felt for her, and I didn't even fully realize it until we were apart for a while. It was little things like the way she would snark about me working out or about my job or if I wanted to visit my family. The way she wished I could be someone I never was. It was like the moment we got married, she wanted me to be someone different. When we decided to break up, that lifted because there was no pressure for me to be that person anymore and she didn't feel pressured to approve one way or the other. We could just be friends raising our girls together.

But it was confusing at the time and explaining it to the girls felt impossible.

"I loved your mother, but I don't feel like we're right together. At first, it was hard to understand that. The most important thing was me being with you guys all the time. I didn't want to miss out on anything. I still don't. We've got a good thing going, raising you together, and I don't know if Alex is the man she'll be with forever, but I think she's happy with him now. You guys should really give him a chance."

They were quiet the rest of the ride. I pulled in front of

their house and turned to look at them. "Is everybody okay? Do we need to talk about this more?"

"No," Audrey said.

"I still don't understand why you and Mom aren't together," Cassidy said. "Did something bad happen?"

"No. Nothing bad happened. We just weren't compatible as a couple and we kept trying to make it work anyway," I said. "People grow apart. It happens. But your mom is so much happier now, and so am I," I added.

"That's so sad," Cassidy said, her eyes filling with tears. "How can you be such good friends and not be a good couple too?"

"I wish I could explain it, but it's something that I don't understand myself. We made each other unhappy when we were together, even though we loved each other. One day hopefully you'll know what I mean when you find someone you're meant to be with...the right person. Hopefully you'll know what's right for you better than we did."

When I walk into the gym, the guys can tell right away that something's wrong.

"You haven't been answering our texts. What's going on? You leave us hanging about the kiss. And now you walk in here looking like your dog has died," Rhodes says.

"I don't have a dog," I grumble.

"Exactly, so what's up?" he says.

"I'm troubled about a conversation I had with the girls last night. Can't get it off my mind. Tru was at the house yesterday to work with Cassidy. She stayed and had dinner with us. It was such a fun night. Everything seemed to be going great. And then Gracie asks if Bree and I will ever get back together..."

"Shit," Bowie says.

"Where did that come from?" Weston asks. "I never knew they were thinking that way."

"Me either, they've seemed great with our arrangement. Well-adjusted. At least, I thought they were. I told them clearly that it's not happening. And they don't understand why. It's hard to explain...feelings. I never want to put Bree in a bad light and I don't feel negatively about her. But I don't love her like that and she doesn't love me like that. How do you say that and still let your kids know that you love their mother?"

"Shit, if you're fucked, we're all fucked because I've never seen two parents co-parent any better than you guys do," Rhodes says. "It's going to be hard for me to talk positively about Carrie to Levi, but I'm going to do my best when he's old enough. But we *don't* get along. He's going to be happy we're *not* together. I guess that's always the risk with getting along well with your ex—it could give the kids hope."

"Yeah, I thought the whole 'we're just friends' thing would be enough, but I don't think so."

"Well, maybe Bree will reiterate that with them," Bowie says. "She's doing good with Alex, right?"

"It seems like it. I think she's into him." I nod.

"Well, maybe the happier they see her with someone else...and eventually *you* with someone else," Bowie grins, "maybe it'll be clear. They'll see that you're different with Tru, for example, than their mom."

"I think the whole thing is scaring Tru off. And I wouldn't blame her. She's already worried about dating me with Cassidy being her student. And hearing that whole conversation did not help my cause in any way. I'm worried about it too, but I...like her."

They all pause what they're doing and look at me in shock before breaking out in grins and whoops.

"Shut up," I grumble. "I don't know that I can do much about it. I just want to get to know her, but it's important that the girls are okay."

"Fuck," Penn says. "Why are kids so complicated? Sam said something last night about his parents never getting along...and that he hopes he never has to be in the same house with them ever again. So it's definitely preferable that they want you together than that scenario."

"Damn straight," I say. "How's he doing these days?"

"He's doing good. He's crushing on a girl named Charlotte. It's pretty fucking cute. I'm trying to convince him to talk to her. He says he gets tongue-tied whenever he tries."

We all laugh.

"Hey, it's been a while since we've updated this." Weston pulls The Single Dad Playbook out of his bag and lays it on the counter near the weight machines.

Rhodes picks it up and writes in it before he starts working out. Bowie takes it next. I'm already lifting, so I'll have to get to it afterward.

When I pick it up after my shower, I write:

It can be so hard to know if you're getting through to your kids.
They can seem like they're on the same page, but then the truth comes out later and you realize you hadn't communicated enough after all.
I don't know the secret or the answer to this. I'm still trying to figure it out, and it may always be a mystery.
All I know is it's important to keep trying.
Keep the lines of communication open.
Be a safe place for them to land.
I have to hope that it all ends up working out.

~Henley

I call Bree when I get home and get right to the topic. "Hey. Did you know the girls are holding out hope that we get back together?"

"What?"

I already feel better hearing the shock in her voice. "Yeah, it floored me too."

"Well, did you set them straight?"

"I tried, but maybe you can solidify the point. Tell them how I drive you nuts or whatever you have to do."

She laughs, but her voice is sad. "I thought they liked Alex. I've tried to ease him into their lives, but maybe he should be more involved."

"Whatever you think regarding Alex, but I thought you should be aware."

"Thanks. I'm glad you told me. I'll talk with them."

———————

Tru is all business with me that afternoon. I had a feeling that her having time to think about that conversation with the girls last night would not go in my favor. And I'm too uncertain of how to proceed that I don't push it.

CHAPTER EIGHTEEN

GETTING TO KNOW YOU

TRU

Henley seemed bold on our text thread, but when I go to his house the next afternoon, he's tentative around me. I guess I'm tentative around him too, even though just looking at him reminds me of the way he kisses and how much I want more of that.

But I'm grateful for the reprieve. I've thought of very little but him and our situation...even trying to muddle through it during English class all day.

My brain is tired. I don't know what the right thing is.

I like what I know about him *so much*. But it's compli-cated. And I'm just not sure I want to start out my time in Silver Hills this way. It'd be one thing if I was doing the temporary thing that my parents do, where they're in and out of a place in no time. I want this to be my home. I want to create memories here. I want to make a life. I don't want to start trouble with my job or with the people here. So, a little bit of time and space in this weird situation seems like a good idea.

But before I leave, Henley jogs out and meets me at my car.

"Hey," he says, smiling shyly. "I wanted to give you this."

He hands me a piece of paper folded over once, and when I start to open it, he reaches out, his fingers skimming over mine.

"You don't have to read it now. I just wanted you to know I meant what I said."

My cheeks heat.

"Okay," I whisper.

He nods and takes a step back. "Have a good night. Thanks again for what you're doing with Cassidy. Today was hard, but I can tell she's hopeful."

It needs to go on the record somewhere that Henley Ward is impossible to resist.

When Earl and I get home, I eat some leftover soup and we curl up on the couch together. The note from Henley is on the coffee table and I pick it up, excitement thrumming through me despite all my efforts to be calm. I unfold it and smile when I see his handwriting. It's nice, just like every-thing else about him.

. . .

Tru,

I still want to know everything, but how about we start out with these three questions…

What is your very first memory?

What made you choose Silver Hills?

Did you know that when you're reading, you twirl your hair around your fingers?

Henley

Well, now I'm really smiling. *Impossible to resist.*

I think about my answers as I wash out my soup bowl and grade papers and later, when I'm in the tub. As I crawl into bed, I pick up my phone and text him.

> You didn't mention the format you wanted me to answer these questions.

He texts back right away.

HENLEY

> By text, over wine, phone call, FaceTime, write me back, on my dock at the lake… however you please.

> Has anyone ever told you you're pretty amazing?

HENLEY

> Hey, I thought I was the one asking the questions… <smile emoji>

> Well, I'll be asking some myself, so get ready…but that question above counts. ^

HENLEY

> Noted.

My next questions for you would be:

When did you first know you wanted to play football professionally?

Do you have any siblings and if so, are you close?

HENLEY

Okay, solid questions and not too difficult to answer, I approve.

By now, I'm practically beaming at my phone. This guy.

Oh...and where did you learn to dance so well? <Wink emoji>

And here are my answers...

Is it weird that I remember chewing on my crib? I also remember climbing out of it.

HENLEY

That's wild and I love it. Do you know how old you would've been?

Maybe a year and a half at most?

HENLEY

So, a climber early on.

Yep. lol

My mom and I drove through Silver Hills a couple years ago when we first moved to Boulder. It was a beautiful day, the middle of winter, but everyone was out and about. There was such a wholesome feeling about the town. Jupiter Lane was so charming with all the cute shops and restaurants. We stopped and ate at Starlight Cafe, and I couldn't stop watching the way everyone interacted with each other. It felt like a community and I have always craved that.

HENLEY

You're in the right place. Wholesome is exactly what I thought when I first came to Silver Hills too. I didn't know I'd love the small-town life, but it's been the perfect balance for me. I hope Silver Hills is everything you hope it to be.

It's far surpassing everything I'd hoped for so far.

HENLEY

Excellent. Let me know what I can do to improve your experience.

You already are.

Hmm. No, I did not know that I twirl my hair when reading.

HENLEY

Your hair is really beautiful, Tru.

I press my lips together. I really like this man.

Thank you.

HENLEY

Thank you for answering my questions. And to answer yours...pretty amazing? No, I don't think so.

I don't believe you.

HENLEY

If it's happened, I didn't hear it until you said it.

You are smooth, Mr. Football Player.

HENLEY

You think so? I just say what's on my mind.

Well, it translates as SMOOTH.

HENLEY

That's a good thing, I hope? Uh...I dreamed of playing football as a kid, and my parents made that possible by sending me to the camps and all that when I was young. I'm fortunate they encouraged it. And I have an older brother who still lives in Minnesota, Jeremy. He's a good guy, does well in finance. We're close, but I don't see him as often as I'd like. He and his family usually come to visit in the summer, and I take the girls there during any holiday I'm free... which can be challenging with games.

I always wanted a sibling. I'm glad you guys are close.

HENLEY

And dancing...funny story. One of our coaches made us take ballet classes for the coordination.

The level of regret I have for not witnessing that class is extreme.

HENLEY

I didn't love it at first, but it actually accomplished what our coach was hoping it would.

I wouldn't mind teaching football players.

HENLEY

Is it wrong that I just growled?

I wouldn't mind hearing that as well.

HENLEY

You are so fucking cute. I have so many more questions, but I know you have an early morning. Thank you for indulging me.

It was fun. Good night, Henley.

HENLEY

Good night, Tru.

Over the course of the next week and a half, when I'm at his house, we share private smiles and furtive glances. And then when I get home, we spend hours texting or talking on the phone. I'd feel like I'm sneaking around, but we haven't kissed since that first day at his house.

It doesn't mean we haven't talked about it though.

One of his questions yesterday was:

Did you know your lips are the sweetest thing I've ever tasted?

I didn't know how to answer that one, but I felt his words

from the top of my head to the soles of my feet and everywhere in between.

But he also asked about my thoughts on Twizzlers—we both love them—so he keeps things both steamy and light, which I appreciate.

It's been easier than I expected with the girls too. Since I keep it all about Earl and tutoring when I'm at their house and we focus on dancing together when they're at the studio, I don't think they see me as any kind of threat.

Part of me feels guilty that my feelings just keep magnifying where their dad is concerned, but I'm all about them when I'm at Henley's house. I see him when I'm there too, but I'm getting to know him more in our phone chats. It's something just for the two of us…and it's secretive, I guess, but I kind of love it.

I walk into my house and set Earl down. He's been thoroughly adored over at Henley's this afternoon and now he's ready to curl up in a basket near the window. I grade papers for an hour or so and then stand up to stretch. My phone buzzes and I pick it up, answering on the second ring.

"Hey," I say, smiling already.

"Remind me why you had to leave?" I can tell he's smiling too.

"Because I'm already at your house almost as much as I'm at my house and you had things you needed to do with the girls."

"I think you should stay for dinner again soon."

"Maybe one of these days, but I want the girls to enjoy seeing me come through the door, not dread me being around all the time."

"There is no part of them that dreads seeing you, trust me. They think you're the greatest thing that's ever come through these doors."

I laugh. "I think you're exaggerating, but that's sweet."

"I don't exaggerate."

"Mmhmm. The other day you and Gracie were talking about catching fish and that story kept changing—the size of the fish kept getting bigger and bigger."

He laughs. "Fishing stories don't count! But speaking of that, you should come fishing with us sometime soon."

"That would be fun. I haven't fished since I was a little girl and I don't remember catching anything."

"Well, then, let's plan on it."

I stretch out on the couch and Earl comes over. He's grown so much. I reach out and pick him up and he kneads my stomach before curling up and falling asleep there.

"You should see Earl right now." I snap a picture and send it to him.

"I wish I was Earl."

"I think I prefer your non-furry massive self, but—"

"Not what I meant and you know it."

I laugh.

When he says things like this, I usually tease him back, but I love every second of it.

"Okay, number one question of the day," he says. "When did you first learn to roller-skate? Or Rollerblade?"

"You assume I've roller-skated."

"Oh, have you never?"

"No, I have. I'm just teasing. But, um, I was probably eleven. How old were you?"

"Three."

"No way. What, you could barely walk and you were put in skates?"

"Blades, actually, and yes...I had to follow my big brother and he liked to skate. I wasn't very good at it at first, but eventually I could Rollerblade circles around him. It was great."

"Do you still Rollerblade?" I can barely get the words out because the thought of him on Rollerblades makes me laugh.

"What? You find this hilarious?"

"I'm trying to picture you on Rollerblades and it's really hard. You're massive. I feel like that doesn't work."

"You think massive people can't skate?"

"No. Just, I feel like you would topple over." I start laughing again.

"Trust me, I do not topple over. Hockey players are large, you know." He's laughing now too.

"Right. As you can see, I don't often think of sports in my logic. I need to learn."

"Growing up, were there any sports you liked to play?"

"I liked volleyball and tennis."

He hums appreciatively. "I can picture that."

My cheeks hurt from smiling so big.

"So, I have a problem with you," he says.

My smile drops. "You do?"

"Yes. Mondays through Wednesdays, I get to see you at the house, and it's torturous, not getting to touch you, but I at least get to see you. And then Thursdays and Fridays, there's this vast void in my life."

I laugh. "I always thought I was the dramatic one in any friendship."

"Are we friends, Tru?" His voice is husky but playful. "Because friends see each other on Thursdays and Fridays. And for longer than mere minutes on Saturdays," he adds. "It's like a tease to see you high-fiving everyone but me on Saturday mornings. And then again, the void on Sundays."

"Would it make you feel better if I high-five you at dance on Saturday too?"

"It might help a little, yes."

I laugh again. "I'll see what I can do."

CHAPTER NINETEEN

SIMPLE THINGS

HENLEY

It's been a lot of fun talking to Tru over the past week. I'm getting to know her, and even though I'd love nothing more than to spend one-on-one time with her, I'm enjoying this process too. I haven't actually done a lot of dating in my life besides Bree all those years ago. And I have to say, even though we're not technically going out, this feels more exciting than I could have imagined. The simple things, looking forward to hearing Tru's voice, waiting to get texts from her, and the conversations we have...I've never had more fun.

It's Thursday night, and like I told Tru last night, these days when I don't see her drag. I feel deprived of her sunshine.

It's been a busy day though. I drop the girls off and head to the grocery store. I need to pick up a few things before tomorrow. After I'm done at the store, I notice Tru's car parked outside Wiggles & Whimsy. On a whim, I stop and park around the back and walk around to the sidewalk, pausing to say hi to a few people in front of Serendipity. I don't see Tru when I reach the studio window, but when I try the door, it's unlocked, and I walk in.

"Hello?" I call.

I hear music in the other room and follow it, going through the main studio and to the back. I didn't even realize there was another studio back here.

She's dancing.

At first, I'm concerned that I was able to just walk in without her noticing. I don't want to alarm her and I want to remind her to lock the door.

But *fuck me*, what a sight to behold.

She's in a black sports bra and leggings, her body perfection as she leaps through the air and twirls with precision.

I don't know how this woman ever thought she wasn't athletic because I've never seen anything more controlled or more powerful than the way she dances. It's breathtaking and awe-inspiring.

I watch for a few minutes, and when the song is over and she seems to come back to earth, both feet on the ground, I clear my throat.

"Hello?"

Her eyes meet mine in the mirror and then she turns to face me. I hold up my hand.

"I'm so sorry if I startled you. I felt terrible about interrupting, and yet I couldn't stop watching. I didn't want to scare you."

She smiles. "Hey, you. What are you doing here?"

"I saw your car out front and I wanted to say hi. It was unlocked. You should really keep that door up front locked, even though Silver Hills is completely safe...you just never know."

She smirks. "Why? So hot, sexy football players can't sneak in and watch me dance?"

I put my hands in my pockets and grin. "Hot *and* sexy, huh? I guess you can keep it unlocked as much as you want if that's the praise I'll get."

Her lips pucker out as she looks me over with approval. "I did mean to lock it, but this is a nice surprise."

My adrenaline is pumping. "I'm really glad I got to see you dance. You are something else, Tru. I don't think you can get more athletic than ballet. And you make it look so easy."

"Really? I mean, *I* think it takes a lot, but I'm surprised to hear you say that, with these muscles and all." She reaches out to squeeze my bicep.

"Dang, do it again. I wasn't even flexing. Give me another second."

She cracks up. "You don't need to flex for me to feel that definition."

I reach out and put my hands around her waist, drawing her close.

"How are you today?" I ask. "I missed you."

Her head tilts. "I missed you too. It's crazy, seeing you. I'm talking to you all the time and when we're around each other, we're so careful. But this afternoon, I felt like I was so deprived."

I lean my forehead on hers.

"And now you're here, touching me," she whispers.

"This okay?" I ask.

She nods, her eyes intense as she looks up at me. And then her smirk is back and she moves around me, picking up the remote and turning on a song that pulses through the room. It's not the classical music she was dancing to when I walked in, but something far more carnal. The surge of lust I feel as she walks toward me is instant.

She holds out her hand. "Dance with me?"

I take her hand and she twirls until she's against my chest. I tug her body flush against mine and we start to move. The thump of the bass is fast and electrifying, but our bodies are languid as we sway against each other. Unlike the night at the club, our hands don't hold back as they explore, our bodies grinding. She slides her leg around my thigh and I grip it there, as her head falls back, her hair dipping to the floor. When I lift her back up, I keep her leg in place, her core against the erection I can't hide, and she pulls my head down to kiss her.

We never step out of the beat for a second, our bodies completely in sync. I move her back into the mirror, our mouths chasing each other hungrily. Her hands slide into my hair, gripping it hard. I lift her to the barre and her legs wrap around my waist. I lower just enough to grind against her warm center and she whimpers into my mouth, letting me know it's hitting her just right, so I do it again and again, until her kisses become erratic and frenzied.

When her head falls back, she cries out my name and arches against me. It unleashes something primal in me. I slide my hand down her stomach and dip below her leggings until my fingers glide down into her wetness. Her eyes flare and glaze over as she stares at me, and I take her plump lower lip between my teeth and tease it as I also tease the little bud between her legs. She gasps and when I dip my fingers inside of her, she clamps down around me, her flutters against my fingers the greatest reward.

I watch her fall over the edge, and it's a fucking beautiful sight. There's a sheen of sweat on her forehead and the sound of her whimpers are so erotic I can't think straight. When her breathing slows, I slow my fingers too, gently drawing them out of her and trailing a line of her arousal up her skin like paint on a canvas. She tugs on my hair, bringing my mouth back to hers and I kiss her long and hard. When we come up for air, I smile against her lips.

"Even your pussy dances in perfect time," I say.

Her teeth press against her lower lip as she laughs.

"You are lethal," she says, smiling up at me.

Her cheeks are flush and she looks blindingly beautiful. She shakes her head and laughs again.

"I can't believe that just happened," she says and she makes a face that doesn't look like regret exactly, more like embarrassment.

I lift her off of the barre and slide her down my body. Her breath hitches when she feels how hard I still am and it takes serious restraint to not strip her bare and have my way with her right here and now. But it's not the time or place.

I bring her hand to my mouth and kiss her knuckles.

"I'm really glad that just happened," I tell her.

Her cheeks flush brighter. "You are?"

"An emphatic yes."

"Me too." Her gaze lowers and her eyes widen. "That looks uncomfortable though." She steps closer to me, her stomach pressed against my dick and I try to stand perfectly still.

"I'm fine, trust me." I smile and brush her hair away from her face.

She stands on her tiptoes and swivels her hips against me and I groan, putting my hands on her waist to still her when she does it again.

"Despite sticking my hand down your pants, I'm trying to be a gentleman here," I say, laughing.

With my hands on her waist, I lift her and place her a foot away from me.

Her eyes are dancing with mischief, and I'm relieved to see more than a little lust in them too.

"It just doesn't seem fair that I feel so good right now and you're left...hanging," she says.

I lift a shoulder. "Life isn't fair," I say.

Her head falls back with her laugh and I take her in. God, she's beautiful. We stare at each other for a long time, the air thick with desire.

"I interrupted you and it's getting late," I finally say.

"I'm glad you said...hello." She laughs again. "I'm done for the night and need to check on Earl. He's in the office."

"I can walk out with you if you want."

"Sure. That would be nice."

We walk back to the office and Earl is sleeping on top of a cardboard box.

"I bought him that cute little bed," she points at the fluffy bed in the corner, "and he keeps going for the boxes instead."

She's smiling as she grabs her bag and puts on my hoodie, shooting me a sheepish look. Fucking adorable. She bends down to pick up Earl. He blinks up sleepily at her and is so damn cute. I pet behind his ears and he leans into my hand.

"He really likes you," she says. "I mean, who doesn't?"

I want to kiss her again, but I keep my distance or we'll never get out of here.

"All right, I think I'm ready." She leads the way down the hall, and I watch the swish of her hair as she walks.

Everything about her mesmerizes me, and I'm not altogether sure what to do about it. I'm not used to being so consumed by a woman.

My girls and football, yes.

Part of me feels bad that I never felt this way about Bree. But it's making more sense every time I talk to Tru and with every interaction we have with one another, that this is something altogether different. This is how falling in love is supposed to feel. It helps lessen the guilt, knowing that Bree has had the same realization about me.

When we open the door, the air is chillier than it was and Tru shivers. I run my hands down her shoulders to warm her up as she locks the door and then she leans her back against my chest. We stand for a few seconds this way and then I lean in to kiss the side of her head.

"Come on, let's get you out of this cold night air." I step back and we walk to her car.

When she clicks the lock, I open the door for her and once she's in the driver's seat, I grin and say, "Good night, tiny dancer. I know who I'll be dreaming about tonight."

I shut her car door and she lifts her fingers to her lips and kisses them before holding them out my way. I smile and watch as she drives away.

Damn. What kind of magic has this woman cast on me?

CHAPTER TWENTY

OH, SO THIS IS...

TRU

I've been floating since that make-out session with Henley last night. I felt bad that I didn't reciprocate, but when I told him so in our text thread after I got home, he insisted he loved every second of what we did do and wouldn't change a thing.

He seemed so chill about it all, and I have to admit that whole thing with him holding back and saying he was trying to be a gentleman...I kind of love it. I love that he still wanted me so much when he said bye but didn't push even a little bit.

I hope he couldn't stop thinking about me all night long. That's selfish, I know, the poor guy needs to sleep and get relief, but I can't stop thinking about him, so we're kind of even. I've always heard you're supposed to leave a man wanting more, so there's that, but I also don't want to send him mixed messages. I think it's been clear all along that I want him. But all my good intentions to maintain boundaries and not date my student's dad are going out the window.

Our conversations alone have been chipping away at my resolve, but the way he made me feel last night...I've never felt like that. Ever.

When it's time for Cassidy's class, I notice right away that something's wrong. I overhear one of the girls talking about her and try to figure out what's going on, but I'm not able to in the short time before class. Afterwards, I'm tempted to ask her to stay behind, but I don't want to bring more attention to her. I end up following her out anyway.

"Cassidy, you got a minute?" I call.

She stops and turns, her eyes glossy with tears.

"Are you okay?" I ask quietly. "Can I help?"

"Those girls are just so mean sometimes. They made fun of me when I had to read something out loud in our class before this and were still laughing at me. I feel so stupid and like everybody knows it."

"You are not stupid, Cassidy. You're actually one of my smartest students," I whisper, "but don't tell anyone else I said that." I wink and I'm rewarded with a small smile. "Don't let them get to you. I know that's easier said than done, but their rudeness makes them small. And *you* are not small, you're kind and smart and lovely."

Her lower lip trembles. "Thank you, Miss Seymour." She blinks up at the ceiling and takes a deep breath.

"It's just the truth. I hope they'll wake up and realize the way they're acting is no way to treat someone, but you just keep being you. Because you're great."

She sniffles and a tear trickles down her cheek when she blinks. She hurriedly wipes it away.

"Okay, you better get to lunch before you miss out on whatever delicacies they're serving today."

She laughs. "Yeah, right. Okay. Thank you." She gives me another smile and looks the tiniest bit happier this time.

"I'll see you at dance tomorrow."

She nods and walks away, and I wish I could haul her out of here and treat her to a decent lunch and positive conversation, anything to keep cheering her up.

During my lunch break, I check my phone and smile at the messages from Henley.

> **HENLEY**
>
> A dancer with hair to her waist did in fact invade my dreams last night.

> **HENLEY**
>
> I'm hoping she'll invade them again tonight. Or even better, that she'd consider stepping out of my dreams and into my house at seven o'clock for dinner.

> How dare she take my place!

> **HENLEY**
>
> You could probably beat her out if you showed up a few minutes early. Drinks at 6:45?

I smile at my phone and then get another text from Sadie before I've responded to Henley.

> **SADIE**
> Hi! How are you? Felicity is coming Sunday to help with wedding stuff, but I wondered if you'd want to get drinks with us at The Fairy Hut at some point?

> Sure, I'd love to!

> **SADIE**
> Yay! I'm thinking 5ish? I've been awful at wedding planning, so I'm hoping we'll be done by then and won't bore you to death with all the details.

> Trust me, I won't be bored. And if you need any help, let me know! I LOVE planning any kind of party.

> **SADIE**
> I knew you and Felicity were two peas in a pod.

> <Smiling emoji>

I switch back to the thread with Henley and there's a new one from him. This man...I've never met anyone like him.

> **HENLEY**
> True confession: No one can take your place.

I press my lips together, but my insides are beaming and doing little leaps around this whole building.

> I'll be there.

HENLEY

And Earl, of course.

Thank you for putting up with my kitty.

HENLEY

I'll put up with your kitty any day, Tru. <Wink emoji>

I snort and glance around to see if anyone heard me, and of course, Mrs. Davenport is walking by at that exact moment. She looks at me with her usual pinched expression and I smile and wave. She just walks on like she can't be bothered by this weirdo and I'm too happy to let it faze me. I'm going to dinner at Henley's tonight and I can't wait.

He opens the door and his mouth gapes. Exactly the reaction I was hoping for. I grin as his eyes wander down my body. My dress is an off-the-shoulder A-line dress with a flowy skirt that hits just above my knees, and it's fire engine red. It shows off the little cleavage I have, and my shoulders and legs are showcased in their best light, if I do say so myself.

He takes my hand and kisses it before placing it on his chest where I can feel his heart galloping.

I smile and he does too.

"You look stunning," he says.

He's wearing a button-down shirt with the sleeves rolled up and jeans, and his feet are bare. His hair is damp on the ends and he smells divine.

"You do too," I say.

He tugs me in and closes the door behind me. I lean

against the door and he leans his hand on it as he comes within an inch of my face, his eyes on mine.

"I'm so glad you're here." He leans in and kisses me once. So soft and sweet.

He steps back and I want to pull him in again, run my fingers through his hair and kiss him until we're both breathless.

But he takes my hand and leads me into the kitchen where I can tell he's been working hard. There's a pile of dishes in the sink, a massive wooden bowl of Caesar salad and bottles of alcohol on the island, with limes and lemon zest in pretty little glass bowls.

I inhale and sigh. "It smells so good in here."

"I hope you meant it when you said you like spinach and mushroom lasagna. I made my mom's recipe."

My stomach does a little flip-flop. "You remember everything, don't you? I think I said that during one of our first texts."

"I remember everything about you." He smirks.

"Are you trying to seduce me, Henley Ward?"

"Is it working?"

Now I'm the one smirking. "Spinach and mushroom lasagna sounds delicious."

"Would you like a cocktail or wine?"

I point to the lemon vodka. "I can't resist anything with lemon."

"One lemon drop coming right up, tiny dancer."

My heart cannot take all this swoonworthiness. Made-up word, but it's entirely how I feel.

"Can I do anything to help?"

"You standing there looking the way you do in my kitchen is *extremely* helpful. Except you're taking my breath away, so I suggest you keep a safe distance. I want to feed you, but these hands have a mind of their own." He holds up his hands and waves his long, thick fingers.

My mind goes straight to the way those skilled fingers worked me over, and I flush. He smiles like he knows exactly where my mind is. It's the sexiest thing when he mixes the drink in the shaker; his forearms make my mouth water. He pours the drink into a pretty glass and garnishes it with a twist of lemon zest.

"You're not having one?" I ask when he hands it to me.

He grabs a glass and lifts a bottle of Jameson. "I'll have this." He pours the amber liquid into the glass and taps it against mine. "To a spectacular date."

"Oh, this is a date?" I can't stop smiling.

"It's absolutely a date." He can't stop smiling either.

"Good to know. To a spectacular date then." I tap his glass again and we take a sip of our drinks. "Oh, that's so good."

He leans over and kisses me. "Agreed," he says. "So good." He points to the table. "Have a seat. You're tempting me with those pretty lips."

I move to the other side of the island but don't sit down yet.

"Cassidy said she had a rough day at school today and you helped cheer her up. Thanks for that."

"I'm glad she talked about what happened. I spoke with Megan, the other teacher they share, to make her aware of the situation. We'll watch things and put a stop to anything we see happening. I want to mention it to Mr. Hanson on Monday as well."

"I appreciate that. It's hard to not be there to protect her."

We sit down and start eating, Earl sliding between our

legs like we're his own personal carwash, and the conversation flows easily from one topic to the next. Our meal is like a long session of foreplay with the lingering stares and flirty touches, everything heightened by the delicious food and drinks.

"This is the best meal I've had in a long time," I say, as I put my napkin on the table. "I'm really impressed that you know how to cook so well."

"Thank you. I enjoy it during the offseason. The girls and I took a few cooking classes in Denver. It's something we like to do together. Once I start playing again, my time in the kitchen is limited so it's a lot of grilling and quick meals." He leans in. "Do you like chocolate?"

"I adore chocolate."

His eyes crinkle as he smiles. "I was hoping you would. I have another true confession for you." His fingers slide through mine. "I'm no baker, but Wyndham and Greer from Serendipity make these hot lava cakes that are so good. It just takes a sec to heat up."

"Count me in, I'm all about it," I say.

He kisses the inside of my hand and stands up, taking our plates as he goes. I start helping him with the dishes, despite him telling me to relax. He works on the cake while I put the dishes in the sink.

When he drizzles chocolate over the top of the cake, I groan. "Oh, this is gonna be so good."

"You just wait," he says. "It's even better than it looks."

He's right. The dessert is next level. I struggle to not moan with every bite and he just laughs as he watches me with amusement.

"You're making it really hard to behave," he says.

"Why should you behave?" I smile as I eat the very last bite.

"Because it's only our first date."

"Did last night not count?" I tease. "It sure seems like it should."

He laughs and stands up, holding his hand out to me. When I stand, he puts his hand on my waist and his other hand slides up my neck.

"You're right. I kind of jumped a couple of bases last night, didn't I?" he says.

"Yes, you did...we did."

His head lowers and against my lips, he says, "Too soon?"

"Not even a little bit," I whisper.

Our kiss starts out slow and soft, but quickly escalates to a tornado. I feel his adoration, his desire, his hunger. His hands cup my face and my hands explore his back, but then they're everywhere. I want to rip his shirt off and crawl into his skin. When I stand on my tiptoes, he groans as our kisses become fevered, the desire for more an aching need. He lifts me up, my legs wrapping around his waist, and we kiss right there for the longest time.

He breaks our kiss, staring at me. "I didn't invite you to dinner to ravage you."

"No?" I poke my bottom lip out and he grins as he leans in to suck it.

"Regardless of how it may seem, no."

"Well, boo."

"I think it's obvious how much I want you...but I know you've had reservations and I don't want to do anything that scares you off."

"I've forgotten every reservation, and consider me completely on board with ravaging." I lean my forehead against his.

"Yeah?" His voice is hoarse and I shiver.

"Yes, please."

"In that case..." He carries me up the stairs, kissing me the whole way.

When we reach his room, he sets me on my feet and puts his hand on my cheek. "I've been thinking about you in my room ever since I kissed you in here...well, that's not true. It was before that." His lips pucker as he tries to hold back his grin. "Okay, since the day we met, I've thought about this."

"I have too."

I turn so my back's to him and look at him over my shoulder, moving my hair aside for him to unzip my dress. He takes a step closer and slowly lowers the zipper, his fingers like feathers down my skin. When the dress slides down my back, he kisses my shoulder and I slowly turn to face him.

He swallows hard when he sees my red strapless bra and matching panties.

"You're so beautiful, Tru." His raspy voice sends a shiver down me, and he notices, sliding his hands down my arms. "I'll warm you up."

I unbutton his shirt and it's a revelation. Did I ever doubt it would be?

"Henley," I whisper reverently, my hands roaming over his chest and down his stomach. His abs are taut, his chest expansive.

I've never felt so small yet powerful, as I do standing in front of this man.

I reach out and undo his pants, loving the quick intake of breath I hear when my fingers brush over his erection. I lower his pants and he steps out of them, standing in front of me looking like a chiseled god out of a mythology. The view of him in his boxer briefs has me gulping down a rush of lust and awe.

I unhook my bra and let it fall to the floor. He curses under his breath and his fingers lightly skim over my nipple. My heart thunders in my chest and my knees hit the back of the bed. He lifts me up until I'm lying in the center.

"Perfection," he whispers, looking down at me.

CHAPTER TWENTY-ONE

RIDE ME

HENLEY

I've never seen such a beautiful sight. My fingers trail over every inch of her body, and I enjoy the way she starts to squirm when she gets hungrier for more than just these slight touches. Her breasts are mouth-watering perfection, her dark, rosy nipples tightly budded and irresistible. I lean in to kiss them, one by one. She gasps when I tongue the tips and then suck them in, taking my time to give them the attention they deserve.

She arches against me, and my fingers glide down her toned stomach. When I reach the red lace, I slide it down her legs and groan when I take her in. My dick jolts and I palm myself so I'm not hanging out the top of my briefs' waistband. She bites her bottom lip...which undoes all my efforts.

"You don't need to hide," she says, leaning up on her elbows and coming so close to my dick, it jolts again. "I want to see you." Her smile is so damn alluring, I'm a fucking goner.

I lean back and take my boxer briefs off and she gasps when my dick bobs.

She pinches her arm. "Okay, I'm not dreaming. But seriously, what is this life? You are..." She shakes her head, as if she's speechless.

"*You* are..." I tell her, equally overwhelmed.

I kiss my way down her body until I'm between her legs and I spread her apart with my fingers. I hear a whimper and look up. She's leaned up on her elbows again, staring down at me.

"You're going to ruin me for everyone else, aren't you," she says, her eyes wide.

"Yes." I nod solemnly. "I fully intend to."

I flick her with my tongue and the sweet sounds she makes will be the death of me. I start out slow and steady, until she can't stop arching against my face, which drives me crazy. And when I dive in, she falls back against the pillow and shakes her head back and forth.

I can't stop watching her as I lick her senseless.

I also don't let up until she's fluttering against my tongue, her whimpers turning into her crying out my name.

It's the best goddamn sound I've ever heard.

When she's like melted butter, I lift my head and wipe off

some of her arousal from my mouth then kiss my way up her thighs and stomach.

"You taste so good," I say across her skin. "Feel so good. Look so good."

She mumbles something I can't quite make out and I smile against her breast, pausing to suck it for a second. She whimpers and pulls my hair, yanking my head up.

"That was otherworldly," she says.

"Otherworldly good?"

"Otherworldly amazing. But I want more of you," she says. "Come here."

I kiss her forehead and shift to get the new box of condoms I put in my nightstand. I open the box and pull one out, sliding it on quickly. She watches me like I'm her own private show, and I have to admit, it's a powerful rush. She looks sated and hungry at the same time, and I want to give her everything she's ever desired and also leave her craving more of me.

When I'm leaning over her, she looks nervous for a second.

"You okay? You still want this?" I ask.

"I want you more than anything. It's just…a little intimidating, seeing how huge you are." Her teeth slide over her bottom lip as she stares at my dick.

"We can take this as slow as you want," I tell her. "And we don't even have to do this tonight."

"No, please. I'm dying to," she says.

I lean down and chuckle into her neck. "Oh, Tru. What am I going to do with you?"

She pulls my head to her and kisses me. And I line up to her center, just nudging into her slightly and already loving how she feels. I groan when she lifts her leg and wraps her thigh around my waist. I inch in a little more with her movement and she gasps.

"Oh, that's really good," she whispers. "Really, really good."

"I can make it better," I say, dipping in more.

Her eyes glaze over and she hums when I pull out and the glide is easier on the way back in.

"You feel this?" I ask. "How perfect we are together?"

I'm trembling with restraint and there's a thin sheen of sweat covering our bodies as I slide in a little deeper with each thrust into her.

"So perfect," she says. She leans up to kiss me and gasps when I make it all the way inside of her. "*Oh*," she breathes.

I squeeze my eyes shut and pause for a moment. "I never want this to end," I say when I open my eyes again. "Let's do this all night."

"Yes, please. I never want to stop."

I pull back to watch as I slide in and out of her, the sound erotic and intoxicating. When I meet her eyes again, she's watching me and the emotion on her face is raw and vulnerable. An overwhelming rush of emotion floods through me. I can't describe it. I just know this is more than fucking.

I flip us so she's on top. "Ride me, tiny dancer. As fast or as slow as you want. God, you're beautiful."

I move her hair back so I can see all of her, and it's almost too much. I could come just looking at her, but the feel of her hips swiveling over me, the way her insides are squeezing me like a vise...it's a constant struggle to maintain my composure.

Her breasts bounce with her movements and then she tenses and tightens all around me. Her orgasm takes her by surprise, and her head falls back, her hair spilling onto my thighs. She shudders and I watch her in awe. When she's relaxed again, her eyes opening with that sated look that I can't get enough of, I hold her backside and thrust into her faster.

"Henley," she cries, her body warming up again.

I flip her onto her back again, and going faster and faster, I sink into her as deep as I can go.

"Yes," she whimpers. "Henley, I'm going to—"

"Me too. Come with me," I say, my voice ragged. "I want to feel you come with me."

One hand holds her backside and the other grips her hip as we both give it our all. My eyes are on hers and she doesn't look away even when she's so close. Her mouth parts and her entire body trembles as she falls over the edge. I have tunnel vision when my orgasm barrels through me, and every pulse and twitch I make, her insides squeeze back in response, making it feel like it lasts forever.

"What. Was. That?" she asks when I've collapsed on the other side of her.

"Best thing I've ever felt."

"Me too."

I take care of the condom, and she lays her head on my chest when I get back in bed. I trace circles over her back and she sighs, her fingers tickling my chest.

"Henley?"

"Yeah?" I smile down at her when she leans her chin on my chest.

"Was that as intense for you as it was for me?"

"Yes," I say emphatically. "And just you saying that out loud and looking at me with those eyes and those fucking lips has me ready for more."

Her eyes light up and she reaches down to feel me. "You're not lying."

"You'll find that I don't."

She sighs, and I jolt into her hand when she grips me tight.

"I like you so much," she says.

I let out a garbled sound when she slides her hand up and down. "I'm so glad, because I really, really like you. It would suck so bad if you didn't feel the same." I rub my hand down my face. "God, Tru. That's too good. Do you see what you do to me?"

"I do," she whispers, "and I love it so much."

"Is it too soon? Because I want you more than anything, but I don't want to hurt you."

"You won't hurt me. I want you and I don't want to wait another second." Her mouth is on mine in the next second and it's *heaven*.

Last night was one of the best nights of my life. I don't think we slept for more than an hour and I wouldn't change a single thing.

After she rides me in the shower, we contemplate whether to get back in bed or to eat breakfast. The only reason breakfast wins is because she has to get to the dance studio soon. I have to pick up the girls for dance today, but their class isn't until later.

I put on my sweats and Tru throws on my shirt. She looks so good in it, I want to strip it right off of her. Instead, I chase her into the kitchen, nuzzling her neck when I catch her.

"I think I'll just eat you instead," I say, burrowing my face into her neck while she cackles. "Oh, did we find another ticklish spot?"

She wiggles around, making me hard as a rock, and when

she turns in my arms, she points at me, looking cute as hell in her glasses.

"Behave."

"Do I have to?" I give her my most innocent expression and she giggles. "When you're all sexy librarian like this, I just want to be naughty."

I lean in and kiss her. Now that I've had a taste of her, I never want to stop.

A shriek startles both of us and I pull away to see where the sound came from. Cassidy stands on the other side of the island, staring at us in horror. She runs out of the room. I let go of Tru and hurry after Cassidy. She's going out the front door when I get there.

"Cassidy, wait—"

She keeps going and runs to the car where Bree is waiting. Bree looks at her and then me in confusion.

"What happened?" she asks. "What is it?"

"Just go, Mom. Just go," Cassidy says.

"Wait, Cassidy. Talk to me." I lean down to see her better and she won't look at me. Fuck.

Bree looks at me with wide eyes and I grimace.

"I'll come pick you up in a couple hours for dance," I tell Cassidy.

"I'm not going," she says through her tears. She lifts up the book she must have left at my house. "I've got a lot of homework."

"Will someone tell me what's going on?" Bree says.

"I don't want to talk about it," Cassidy says. "Please, Mom, just take me *home*."

"Cassidy, we need to talk about this," I say. "When I drop Audrey off after dance, you and me...okay?"

She stares straight ahead and I feel like shit. I don't regret a second of being with Tru last night, but this is exactly what

Tru was worried about. It would've been so much better to ease the girls into this.

"All right. I love you, bunny. I'll see you in a little while." I tap the car and nod at Bree. "I'll explain everything later," I say under my breath.

When I get back in the house, Tru isn't in the kitchen. I find her in my room with her clothes on and she's fumbling around, holding Earl and trying to get her shoes on. She looks panicked. I put my hand on her arm and she jumps.

"Tru. Are you okay? I'm so sorry that happened."

"I'm the one who should be sorry. I knew better than to let this happen. Cassidy shouldn't have to deal with this and—"

"I agree, I wish I'd talked about us with the girls first, but it'll be okay. I don't regret anything, Tru." I try to meet her eyes and she won't let me. "Hey, look at me."

When she does, I'm concerned with what I see there. Or what I don't see is probably more accurate. The walls are back up and she's shut me out. The vulnerability between us all night is there, but it feels like we're both on separate islands.

"Last night was—" she starts.

"Unbelievable," I finish.

Her jaw clenches. "But it shouldn't have happened. Not yet. I'm making such great progress with Cassidy and I might've just ruined it all."

"No, I just need to talk to her. She was upset, but it'll—"

She turns and puts her hand on my chest, stopping me. Her eyes are glassy when she looks up at me. "I'll never forget last night. Ever. It was..." She shakes her head. "Well, I've never experienced anything even close to that, so trust me when I say it was unbelievable for me too, but this is exactly what I was afraid of. Your girls are the most important people in your life and they should be. And I'm an important role in her life right now for this limited time, and I don't want to mess any of it up."

She turns and picks up the shirt of mine that she discarded in her rush to change. And then she walks toward the door, Earl still tucked close.

"Don't go. Let's talk about this. It feels like you're ending things before we've even fully begun." I follow her to the door and she looks at me over her shoulder.

"I'm pausing things...not ending..."

I exhale, my shoulders sagging in relief. "Good."

"But it's probably best that we don't see each other until the summer...if then. We can see how the girls feel about things then."

"That's a couple of months away." After the elation of last night and how right everything felt, I don't want to be away from her for a day, much less *months*.

She nods, swallowing hard. "I'm glad we had last night."

CHAPTER TWENTY-TWO

ALREADY LOST

TRU

I've never had a night like the one I just had.

It was pure magic. I felt like I was living in a dream, floating on air...and like I would never come back to Earth.

The connection Henley and I share.

The intimacy that's so easy and comfortable, while also being electrifying and mind-blowing...I didn't even know that was a possibility, to have it all.

We stayed up all night, learning each other's bodies, and

he made me feel things I've never felt. He handled me like I weighed nothing, moving me into various positions and angles, doing most of the work, while I turned into a pleasure-filled puddle.

I still hear the way his voice rasped when he said, "Wait, don't come yet."

It was the time early this morning before we fell asleep. I thought for sure I was so wrung out with pleasure, I wouldn't be able to orgasm even one more time, but I held on and he made it so good. It was wild and frantic and perfect, and I came twice. And again, later in the shower.

But wow, did we come crashing down.

Talk about a severe reality check.

The look on Cassidy's face when she saw me in her dad's shirt, cuddled up to him…I think it will haunt me forever. She looked devastated and shocked and so hurt.

I'm talking to Jacklyn and a few of the girls when Henley walks into the studio with Audrey.

No Cassidy.

Our eyes meet…I can't look at him without thinking of all the things he did to me last night. All the things we did. My cheeks heat. He smiles like maybe he's thinking about the same things. My smile drops quickly and I try to focus on what's being said around me.

I want to rush over there and ask him about Cassidy, but if I talk to him, it feels like everyone will know what we did. I can't even look at him without flushing right now, and all the mothers already watch him like a hawk as it is.

I want him to hug me and tell me everything's going to be okay. I want to take back the things I said about putting everything on hold, taking a break. I hated the whole *Friends* plot where Ross and Rachel were taking a break. It made me never like Ross again. And what I'm doing feels even more risky because we don't have years of friendship behind us like Ross and Rachel.

And why in the world am I comparing us to a 90s sitcom?

Henley and I are on shaky legs at best. What we shared last night was life-changing for me, but maybe he has nights like that with random strangers or maybe it used to be an everyday occurrence with his ex-wife for all I know. What felt special to me might not be as special to him and we could have risked his relationship with his daughters over something that was meant to be nothing more than a fun night together.

What if Bree is upset that he's sleeping with her daughter's teacher and goes to the school? I could lose my job...

I feel sick.

I watch as he lingers, looking like he wants to speak with me, but it's time for class to start. I move to the front of the class and watch as Audrey lines up with the rest of the girls. She waves at her dad and he lingers a few minutes more before ducking out of the studio.

I don't watch him walk away even though I want to more than anything.

This already hurts and we barely even got started.

After class, I hurry to the office, hoping to avoid seeing him again. I'm surprised he wasn't here waiting at the end of class, like he usually is, but maybe he wants to avoid seeing me too. I get through the rest of the classes in a blur.

Jacklyn asks if I'm okay, and I smile and nod. "I'm just tired. I didn't sleep much last night. Sorry if I'm acting like a downer."

"No," she tsks. "You're fine. Just not your usual smiley self."

"I'll be okay. I'm going to get some rest this weekend."

"Sounds good."

After we say bye, I'm still not ready to go home. So Earl and I wander through town, him happy hanging out in my hood. He's almost getting too big to do that now, but not quite, although he is peeking out way more than he did in the beginning.

"Do you think you'd like walking on a leash?" I ask him as we pass one cute dog after the other. Silver Hills seems to be the dog mecca. I've seen every kind of cute dog imaginable here and it makes me wish I had one. Although Earl is doing plenty to keep me busy.

I pass the cute bookstore, Twinkle Tales, and decide to go in, making sure to tuck Earl lower into my hood. I'm startled when something rubs against my leg and look down to see a massive orange tabby.

"Why, hello," I say, looking down. "Aren't you beautiful and huge!"

A girl laughs as she looks down at me from a ladder. She's beautiful with mahogany skin and natural curls held back with a colorful bandana.

"I hope you're okay with cats. That's Hank. He's got a loud bark, but he's friendly."

"Ooo, a cat that barks. I'm intrigued. I hope it's okay I brought this guy." I turn and show her my hood, and Earl's head pops out. "This is Earl. I have a hard time leaving him at home."

"Oh my goodness," she croons, lowering herself off of the ladder. Now I can see that she's probably more my age than I'd originally thought. "What a cutie. I haven't seen him yet. I haven't seen you yet either. Who are you?"

I laugh. "I'm Tru. I just moved into town not too long ago and I'm loving it. I actually came into your shop once with my mom when we were driving through and have wanted to come back ever since I moved here."

"I'm really glad to hear that. You would've met my aunt probably, when you visited before. I just recently took over the shop." She makes a face. "It still feels weird to say that." She lifts her hands. "She insists I call it my shop, but I think it'll always be my aunt's in my head."

I nod, grinning. "I get that."

"I'm Calista, by the way. Oh! Hey!" She brightens up even more when another gorgeous girl walks into the shop. Her cheeks are flushed from the wind and her dark hair is in a high pony but still looks long over her shoulder. "And this is my bestie, Elle." She gets a sly look on her face. "Maybe you can take the place of being my other bestie since I'm always sharing this one with Rhodes Archer." She rolls her eyes, but sings Rhodes' name, and I laugh when Elle groans and rolls her eyes back just as dramatically.

"Oh, I've met Rhodes!" I say brightly, and the two of them look at me with interest.

Elle nods at me knowingly. "You do look like his type."

"Oh, no. I'm not. We don't. I-uh, no." I put my hand to my face and laugh awkwardly. "I met him at Sadie and Weston's house."

"Aren't they great?" Elle says. "But I assure you, you *are* Rhodes' type."

"Isn't everyone?" Calista snorts. "Sorry, I didn't mean it," she adds when Elle glares at her.

"I'm not...Rhodes' type. Well, I mean, I don't think...he didn't act...I like one of his friends," I spit out. And then I cover my face in horror. "Oh, God. This is why I need to always be on the move. Apparently, I don't know how to keep my mouth shut."

I feel a hand on my shoulder and lower my hands to look at them. Both girls stand there smiling at me, barely able to contain their delight.

Calista's hand drops. "Tell us everything. I'm dying to know which friend you're talking about…"

The door opens and Sadie walks in. My cheeks flame and I fan them as I try to act casual but friendly.

"It's a party," Calista sings. "Hi, Sadie. Where's Caleb?"

"Hi!" Sadie says. "Ahhh, you met Tru. Don't you love her?"

Calista and Elle both say *yes* at the same time and my insides flood with warmth. Sadie hugs all of us and then leans on the counter next to me.

"Weston took him swimming at Bowie's. He has the indoor pool."

Calista and Elle both turn to look at me, trying to gauge my reaction and I laugh, shaking my head.

"What did I miss?" Sadie looks at me.

"Tru was just telling us she'd met Rhodes at your house… and she insists she's not his type, but she likes one of his friends…" Calista says. She makes an apologetic face. "Sorry, there's a reason small towns are known for the gossip."

Sadie looks over at me and winks. "I think I have a pretty good idea."

"My bet is on Penn," Calista says. "That boy is fine. A little too pretty for me, but *fine*."

Elle shakes her head. "I think Bowie. He's hot and so mysterious. You never fully know what he's thinking, but know he would lift a car off of you if he had to."

We all crack up at that.

"Lift a car off of you?" Calista repeats. "Is that what every woman wants?" She lifts her hand. "Yes, please. I do."

We laugh again.

"You've already got a man who would do that." Elle

moves a stack of books and pokes Calista in the side. "Javi worships the ground you walk on, and he's hot as hell."

"Oh yeah, that's right." Calista grins.

Sadie smiles at me again.

And I don't know if it's because I miss my mom, or if it's because these girls are so fun and sweet and easy to be around, but I open my mouth and start talking.

"It's Henley. But we can't be a thing. We can't. And it's too late to even say that because from the moment we met, there was an instant spark, but I'm his daughter's English teacher, and I also teach the dance class two of his daughters are in...and it's just...I'm making progress with..." I shake my head. I'm talking *way* too fast. "It just can't happen again."

"Damn," Elle says, staring at me. The grin on her face just keeps growing. "I am in awe of you, girl. Henley Ward has been putting out the off-limits vibe for as long as I've known him. I've seen what happens when he goes out with the guys. The women swarm Henley, and I've never seen him pay them any attention. So when you say there was an instant spark, and it sounds like something has *already happened*, my hat is off to you."

"Oh, there's a spark between them all right. More like a raging bonfire," Sadie says.

I fan my face, laughing.

Calista claps her hands. "I mean, I would have said Henley first, except exactly what Elle is saying. That man is so hot and he just keeps getting better. And look at you with this little age gap thing going. That is so sexy," she says.

We all laugh and I put my hands on my fevered face.

"I need to forget about the sparks we might have because his daughter caught me at his place this morning. And I put an end to whatever we had just started."

"*No*," Calista moans.

"Aw, Tru," Sadie says. "You guys can work it out, right?"

"I'm not sure. I think the timing is all wrong." I lift my shoulder and try to act nonchalant about it, but I can tell they see through me.

This whole conversation is so much better than the tears I would've been shedding if I'd gone home instead.

I do see that in my future tonight though.

CHAPTER TWENTY-THREE

PEACEFUL BADGERING

HENLEY

I shoot the guys a text before I leave for Bree's house. She ended up picking up Audrey from dance, so I still haven't talked to her about anything.

> I need a meeting ASAP.

PENN

> I can be there in ten.

I can't actually meet right now. Just putting it out there that it needs to be soon.

RHODES

Name the time and we'll come running.

BOWIE

You okay, man?

Yes and no.

WESTON

You sure you can't meet now? Caleb and I are at Bowie's right now. Come over.

I have to talk to Cassidy. She caught Tru at my house this morning. Tru was wearing nothing but my shirt...

RHODES

Shit. I mean, my first thought is that's hot as fuck. But not the Cassidy part.

Right. Not the Cassidy part. And don't be thinking about Tru in nothing but my shirt.

RHODES

LOL. Okay! I like jealous Henley!

PENN

I don't know what to say. Kids are hard, man. Sam is moody as fuck. Right when I thought we had some things figured out, I take him out for chicken last night and he was mopey.

WESTON

Remember how you felt between ten and fifteen?

PENN

No

WESTON

Well, think about it for a minute and get
back to me.

PENN

<eye roll emoji> That's what you guys are
for, so I don't have to be all wise and shit.

RHODES

LOL You said it, not me. We have it in
writing that you think we're wise. I like how
this day is turning out. Sorry, Hen. I'm not
discounting your feelings, man. Let us know
how your talk with Cassidy goes.

Will do. I'll see where you guys are after this.

I knock on the door and am about to knock again when
the door opens. Gracie is standing there in the outfit she wore
to the last Super Bowl, a white tux with a turquoise bowtie.

I lift my eyebrows. "You're looking great. Going somewhere, peanut?"

She smiles coyly. "Nope. Come in, Father."

"Father..." I make a face at her and she presses her lips
together to keep from laughing. "Who are you and what have
you done with my daughter?"

"I'm Gracie!" she insists. "Come on." She turns and
waves her hand for me to follow.

We walk through the house and to the back door, which
she opens with a flourish. A ballad plays over the outdoor
speakers. Audrey is standing in front of a table set for two
and is in one of her pretty dresses. Electric candles are lit all
over the deck and table.

"Hi, Daddy." She smiles and holds out a chair for me, motioning for me to have a seat.

I move toward her and kiss her cheek. "Hi, pumpkin. You look lovely."

"Thank you." Her smile widens when I sit down and she puts a napkin over my lap.

"Wow. What did I do to deserve all this?"

A throat is cleared and I look up to see Cassidy, who is also dressed up. I smile at her and am relieved when she smiles back. It's only then that I notice Bree is standing behind her, looking like she just swallowed something painful. I get a sudden sense of dread.

"What's going on, girls?"

"We wanted to do something nice for the two of you," Cassidy says, moving aside and motioning for Bree to sit down next to me. "Since you both do so much for us."

I'd foolishly thought maybe the other place setting was for Cassidy and me to talk things over.

"Girls," Bree starts...

"Wine?" Cassidy interrupts, holding up the bottle of chilled wine out of the ice bucket. She pulls out a bottle opener. "I looked up how to do it online."

"I'll do that." I take it from her and open the bottle. "Would you like some?" I ask Bree.

She nods and I fill our glasses.

"What is this really about?" I ask Cassidy and then Audrey and Gracie. Their looks are fleeting before also turning toward Cassidy.

"What I said," Cassidy says, her smile faltering for only a second. "We wanted to do something nice for you guys."

"I do need to talk to your mother, but then I want to talk to all of you," I say.

Cassidy gulps and nods. "We'll bring out the food and

you can take all the time you need to talk and...and enjoy being outside on this nice day."

"Smell the flowers!" Gracie yells across the deck.

Audrey giggles and goes into the kitchen. Cassidy and Gracie follow her inside and Bree and I are left to look at each other in concern.

"Are our daughters trying to matchmake us?" Bree whispers. She picks up her glass of wine and takes a long gulp.

"It looks that way." I take a long drink myself.

"What happened this morning? Cassidy wouldn't talk about it and then they've been super secretive all afternoon, shooing me out of the kitchen any time I tried to go in."

"There was a woman at my house when Cassidy came in this morning." I scrunch up my nose. "Not the way I wanted to tell any of you about this."

"Oh. *Oh*." She looks at me with interest and then clinks my glass. But then her shoulders deflate. "Wait, what exactly did Cassidy see? Because she was upset." Her eyes widen. *"Did she see you having sex with someone?"*

"*No*. No, she didn't." I look around to make sure the girls aren't nearby. "But a heads-up that she was coming inside would've been nice. I don't want them to ever feel like they have to knock when they come to my house, but...yeah, it could've been much worse." I shudder thinking about it.

"Well, who is it?" Bree waves her hand to hurry me along. "And you still haven't said what she saw."

"It's Tru Seymour and she was in my shirt."

Bree leans back in her chair and then picks up her glass and empties it in one long gulp.

"You would pick the one person who makes it complicated," she groans.

"I don't really get why it has to be—"

"She's her teacher, Henley."

"I met her before she was her teacher."

She stares at me in shock and then shakes her head. "I should've known. I thought you were dressed extra nice for a teacher conference." She snorts and then sits up straight when the girls bring out salads and dinner rolls. We thank them and start eating, talking quietly so the girls don't hear us.

"I'm glad you're dating, Hen. Not who I would've picked, but—" She lifts her shoulder.

"Good thing I wasn't asking you," I say dryly and she smirks.

"Touché. And I didn't mean anything bad about it. Just… it is complicated with her being Cassidy's teacher. They're working so hard together on the reading stuff…" She leans in. "And she's, what? Early twenties?"

I scrub my hand over my face. "God, Bree. You don't have to make it sound so dirty. She's twenty-four. Yeah, she's young. But she's brilliant and funny and we click."

"You really like her," she says, her eyes assessing me shrewdly.

"Yes, I really like her. But this conversation might be pointless after she went running out of the house today, traumatized because *she* had traumatized our daughter. She didn't want to do this yet, get involved with me. So, it's probably a non-issue. I'm pretty sure she dumped me this morning."

"What? Already? Why? I'm sorry. No, I'm sure she'll come back around. She was probably just embarrassed and—"

We stop when the girls bring out steaks and baked potatoes.

"Steak! What is this?" I look up at the girls who are all standing shy but proud near the table. "Someone's been holding out on their cooking skills before now."

Cassidy lifts her shoulder in a shrug that looks just like

her mother and I laugh. "We've been watching cooking shows."

"And lots of YouTube videos," Audrey adds.

Gracie starts to say something and Cassidy motions for them to follow her back into the kitchen. They scurry off like little elves.

"This is weird," I say under my breath. "What are we going to do about this?"

"We need to have a talk with them. Tonight. But first, I want to eat this steak and have another glass of wine in peace."

I chuckle. "Oh, this is peaceful for you? Maybe I can badger you a little bit about Alex to even it out a little bit."

She frowns and then laughs. "Is that what I'm doing? Badgering? Ugh. Sorry. It's just…you haven't really dated anyone and it's an important decision, who we have in the kids' lives."

"I know it is, and I don't take it lightly. I don't just bring anyone into my house…Tru's different."

"I can see that." She smiles. "I'm happy for you, Hen. If you're happy, I'm happy. And the girls will get on board too."

"As I said, I think it's all up in the air, so—"

Surprise flickers across Bree's face as she takes a bite of the steak. "Not bad."

I agree. "I'm going to put them to work cooking more often."

When they bring out the dessert—vanilla ice cream with strawberries and chocolate syrup—I ask them to join us at the table. They're so quick to bring it out that it's obvious they'd already prepared their somewhat heartier portions of dessert.

I point at Gracie's bowl and then mine. "Did you accidentally give me the baby bear portion and take the papa bear portion?"

She frowns and shakes her head. "They look the same to me."

"Mm-hmm," I tease and she hurries and takes a big bite of her ice cream. "So, your mom and I want to talk to you. Thanks for this amazing dinner. It's all been delicious and we're both going to have you start cooking more."

We laugh when they look at each other like *Oops, what have we done?*

"But we need to talk about why you guys did this for us. I think maybe because your mom and I are such good friends and that's unusual to see with some divorced parents, it could seem like maybe there's hope of us getting back together." I look at each one of them in the eye and my heart hurts with how closely they're listening and how hopeful they look. "Your mom and I stayed together longer than we probably should have because of wanting to make sure we provided a good home for our little ladies. We still want that for you, but like we've said before, we're not getting back together."

Gracie's lip pokes out. "But why?"

"Because we're better like this," Bree says. "We're better as friends. We can love you better this way. We can love each other better this way. And there will be other people in our lives." She looks at me and I nod.

"Exactly. Your mom is dating Alex and happy with him. Whoever we're with, you guys are always taken into consideration."

Cassidy's face falls. "But my teacher? You're really going to date my teacher?"

"Wait, what?" Audrey says. "What do you mean?"

"He's with Miss Seymour," Cassidy says, flinging her arm my way.

I hold up my hand. "I wish I'd had a chance to talk to you all about it before you found out, Cassidy. I like Miss

Seymour. Tru. I like her a lot. But she's had reservations about being with me because she's your teacher too, and I don't know what's going to happen with her. But we need to first establish that your mom and I are *not* happening. We decided that a long time ago when we got divorced, and that's not changing."

Audrey nods like she expected this. "I think it's cool that you guys get along so well. Briana's parents are divorced and they hate each other. And they always make her feel bad when she goes to the other parent's house. She says it's the worst."

"I think it's cool that you get along too," Cassidy says, "but I still don't understand why you're not perfect for each other. It seems like you are to me."

"I *like* Miss Seymour," Gracie says. "I like her a lot. I didn't know you were dating her. It's weird, but if you were going to date anybody, I guess she's the best one it could be besides Mom." She looks at Bree like she's making sure that's okay to say.

Bree smiles reassuringly at her.

Cassidy groans. "No, it's wrong. It's weird. And I don't like it."

"Your dad is being gracious to talk this over with all of us. When I started dating Alex, I didn't ask your permission, and your dad doesn't have to ask our permission about Miss Seymour either. Tru," she adds, smirking at me.

Cassidy starts crying. "It's so embarrassing. I already get made fun of at school and now everyone will talk about this."

"No one will kn—" I start, but she runs inside.

I follow her, but she's faster and when I knock on the door, she yells.

"I don't want to talk about it anymore."

Fucking hell.

Penn and Rhodes meet us at Bowie's. Weston runs Caleb home to hand him off to Sadie and when he walks in, he slaps The Single Dad Playbook on the table. We talk about the way my night went right off the bat. They look as bewildered as I feel.

Weston points at our notebook. "I'm sorry we don't really have the advice for you on all this, Hen. We're looking at you to lead the way through the teenage years."

I shake my head, as I let out a long exhale. "And hopefully none of you will ever have to go through a divorce." I give Bowie an apologetic look because what he went through with his ex-girlfriend over Becca was worse than any divorce. He squeezes my shoulder in response. "But guys, I think it might be the Wild, Wild West when it comes to teenagers. I called Jeremy on the way over here and he alluded to as much. No help whatsoever." I chuckle as I see the concerned looks on their faces. "It ended okay tonight. Cassidy's gonna take a while, but I think she'll come around."

"What about Tru? What's happening with her?" Rhodes asks.

"She ended things...or paused them, I guess." I lean forward, my elbows on my knees and looked down. "After the best night I've ever had. I don't know...I'm going to respect her wishes, but fuck, the last thing I want from her is space."

CHAPTER TWENTY-FOUR

SUFFERING

TRU

I've managed to get through a day and a half of not texting Henley. I feel the void like an aching hole in my chest because we've been talking more and more every day. I feel sick about the way we ended things. I thought I'd hear from him yesterday and am surprised...and a little hurt that I still haven't.

But you ended it, I remind myself. *You said it was best to not see each other until the summer, if then.*

But why did he have to go and listen to me?

I park in front of The Fairy Hut to meet the girls and am glad for the distraction tonight. Sadie invited Calista and Elle while we were together at the book store yesterday and I'm excited to spend time with all of them again, Felicity too.

When I walk in, Sadie and Felicity are already at a table and they wave me over. Felicity stands up to hug me and then I hug Sadie too before sitting down.

"This is such a cute place." I look around, taken in by the whimsical decor.

The doors and windows are arched, and it looks like it could be the same builder who designed Henley's kitchen with the unique wooden turrets.

Calista and Elle come in while I'm laughing about the menu. The names are hilarious.

"Don't be scared off by the names of things," Elle says, when I repeat *Cow Slobber Soup?* under my breath.

"Beyond the Goat Hollow has become my signature drink," Sadie says, laughing. "I couldn't tell you what all is in it…too many things to remember…but it's delicious."

Sadie and Felicity talk about their day with the wedding plans and both have us laughing hysterically over Felicity's Type-A level of organization and Sadie's go-with-the-flow, keep-things-simple mentality. They're a riot together and I love that they're gonna be sisters-in-law because you can tell they adore one another. Henley has told me just a little bit about Sadie. She lost her sister unexpectedly, so I'm really glad she has people she cares about in her life who have helped her through this healing process. They all seem like such great people. I find out too that Rhodes has a little boy named Levi who Elle is crazy about.

"So you guys are best friends, or is there maybe more?" I ask.

Everyone stops and looks at Elle as she shakes her head and laughs.

"No, we're just friends. We've always just been friends. And we'll only ever be friends. He's always been hands-off, but now that I'm trying out for a spot on the Mustangs cheer team, that settles it!" She laughs and does a little dance in her seat. "The cheerleaders can't associate with the players."

"What? I didn't know you're a cheerleader! It makes sense though. You are *hot*," I say.

They all laugh, and Elle's cheeks flush. "Thank you. We'll see if I get far enough. And I'm surrounded by hotties," she says. "I've been in a relationship for a long time with Bernard, but—" She and Calista exchange a look.

"But we're trying to talk her out of that one, me and Rhodes," Calista says. "Have been for a while."

Elle makes a face. "Yeah, she's not lying. He's not their favorite. And not mine right now either." She shakes her head. She's quiet for a few minutes after that and the conversation turns to Henley.

"Have you heard from him?" Sadie asks.

"No, nothing, but I can't blame him. I told him we should end things." I swallow hard. "It's my fault and I knew we were a bad idea to begin with, but—"

I hear a loud burst of laughter coming through the door and turn to see *the* five men from the Colorado Mustangs walking in together, looking like every woman's fantasy.

Every woman in the restaurant turns and looks their way. It's like a collective pause that takes place, the noisy chatter dying down to a bated breath of anticipation. I watch as they sit down not too far from us, and Weston and Sadie make eye contact. He blows her a kiss and she blows one back.

"Did you plan this?" I ask her.

"No, I swear I didn't," she says, laughing. "But there are

only so many places you can go in Silver Hills without running into someone you know. I did plan the other time… and the time before that." She laughs. "But not tonight, I promise."

I'm laughing when I look at Henley and he catches me staring at him. He looks serious and like he hasn't slept since our night together. I haven't slept much either, so I know the feeling. He still looks so good, but I feel the weight of his sad eyes on me and stand up suddenly, moving toward the restroom. I need to get away from here or I will be tempted to jog over there and crawl into his lap.

I rinse my face with cold water, shake my hands out, jump around, wiggling my arms as I try to psych myself out in the mirror.

"You can do this. He's just a very hot, sexy man that you like so much and had a life-altering night with. You can be in the same room with him and not jump him. You can be in the same room with him and not look desperate. You've got this."

I point at myself once more emphatically before I walk out and run right into Henley Ward.

Damn, he feels so good.

"Hey," he says, looking down at me.

His hands steady my shoulders.

"Hey," I say back.

"You look beautiful."

"So do you."

"I miss you."

"It has felt like a long day and a half." My voice is half tease, half earnest.

He smiles. "The longest." He leans in close and whispers, "I don't want to wait until summer."

"I don't either."

"It's been torture not talking to you for the past...*longest* day and a half."

"I know. I've hated it." I stare at the scruff he's grown over the weekend, thinking there's no way this man could ever look bad. "But our situation hasn't changed."

He groans. "I know. The girls planned an elaborate setup for me and Bree last night. Steak dinner on the deck, candles, flowers, the whole works. We had a talk. I think they get the message that their mom and I are not gonna be together. But things might take a little longer for Cassidy to be on board with me dating you. And it's not because she's not crazy about you. I think it's because she *is*."

"It's okay. I get it. I would be worried about the whole thing if I were her. Especially at that age, it would have been a lot to take in. I don't blame her for feeling weird about it."

Someone walks past us and he takes a step back until they move into the restroom and then he steps closer again.

"It's hard to be this close to you and not touch you," he says.

"Believe me, I'm struggling with not climbing your body like a tree right now."

He groans. "You can't say things like that to me and not expect me to kiss you senseless."

"I don't feel your lips on mine." I lift my shoulder, smirking.

"Oh, you're trouble, tiny dancer. How about this? We don't have any public tree climbing or declarations. But what happens at my house or your house...or when we're alone in a dark alcove at The Fairy Hut stays between us."

"I may or may not have told my new girlfriends about my crush."

"Is that what we're calling it? Because my guys know and

have from the beginning. The very first day I met you, I told them about you."

"You're kidding," I say, intrigued and a little dizzy from all the swooning going on inside. "But okay, I can agree to those terms. We keep this a secret except between our close friends for now. Are you really okay with that?"

"I don't like Cassidy not being on board with this," he says. "But I feel like she just needs time and we can give her that while we see where all this can go between us."

I nod, feeling winded just being near him. "Okay, I can do that. No pressure, just the two of us privately…seeing what happens."

"Can I see what happens at your place tonight after this?" His lips lift and I laugh, looking away from him because if I don't, I won't be able to resist him.

"I think we need to sleep through the night. You at your place and me at mine," I add, when he starts to insist we *will* sleep. "I already don't know if I can look Cassidy in the eye tomorrow. If we spent the night together tonight, I…" I shake my head and make a face.

He lifts his hand to my cheek and glides it over my skin softly. "Fair enough," he says. "I'll be thinking about you all night long though. You invaded my dreams last night and woke me up multiple times. This body is suffering from the loss."

I laugh, thrilled by the things he's saying. Knowing I have this effect on him makes all the suffering I've dealt with since yesterday morning worth it.

"You'll survive," I tell him.

He shakes his head. "I'm not sure I will, but this tonight has been almost exactly what I needed."

We grin at each other like two whipped puppies and I take a step back.

"Oh...how about I meet with Cassidy at school this week, just to make it a little easier on all of us?"

"That doesn't sound easier for me at all, but I'll agree to whatever you say."

I nod. "I think that would be the best. We can gradually move back to house sessions if she gets more comfortable, but for now, let's do this."

"Okay, I'll follow your lead."

I lean up and kiss him on the cheek and he turns at the last second so our lips brush against each other's. I suck in a breath and meet his eyes, feeling a rush of adrenaline so powerful it makes me woozy.

"I'll just go sit down now with my friends," I say, breathlessly.

He holds his hand out gallantly. "After you."

When we get back, a table has been pulled up to ours and the guys are sitting there. Henley ends up next to me, his thigh touching mine. He slides his hand up my leg and looks over at me.

"Things are looking up, tiny dancer."

CHAPTER TWENTY-FIVE

NEW NORMAL

HENLEY

The next day, I'm in the school parking lot, tapping the steering wheel and wondering whether I should go in and see what's taking Cassidy so long. Her tutoring session with Tru was supposed to end ten minutes ago. I turn on the radio, trying to chill because I know part of this impatience is that I want an excuse to see Tru.

But I also really want to make sure both of them are okay in there.

Finally, Cassidy walks out of the building and saunters to the SUV. It's a weird phenomenon that happens when kids get to a certain age. They go from running everywhere to experimenting with the speeds of turtles.

She gets inside and slumps back in her seat.

"How did it go?"

"Fine, Dad. It went fine. Okay? I wasn't rude. I didn't act like a child the way you expected me to."

I touch her shoulder, and when she doesn't look at me, I tilt her chin so she meets my eyes.

"Bunny. I know you're not a rude person. I didn't expect you to act like a child. I'm asking how it went with the reading." *And okay, yes, how it went with Tru.* "I've been in on this process for most of the time you've worked with Miss Seymour. I want to keep hearing about how it goes even if I'm not around some of these tutoring sessions for a while."

She waves her hand. "That part was normal. I don't know…it's helping, I think. But I felt dumb. Like I made it weird the other day. I didn't *want* to be weird. I like her. You know I like her *so much*."

She looks at me and empathy floods through me. My girl is trying so hard and it's fucking hard to grow up and deal with all the things.

"I know you do. I know all of this is strange. And weird and uncomfortable. But your sessions with her are important to me and I know they're important to her. I don't want anything to get in the way of that."

"It won't. She was nice. She acted even better than normal." She sighs and lets her head fall back against the seat. "She's really great, okay? I'm sorry I'm being mean about you and her."

"You don't need to apologize for anything. In fact, you don't have to think about me and Tru at all. Focus on your schoolwork. Focus on being who you are. Being the great sister and daughter you already are. And I'll focus on my… stuff too," I finish lamely.

I try not to swear in front of my kids, but the battle is uphill a lot of the time.

"I love you, bunny."

"I love you too."

"Okay, let's get home. Your sisters are anxiously waiting for you so you can play this new game we got…about cats."

"How about you just *get* us a cat instead of giving us a new game about cats?"

"Very funny, har-har."

"I missed seeing Earl…since we met at school instead of the house…"

I don't say anything but file that away for later. Maybe keeping things quiet won't have to last very long.

I want to call Tru. I'm tempted to stop by her house, but I don't. I'm trying to take things slowly, which is what I think she wants. But damn, it's hard. When I get home from dropping the girls off, Tru texts, and I feel like a kid because I'm so excited and relieved to be hearing from her.

TRU

Things went well with Cassidy today.

Cassidy thought so too, and I'm really glad you also felt that way. She reiterated again how much she likes you, and she's sorry for being mean, which I told her she's not. She's just human, and this is a weird situation, but I think she's already softening toward the idea. I really do.

TRU

I'm so glad to hear that. We had a productive day, and I think it's a good move to keep working at the school for now. I told her I was sorry she saw anything that might make her uncomfortable and she turned bright red and said she's totally fine. I don't fully buy that, but we both did our best to act normal, and by the end of our session, it felt close to it! But I do miss seeing your face. So much.

Not as much as I miss seeing yours. You're welcome over here anytime. You know that, right?

TRU

Yeah, I do. And believe me, I'm so tempted. But I'm just trying to pace myself, you know? I haven't had many nights like the one we had, Henley. Zero, if you want the truth. And another true confession: I've been lonely for a long time, but I don't feel that way as much now that I'm here. But I don't want to lose myself in us. I've seen that with my mom and dad's relationship my whole life, and I don't want to follow that path.

Give yourself credit, tiny dancer. You're much too independent and wise for that to happen, and I'm too in awe of who you are to let that become us. There's no rush. I want to be with you and learn everything about you, but we can take all the time you need.

TRU

Has anyone told you you're the best man ever?

Nope.

TRU

Wait. I feel like maybe I've told you this before.

Not today you haven't. <Smile emoji>

TRU

Okay, Mr. Football Player.

I set my phone down, smiling…something I've done a lot of since Friday night, despite how things went haywire afterward.

I can't help but feel like things are gonna work out with us. The fact that I'm excited about someone is huge. I didn't think I would get invested in a relationship ever again really. The fact that I'm feeling all these feelings….it's just fun.

I laugh out loud at myself and take a long shower after I've worked out.

The guys start texting one by one, checking in to see how things went with Cassidy and Tru this afternoon. When I'm in bed, I text them back.

It went well. Cassidy and Tru both said so. I think things are gonna be okay, guys. Thanks for hanging out with me this weekend and walking me through it.

PENN

You're always there for us and we'll always be here for you too.

BOWIE

What Penn said.

RHODES

I'm just glad you're getting laid. It's about fucking time.

WESTON

<laughing crying emoji> Leave it to Rhodes to say what we're all thinking but would never say.

RHODES

You're welcome.

Well, it was one night, albeit one fan-fucking-tastic night. But it's not like I'm living the sexed-up life most of you are living. It's a start though. LOL.

BOWIE

Most of you, he says. Way to make me feel left out, dude.

He sends an Eeyore gif.

BOW, you and I have purposely chosen the drought. I thought mine might last forever, and I'm still not out of the woods.

RHODES

Your time is coming, Bowie! And you've just gotta take what you want, Henley! < And you guys know I don't use exclamation points unless I'm FEELING it.

I love you guys.

WESTON

^ If you hadn't told us you'd had sex, we'd know it by that right there.

I tell you guys I love you!

PENN

Uh, it's rare. Weston and I are the showy-feely types. The rest of you, not as much.

RHODES

Dude, I resent that.

PENN

It's the truth and I love you anyway.

RHODES

I say it in other ways.

PENN

I dare you to tell me at the gym tomorrow.

BOWIE

I'll tell you. I'm not afraid of showing my feelings.

RHODES

NEITHER AM I.

WESTON

Sadie wants to know why I'm snorting every other second.

Tell her it's a frickin' love fest on here. That I started, by the way.

WESTON

She says she loves you too. <Wink emoji>

PENN

I love that woman.

BOWIE

Tell her I love her more.

RHODES

I'm the one that loves her most and she knows it.

I love her and that little boy.

WESTON

I'd be jealous of how fast you piled on about how much you love her if I didn't love her so much too. I get it.

Night, guys. See you at the gym tomorrow.

CHAPTER TWENTY-SIX

I HOPE YOU'RE HAPPY

TRU

The week drags by and besides being busy with school, and tutoring Cassidy, and hanging out with Earl while I grade papers, it feels like everything is going in slow motion. I miss seeing Henley and yet, I'm nervous to be around him. Nervous that I feel so much so soon. Nervous about his daughters and what it could mean for them. Nervous about how it affects my job, although now that things are going smoothly with Cassidy again, I feel less of that, but it just all feels so *big* and I'm not used to any of that.

Friday afternoon, I don't have to tutor Cassidy or go to the dance studio, so I linger at school longer, cleaning my classroom and getting organized for next week. I jump when I hear a knock and look up to see Henley standing in the doorway.

"Hey." I smile. "What are you doing here?"

He walks in, looking me over with appreciation before his gaze settles back on my face.

His eyes are smiling and he looks all man when he says, "I just missed you. I needed to see your face and I'm glad I went for it. You look amazing today."

I hold one side of my skirt to the side. "Thank you very much."

I let the material fall back down and he watches, licking his lips. The material falls chastely at my knees, but the way he looks at me makes me feel like I'm wearing the sexiest negligee ever. He steps inside and closes the door, stalking toward me. I move forward at the same time until we collide. His hand lands on my cheek and I lean into it.

"It's really good to see you," he says.

I lean up on my tiptoes and kiss him softly, just once, and then stand back on solid feet…but feel woozy. He makes me feel drunk just being in the same room with him. His hand glides to the back of my neck and he comes in for another kiss.

This one is demanding, hungry, and oh so good.

I moan into his mouth and he answers with his own, his tongue diving deeper, tangling with mine. His hand squeezes my hip, and with his other, he tugs on my hair, pulling my head back so he can get better access.

I arch into him, trying to get as close to him as I possibly can. He pulls away, kissing down my jawline and my neck.

"I better go before we do something crazy and fuck right here."

My breath hitches. I kiss his cheek, his head, and my hands tug his waves when he leans down and tugs my shirt to the side so he can kiss my breast.

"Tell me when we can be together again," he says. "I don't care when it is. I just want to know it's coming. I think about you all the time. I'm trying to do things at your speed. But I'm going crazy for you." He pulls my leg over his thigh and thrusts into me and I gasp.

"I think about you all the time too," I whisper.

He backs me into the wall and then notices the little closet of supplies. The naughtiest grin takes over his face and I lose my breath. He looks so dangerously hot right now. He lifts me up and my legs wrap around his waist as he carries me into the closet. The door stays open, but it's darker in here, the light from the classroom trickling in.

"Is this okay?" he asks.

I nod, leaning in to kiss him. He sets me on my feet and gets on his knees.

"Henley," I whimper.

"I'll make you feel good and then I'll go," he says, looking up at me.

I open my mouth to tell him I want to make him feel good too, but then he lifts my skirt and moves my panties to the side, and that first swipe of his tongue is so perfect, my toes curl.

He groans, praising the way I taste, the way I feel, the way he's thought of nothing but this since the first time, and my head falls back on the shelves of school supplies as he turns my world upside down. My knees buckle when he adds his fingers and he tells me to hang on when I get close. I do, and it's a good thing because he works me over until I'm boneless.

While I'm still catching my breath, he stands, wiping his mouth with the back of his hand. His eyes are glazed over, but he's smiling and more than a little smug.

"Thank you," he says.

"I should be thanking you," I say, cheeks flushing.

I move toward him, needing to touch him, wanting to make him feel as good as he's made me feel, but he shakes his head.

"I said I'd make you feel good and then go. I want to keep my word."

I reach out and touch his chest. "I know you're good for it. Come home with me?"

His eyes drill through me. "Are you sure that's what you want?"

"I am. Very sure."

I move past him and turn to look at him over my shoulder, catching him adjusting himself. When I smirk, he groans and points at the massive bulge in his pants.

"I've been like this since the day I met you. I hope you're happy."

I laugh. "Yes, I am."

I grab my bags and move toward the door of the class-room. He's still standing in the doorway of the closet, watching me.

"You coming?" I ask.

"Not soon enough." He grins when my mouth drops open and moves toward me. "Ladies first." He motions for me to go out the door when I stare at him and his double-entendre self.

I should be worried about getting caught and losing my

job, and I *am*, but damn, this man. I'm giddy as I drive home, happy that I left the house in good shape when I left this morning, happy that Henley is coming over, just happy, period.

My mom calls as I'm pulling onto my street, and I put her on speakerphone.

"Hey, Mom. Can I call you—"

"Tru," my mom's voice cracks.

"Mom! What's wrong?"

She sounds far away and I'm not even sure she hears me. She's saying something, but I can't hear her.

"Mom, I can't hear you. What's going on?"

"He's having an affair." She barely gets the words out, she's crying so hard. And then she takes a deep breath and her voice comes through clearer and more biting than I've ever heard her.

"I've given him thirty years of my life, moved from kingdom come all over this world, and he's sleeping with a woman he just met. He doesn't even act sorry!" Her voice has risen an octave, and I pull into my driveway and park, wiping the tears that have started to fall.

I take her off of speaker as I move the phone out of the holder.

"Mom, where are you? Are you home?"

"I followed his phone. Found him at a restaurant last night with her. He's always told me he doesn't like PDA." She starts laughing and now I'm really worried. "He couldn't stop touching her. He kissed her at the table!"

"Mom, I'm worried about you. Where are you now?"

"I followed them from the restaurant to her place. He called me while he was in her condo to tell me he'd be pulling an all-nighter at work. I'm so stupid."

"Did you drive there? Are you still outside her condo? Can you get in the car and just talk to me? I'm right here."

There's a noise outside my door and I look up to see Henley. He sees my face and frowns, moving to open the door.

"What's happened?" he asks.

"My mom," I whisper.

I step out of the car and he puts his hand on the small of my back as I stumble my way into the house.

"I'm driving home," she says. "And I'm throwing all of his things outside."

"I know you're angry, and you have every reason to be absolutely livid…but can you just take a breath? Maybe go to a hotel while I look into flights for you. What time is it there?"

She takes a deep breath. "I don't know. Four or five in the morning. Tru?" Her voice cracks again and she's crying.

"I'm here, Mom. I love you."

"I love you too. Would you really be okay if I come there?"

"I've been wishing you were here from the very beginning."

"Just for a little while until I figure out what to do."

"I already know I'll want you to stay forever. Just get here, okay? Don't stay in that house. Remember your most valuable things are in storage anyway. Just get your passport, money, license, and get here. I'll text you about flight times when I get them."

"Okay. Thank you, honey."

"Call me when you're at the hotel or airport, depending on how soon I can get you out of there."

"It'll be a fortune."

"That's what credit cards are for."

That makes her laugh a little bit. She's used that line on me countless times, teasing me for being more frugal than her.

"Okay, okay." Her breath hitches. "I'll be okay."

"You will. He's never deserved you."

She breaks into a sob and Henley puts his arms around me when I do too.

"I'm almost to the house," she finally says. "I'll go for now and try to get out of there fast."

"All right. I love you, Mom. So much."

"You are everything to me," she says. "I'll talk to you soon."

I feel ragged when I hang up. I put my forehead on Henley's chest and let the strength of his arms soothe the hurt. Earl comes over and glides between my legs, meowing pitifully until I pick him up. Henley brushes my hair away from my face and I look up at him. He thumbs away my tears, his face so full of compassion, a few more tears fall.

"God." He rubs his chest. "It physically hurts to see you cry. What can I do to help?"

"You're already doing it." I let him hold me another few seconds and then lift my head. "I need to find my mom a ticket out of there as soon as possible."

He runs his hands over my arms and nods. "I'm good at that, and I have a friend who works for a travel agency."

I'm about to make a remark, something like I'm sure he knows a pretty woman who will help him or some other stupid comment, when he adds, "Let me call him."

My heart eases.

He's not your father.

"She's in Sydney, right?" he asks, already dialing the number. "Hey, Stan, it's Henley. I know, it's been a minute. Oh, yeah, you're welcome. I'm glad you were able to make the game. I'm doing well. How about you? Great. Listen, I have a favor to ask, and just tell me if it doesn't work to help us. I have a friend whose mom is in Sydney, Australia, and she needs to get out of there in a hurry. We'll pay whatever it takes."

He shakes his head when I open my mouth to protest.

"To Denver, Colorado," he says. He pauses for a second and his features relax into a smile. "One sec, let me see if that's possible." He looks at me. "A flight leaving there at 9:30 AM?"

"Let me make sure she can leave that soon."

He tells Stan I'm checking and they chat about the Super Bowl while I call my mom. She sounds more focused and says she won't stay in the house long at all. She'll make it to the airport with time to spare.

I put my hand over the phone. "She can make it."

He relays that to Stan and I'm handing him my credit card when he says, "Yes, the one you have on file. Thanks so much, Stan. Okay, I'll tell her to put that info in the Delta app. You're a lifesaver, man. Let me know the next game you want tickets to, and I'll make sure you get them."

We both hang up at the same time and stare at each other.

"She'll be here by 12:30 tomorrow afternoon." He pauses for a second. "Do you want to talk about it?"

"Can we make dinner? I need something normal to process."

He smiles and my heart turns over. "Lead the way to the kitchen, tiny dancer."

While we make tortilla soup and a salad, I tell him about my parents and how the way my dad treated my mom and me instilled distrust in me about other men.

"Seeing the way you love your girls, the way you treat them with such respect...the way you treat *me* with such respect…it's been so eye-opening, Henley." I swallow the lump building in my throat. "I want that for my mom too. And I'm just glad for the chance to know for myself that all men aren't like my dad. I have you to thank for that."

He lifts my hand to his lips and kisses my palm.

And I fall even harder for him.

The fact that I trust Henley enough to share any of this speaks volumes to the kind of man he is.

CHAPTER TWENTY-SEVEN

LITTLE KOALA

HENLEY

It's after midnight and we've talked for hours. We took a shower earlier, where I tended to her. It was a helpless feeling, watching her cry. But I washed her hair and slid her vanilla honey body wash over every inch of her skin, trying to soothe away her pain in the only way I know how. Now we're in her bed, naked, but I'm keeping my hands in the safety zone. We're in a queen bed, smaller than what I'm used to, but I love the way she's wrapped around my body like a little koala.

My dick is obnoxiously hard and has been all night, but I've done my best to ignore it.

She needs more than sex from me tonight.

Her father sounds like a spineless prick. I haven't heard a single decent thing about him. Normally, I'd acknowledge a dad's part for the way his daughter turned out, but something tells me Tru is as wonderful as she is all on her own and because of her mom, Stephanie.

"Henley." Her voice is a caress.

Her fingers glide over my chest, tracing soft tickles over my skin.

"Yes?"

"Thank you for everything tonight...today. Since the day I met you. It's not like me to jump into anything fast. And I know from what you've told me that it isn't like you either. But I think you're so special. And I'm glad you're here." She leans up and rests her chin on my chest. "You don't have to treat me with kid gloves anymore."

I kiss her hair.

"I just want you to be okay. I don't want you to be dealing with all this, but I know you can't help but be sad right now. And I'm here. Whatever you need."

"I need *you*," she says, kissing my chest.

My dick is already thoroughly stirred to life, but it jolts at this new contact. Her hand reaches down and slides over me, gripping me tight.

I suck in a breath.

"Come here," I say, pulling her on top of me.

She reaches over and pulls a box of condoms out of her nightstand. "I bought these the other day just in case this opportunity ever happened again between us."

My hands grip her hips and I grin up at her. "As you can see, I'm ready for you."

"It's been distracting me since the shower...and before."

"Sorry." I laugh.

"No, I just thought you were never going to do anything about it." Her smile is sweet and seductive as she leans down to kiss me between her words.

"I wouldn't have tonight, but not because I don't want to." My fingers play with her nipples, and I reach up to encircle my mouth around one. "I will always want to do this when you're anywhere near me. I want you with everything in my being." I laugh at how emphatically I say it.

She leans down for another kiss, her breasts sending fire to my skin with the contact.

"You're so beautiful, Tru. I feel so lucky to be here with you."

"I'm the lucky one," she says. "Have you seen yourself? Have you been around you? You're willing to forgo sex to wash my hair...if that's not the best kind of man, I don't know what is."

She gasps when I shift her so she's centered on top of me, her wet heat against me.

"You feel too good," I warn her. "And I'm going to have this image burned in my brain from here on out. You on top of me like this."

She opens the condom packet and slides it on me before positioning herself over me. And then she begins to take me so slowly, her hips undulating as I inch into her. I remain still, letting her take her time. I don't want to hurt her. My fingers glide between her legs and I rub her with just the right amount of pressure until she's so wet she sinks onto the rest of me with ease.

"I already feel so close," she says, gasping. "How do you do that?"

"Tell me what you like," I say. "Show me."

"I like everything you do."

We don't speak for a few minutes as we rock back and forth. But our eyes never lose sight of each other. I move my mouth up to her breast in a hot trail of teeth and tongue and lips, but keep the steady momentum going between her legs too. I feel how every touch of her sweet bud sends reactions inside of her, which in turn makes me feel every shift, every flutter, every squeeze. She's so swollen and greedy for me, I fucking love it. It doesn't take long before she throws her head back and comes so hard, it's a challenge not to lose it right along with her. I watch her in awe.

When her body relaxes, she leans down and kisses me, her insides still gripping me tight. I flip her over so she's on her back.

"Oh," she moans. "Yes, please. You feel unreal. Go as hard as you want, Henley. I want it all."

"Oh, tiny dancer. I have so much to give you," I tell her.

"Yes! You're so big and I love how you know exactly what to do with it," she cries.

I laugh into her skin. I wasn't referring to my size, more the way I want to inhale her and give her everything I've got, but I'm glad she thinks I know exactly what to do with my dick.

It's such a powerful feeling, the way she responds to me. Our hands trip over each other, desperate to touch every-where. She opens her legs wider, arching up into me and meeting my thrusts so I'm even deeper inside of her. I love her sounds. I love the way her tits bounce with how hard we're fucking. Her dark hair against her pale pillowcases looks like waves of ocean water in the night. My siren, calling out her siren song. The sounds of our skin slapping together, the creaking of her bed, it's building the urgency in both of us to a frenzy.

"Faster," she cries. "Ahh, you feel so good."

Her nails dig into my skin, and I move my hands to her ass so I can grip her tighter as we move faster. She grips mine too. Our skin is slippery, fevered, and when her walls start clamping around my dick, I go off with a raspy yell.

"Henley, Henley, Henley," she chants.

We're a fucking tidal wave that just goes on and on and on, higher and higher, until it feels like we've reached the depths of heaven and earth together. I lean back, my hands on her face. I push her hair back, and she blinks up at me, her eyes sleepy and sated and sparkling. Even in the dark room, I can tell they're sparkling.

I kiss her and it feels like our sex. Powerful, deep.

"We're incredible together," I tell her.

"We are," she says. "Is it always like that for you?"

"No, not even close. This feels like brand-new territory. And I want you to know I'm here for it."

"I am too," she whispers.

I lean my forehead against hers and eventually, I carefully pull out of her. We both wince at the loss.

"I'm sorry." I kiss her nose.

"I wish you could stay in there forever," she says.

I grin and kiss her again. "Me too, trust me."

I take care of the condom and get back in bed, and when she comes back from the bathroom, she crawls next to me and puts her head on my chest.

"I don't know if I can keep this a secret," I tell her.

"I know, but it won't be long, right? We can do this."

"I feel like I'll be obvious the minute anyone sees my face when I'm around you," I admit.

"Let's just give Cassidy more time to get used to the idea and keep having nights like this." She giggles against my skin. "I don't think I can get enough of you, Henley Ward."

"Well good, because I can't get enough of you either."

We fall asleep, and when I wake up the next morning, spooning her and hard as a rock between her crack, she looks over her shoulder at me.

"Morning," she says.

"Good morning. Did I wake you?"

"I'm not sure if it was this..." She tilts her ass back, encasing me even more, and I groan. "Or if it's all the light coming in." She smiles. "Either way. I like waking up with you here."

"Mm-hmm," I grumble sleepily. "You're so sweet. You smell so good."

"Well, don't get near my breath," she says, turning her head back to face the other way.

I thrust against her, and she tilts back into me again, gasping. I lean over and grab one of the condoms from the table and slide it on, my fingers reaching between her legs to see if she's ready for me.

"I like how you're so wet for me," I say in her ear.

"Always," she says.

I enter her slowly, and it's perfect.

I could really get used to waking up like this.

CHAPTER TWENTY-EIGHT

THAT AGE-OLD QUESTION

TRU

It's hard to tear myself away from Henley, but I finally manage to get out of bed. I clean the house a little bit, put clean sheets on the guest bed, and check to see what I need to pick up from the grocery store. Henley is being helpful too, vacuuming the living room.

I gave Jacklyn a vague idea about what's going on and she said to just take the day off. I had offered to come in for a little while and leave early to pick up my mom, but she knew

I would probably need to get ready for her. I'm grateful for the time. When Henley's done vacuuming, he asks what he can do next.

"You're so good," I tell him. "I'm not used to a man like you. It's going to take me a while to get acclimated."

He laughs. "Okay, I'll be around. Do you want me to mop the kitchen?"

"Are you for real?"

"Yep. You remember I've got three kids and kids are messy..."

"But so are men, right?" I say, laughing.

"Some are, for sure. Tell me what you need."

"I would love for you to mop and then I can run to the store, pick up a few things, and head to the airport."

"Or you could let me run to the store and I could even take you to the airport."

"Don't you need to take the girls to dance?" I ask.

"Bree had already offered to take them. She had some shopping to do on Jupiter. I'll see the girls later today."

"Well, I might just keep cleaning a little bit. I need to take care of Earl's litter box..." I stop and look at him apologetically. "I feel bad taking you from the girls. You don't need to go to the store or the airport, but thank you."

"Are you sure? Don't say what you think I want to hear."

"No, I'm sure. I think it will be good for my mom and me to have some time together when she gets here. I can't wait for you to meet her...but today is probably not the day."

"Yeah, I understand. Okay, mopping it is. And then I will get going."

I walk over and kiss him and he shakes his head. "Nope, none of that, or we won't get anything done."

I laugh and smack his bum. "Good point."

I'm waiting for my mom at the first possible spot when she gets through the gate.

I hardly recognize her at first. She's normally so put together that it's hard to see her like this. She looks so thin and weary. Her hair is going everywhere. She collapses into my arms and doesn't cry, but it feels like she needs help even standing.

"Oh, Mom, I'm so glad you're here, and I'm so sorry this has happened."

She nods and studies my face, her hands on my cheeks.

"You look beautiful," she says. "I am so glad to see you."

"Let's get you home. Did you check anything?"

She nods and we move toward baggage claim where her bag is already waiting.

"Just one bag?" I ask.

"Yeah, I didn't bring much. I got out of there as fast as I could."

"We can pick up whatever you need. Or go to the storage unit whenever you want."

"I'm just glad to be here," she says, her shoulders straightening. "I didn't feel the need to bring much of anything. Fresh start." Her shoulders lift as she takes a deep breath. She tries to smile, but it's wobbly.

"I hate the reasons for it, but your being here is making me so happy. The thought of you being here in Silver Hills with me for more than just a visit—I don't want to jump ahead of things—but I want you to know you could stay forever and I would be thrilled."

"Thank you, honey."

I can tell she's at a loss for what to even say and it breaks my heart to see her so sad.

"Well, let's get you home."

She smiles and it almost reaches her eyes.

My mom dozes on the ride home and perks up when she sees my little house and Earl.

"Well, hello," she says to Earl.

I pick him up and she pets him.

"He is so cute. And your place is darling, Tru. You've got it decorated so cute. I love the architecture. It's so whimsical."

"Thank you. Whimsical is a good word for everything in this town. Definitely the theme. Your bedroom is back this way." I show her to the room and then the rest of the house, taking her upstairs to my room last.

It's a small house with two bedrooms downstairs and one up, but I didn't need much room with it being just me. Now I'm really glad that it's as big as it is. I think we can both be comfortable here.

Her phone is buzzing when we come back downstairs and she goes to pick it up, checks it, and turns the sound off. I can tell by the way her jaw clenches that it's Dad, but she doesn't say anything.

"You must be so exhausted," I say. "Are you hungry?"

"I am exhausted, yes. But I'm hungry too, and I feel better just seeing you."

"Why don't you take a long bath while I make us some food?"

"That sounds perfect. Thank you, honey."

When she comes out, she looks human again. Her long dark hair is wet and brushed, and she's wearing a soft matching sweat suit.

I've made soup and sandwiches for us, and we sit down at the table to eat. Earl purrs down by my feet. I look at my mom out of the corner of my eye, wondering whether I should bring up Dad or to just let her talk about it when she's ready.

But she starts talking about it right away.

"I'm just so glad that I saw him kiss her," she says.

I look at her in surprise.

"If I hadn't seen it with my own eyes, I might have come up with excuses like I have for everything else about him." She sips her soup and shakes her head. "You must think I'm so weak."

"I don't. I don't, Mom. You're the strongest person I know. I haven't understood why you've stayed with him, but I've never thought it's because you're weak. It's been more that you want so badly to see the best in him."

She looks down at her plate and her eyes fill with tears. "That's true. It was almost like I was just determined to make our life be what I *wanted* it to be…all the while knowing it never would be. I don't know why I did that."

"Because you loved him," I say, softly.

"Yeah, I did. And I wasted thirty years on a man who has never really loved me back. That's a rude awakening." She laughs and it sounds brittle and so unbearably sad.

I reach out and put my hand on her arm. "I wish more than anything that I could take away this pain…and I know it's too soon to say this, but I'm so glad you got out of there."

I'm afraid to say too much because what if she goes back to him? But I can only hope that this has opened her eyes for good.

She talks about how it's been since they moved to Sydney. His late nights working, how abrasive and cold he's been, even more than usual. He's berated her over the smallest things and he's never home.

"I'm not sure why he even wanted me to move there with him. But I'm done, Tru." She looks me in the eyes and sets down her spoon, reaching for my hand. "I'm not going back to him. I know now that I can't live this way another second. It's killing me. I don't even recognize myself in the mirror anymore. And I don't want to be that kind of example to you…*or to myself.*"

"I love you, Mom." I bite my lip as the tears start falling down my cheeks. "I love you so much and I know you can do this. You can have a life without him and *thrive.*"

"I don't really know what I'm going to do with myself, but I'm going to do something," she says, trying to laugh again.

"You've always been brilliant. Now it's time to think about what *you* want."

"I'd rather talk about you. But thanks for listening." She leans in. "Now…tell me everything I've missed from living across the world from you."

"Well, I've made some new friends. I told you about going to Sadie and Weston's and then out with Sadie and her soon-to-be sister-in-law. Did I tell you about Elle and Calista yet?"

"No, you haven't mentioned them."

"Remember that cute bookstore we went in when we drove through here? Twinkle Tales? Calista works there. It was her aunt's shop and now she's running it. And Elle is her best friend…who's also best friends with one of Henley's best friends." We both laugh at the way my hand is jumping with the imaginary arrows. "And I can't wait for you to meet Clara from Luminary Coffeehouse. I think the two of you will hit it off. And Weston's mom, Lane. She's great too."

"And then there's Henley…" She lifts her eyebrows and grins.

I lean back in my chair and smile back at her.

"Yeah, Henley. He is…" I let out a loud sigh and we both laugh.

"When do I get to meet him?"

"He would've been here today to meet you if I hadn't said let's wait. I wanted you to get settled in and all that. And… we're still going to keep things under wraps a while longer. Hopefully his daughters will have a chance to warm up to the idea."

Images of the way he looked above me, his muscles straining, his hair over his forehead, the intensity in his eyes when he touched me…and then the conversations we've had on the phone and texting, in person too…where we've covered a lot of ground. It feels like we've gotten to know each other pretty well in a short amount of time.

"I can't wait to meet him. I've never seen you light up about a guy before, but you do about him." She pats my hand and I squeeze hers back.

That night after my mom has gone to bed and I'm getting in mine, my phone buzzes.

HENLEY

How's it going over there?

She's sad, but I think she's going to be okay. She's actually doing better than I expected her to be. A lot has been going on in Sydney between them and she says she's done. She's never said anything close to that about my dad before, but I believe she means it.

HENLEY

It sounds like a great first step. I'm glad, but I'm still sorry. Going through a divorce is never easy.

I can only imagine. I'm sorry you've dealt with that.

HENLEY

I'm all good. It was hard, but I feel very lucky that Bree and I remained friends throughout the process. And I feel even luckier about the night I had last night...with you...in case there was any doubt.

My cheeks flush. I lay back in my bed and grin at the phone.

Yeah?

HENLEY

I've been able to think of little else all day long. It's a good thing it's the offseason or I'd be a mess.

Well, we're gonna have to figure that out before you start playing again. When is that again anyway?

HENLEY

Things are about to start picking up with more regulated workouts. But the mandatory minicamp isn't until June, so there's a little leeway until then for me. Coach Evans goes easier on me than a lot of the other players, but I still try not to miss.

I'm excited to see you play.

HENLEY

You are?

Yes! I hear you're kinda all that.

HENLEY

Tiny dancer, on the field, I am definitely all that.

I shiver and laugh out loud, feeling the heat of his words like he's in bed saying them in my ear.

I just might pass out from lust, seeing you in those tights.

HENLEY

LOL. You make me sound like Robin Hood. They're pants though.

Mm-hmm, those things are leggings at most.

HENLEY

I guess this brings up that age-old question: Are leggings pants?

On females, yes. Especially if they're dark enough to hide underwear, otherwise they just seem like tights. But on men...I'm not so sure.

HENLEY

Maybe it'll take you seeing me on the field to believe.

I cannot wait.

CHAPTER TWENTY-NINE

WATERING THE BUSHES

HENLEY

I walk into Luminary to meet the guys and am surprised to see Tru with a woman who *has* to be her mom. They favor each other so much, it's easy to see what Tru will look like in the future.

Tru must've had the day off.

They're at a table near the front, and Clara and Lane are standing there talking with them. Tru says something and they all laugh, which causes Marv and Walter, sitting at the table next to them, to pause their grumbling to see what's so funny.

Tru stills when she sees me, her eyes bright and smiling. Her mom turns to see who has her attention and her eyes widen. *So she has told her mom about me.* The thought warms me. It's been a few days since Stephanie got into town and I've been trying to give them space to work through things, but I've missed Tru like crazy. We've been Face-Timing late into the night, and I'm dragging as much as my teenager in the mornings.

All worth it, though.

I walk over to the table and when Clara and Lane see me, they hug me, and then I'm face-to-face with Tru and her mom, suddenly nervous.

"Hello, I'm Henley Ward, a friend of Tru's." I hold out my hand and she gets up and hugs me.

"Hi there. I'm Stephanie. I know I have you to thank for that incredible first-class pod. Thank you. I really appreciate it and the way you've been here for Tru."

"It was no problem at all. And any chance I get to be around Tru—well, I'm the lucky one. I hope you're getting adjusted to the time difference and liking Silver Hills so far?"

"I love it," she says, smiling warmly. "We'll have to have you over for dinner to thank you properly...and I'd like to get to know Tru's friends."

I look at Tru then and she's eyeing me with what I can only describe as hunger. *I know the feeling, tiny dancer.* She flushes and my eyes fall to her lush lips wishing I could bite that lower one right now. She lets out a whimper and it pulls me out of my lust cloud. I blink and look at Stephanie again.

"I'd love to come over for dinner."

"Excellent. Tomorrow night?" She looks at Tru to see if that's okay.

Tru laughs nervously. "Or whenever works for you. He's busy, Mom."

"Not too busy for you...or dinner." I smile at them, and when I look at Clara and Lane, they're beaming at me like two proud moms.

It lets me know that it's obvious how into Tru I am, but it also reminds me that I need to call my mom back. We talked yesterday about nailing down the details of their upcoming visit, but I've been so preoccupied with the girls and thoughts of Tru, I haven't touched base with Mom again today.

"Excellent," Stephanie says.

"You're filling up your social calendar quite well," Tru says to her mom, teasing but proud. "Coffee with the girls tomorrow morning." She grins at Clara and Lane before smiling up at me. "And she's meeting Sadie, Elle, and Calista Sunday night."

"My girl's keeping me busy, and I love it," Stephanie says.

"I'm glad. And I'm looking forward to dinner. I'm sorry to cut this short, but my phone is going off like crazy..." I hold it up and chuckle. "The guys are waiting for me in the back, and patience is not their strength."

Everyone laughs.

"You better get to your Single Dad Players...Playbook Meeting? What's it called again?" Tru teases.

Now I'm flushing. I wave my hand. "The name's not important. It's just some dads on the team talking about their kids. I guess we can't call it single anything anymore since Weston's on his way to getting married."

"I've heard the conversation leans more toward women than kids," Lane says with a wink.

"Lane Shaw, are you giving away our secrets?" I tease.

She fans her face. "It felt like we were in safe company,"

she says, laughing. "But when you guys turn that charm on, I don't know how any of you stay single."

I feel Tru watching me, scalding over my body with heat. I can't help myself, I look at her and her eyes are roaming over my body. Her tongue stretches out to lick her lips and just like that, my jeans are way too tight. Time to get out of here before I embarrass myself in front of Tru and the moms.

"I see what you mean, Lane!" Stephanie says. "If they're all as charming as Henley, the women in Silver Hills are in trouble!"

They all look at me with appreciation.

"You better get to your Single Dad meeting before you get the big head," Tru says, trying not to laugh.

She's not wrong. The guys are blowing my phone up, and my erection is about to hit twelve o'clock.

"Well, this has been nice," I say, grinning. "Thank you, ladies." I nod at Tru. "Let me know what time you want me for dinner."

Her mouth drops with my words and I walk away, smirking, and okay, with the big head...two of them, to be exact.

When I walk into the room, the guys are laughing their asses off. Rhodes is holding The Single Dad Playbook and wiping his eyes.

"What did I miss?"

Bowie waves me over and Rhodes hands me the book.

"Read it," he says.

"I guess I've gotta stop singing Cardi B around the house because Caleb's singing it now?" I read Weston's entry out loud, laughing.

"No, the one underneath," Penn says, cracking up.

"I almost didn't put it in there, but I needed to vent," Rhodes says.

It's longer, so I read it to myself and am laughing before I get very far.

Recently, I made the mistake of taking a wee in our yard when Levi and I were out all day and not close to the house. I didn't feel like hauling him inside in a hurry when I had to go that bad, so I chose a tree and went.
Big mistake.
Now, he wants to go every time we're outside...and not just at home.
So far, he's been in the parking lot of Elle's dad's church, the tree at the library, and the park. This morning, we took a walk around the block and before I could stop him, he ran over to Mrs. Hammond's yard and answered nature's call all over her rose bushes. She ran out and shooed us off with her newspaper.
I apologized profusely, but I don't think she will forgive us any time soon.
Moral of the story: Don't let your son see you take a leak outside until they're old enough to know it's a once-in-a-while thing used only in emergencies and never, ever in Mrs. Hammond's roses.
~Rhodes

I'm laughing as hard as they are by the time I'm done.

"Why didn't you tell us about this?" I finally ask. "This is too good."

"Because of the shame," Rhodes says. "I'm trying to raise a dignified little boy here."

That just makes us laugh harder.

"He'll grow out of it. My brother and I did," I tell him. "Well, that was mostly because my mom was like Mrs. Hammond. Watering the yard was a no-go for her too." I laugh again and then shrug. "This is the plus of having three daughters, I guess."

"Levi is a dignified little boy," Weston says. "He's a little gentleman."

"Becca loves how he tries to open the doors for her. I don't know another three-year-old like that," Bowie says.

"If anyone is messing up, it's me. It's not just Cardi B. Caleb heard me singing "Nasty" by Tinashe to Sadie and he's been going around singing, "I've been a nasty girl…""

We lose it at that.

Weston clears his throat and then adds under his breath, "He's also heard "Lunch" by Billie Eilish, so yeah, I am not winning any awards in the dad department."

"We need to work on your music selection," Bowie says, wheezing.

"I love those artists too, man," Rhodes says. "He'll be well-rounded."

We all laugh again.

I sit down and Clara sticks her head in the door, holding my Solar Latte.

"Sounds like too much fun is going on in here." She grins before backing out again.

———

The next night I show up at Tru's with a huge bouquet from The Enchanted Florist. It's a hit—Tru and Stephanie both ooh and ahh over how pretty it is. I'd offered to bring dessert too, but Tru shut me down on the phone last night, saying I've cooked for her, it's time she treats me to a good meal too.

"You look nice," Tru whispers when it's just the two of us in her tiny kitchen.

"You look good enough to eat," I whisper back.

"Oh, how I wish," she says, pure mischief.

I groan. "Do you want to torture me now when I can't put my mouth on you?" I ask, backing her into the stove, my hand on her jaw.

"Yes," she says.

I sing the first line of "Watermelon Sugar" by Harry Styles in her ear. Weston isn't the only one who can turn to song.

She ducks under my arm and points at me, but I'm momentarily distracted by the way her nipples are standing brazenly in her soft, pink, silky blouse.

"Behave," she whispers, biting her bottom lip.

"I can't remember which one of us started it."

"I think we're both in a way," she says, laughing.

I put my hands on her waist and lean in to kiss the back of her neck. "I miss you being in my bed. Or being in your bed. I don't even need a bed…"

She laughs again and picks up the huge salad bowl. "I'm missing you too."

Stephanie walks into the kitchen and points at the bowl. "You got it. That's the only thing we're missing, I think. You two ready to eat?"

"So ready," I say.

Tru shoots me a look.

What? I mouth at her as we walk to the table.

Dinner is excellent. The food is delicious and the company is even better. We bounce around topics and Stephanie is great. She touches briefly on what she's going through, just saying she's making some big changes and getting out of her marriage of thirty years. I expect to see tears, but there aren't any. She actually seems excited about the future, which feels really hopeful.

Everything flows so easily, but I think I still catch them by surprise when I look at Stephanie and say, "I really like your daughter."

"Oh!" She laughs. "I'm so glad to hear that. I really like her too."

Tru puts her hands on her face and shakes her head, laughing.

"Oh my goodness. I did not see that coming out of your mouth," she says. "This guy is full of surprises," she tells her mom, and I grin.

"I feel like the most predictable guy in the world, but I'm glad if I'm keeping you on your toes in a good way."

She laughs. "You definitely are."

I look at Stephanie. "I just wanted to let you know that I think you've raised a great human, and I like everything I know about her. Every day I learn something new, and I just like her more."

"Well, you know how to make a mom feel good," Stephanie says, clutching her throat.

Now her eyes are filled with tears, as she beams at the two of us.

"You told me he was sweet, but wow," she says to Tru.

"I know," Tru says. "You should see the way he is with his daughters."

Stephanie looks at me. "I really love hearing that too. Tru says you've got three beautiful girls."

"I do. They're great kids. And they all really like Tru a lot. My oldest, Cassidy, is her student, and she's struggling with the thought of me dating her teacher, but she's crazy about Tru, so I think it's all going to be fine. But we've kept things kind of low-key because of that…and also just trying to take our time getting to know each other."

"I think it's commendable that you're putting your girls' feelings into consideration," Stephanie says.

"But I want you to know I'm also taking your daughter's feelings into consideration. And I want to do right by her too." I reach out and take Tru's hand and squeeze it.

She looks like she might cry too.

"I didn't mean to make you get teary…I just wanted to be open about the whole thing."

"Thank you for that," Stephanie says.

I smile at her and then reach down and kiss Tru's hand. And then we move on to dessert.

CHAPTER THIRTY

FOREPLAY TIGHTS

TRU

The school year has come to an end, and I can finally breathe a little bit. It's been really hectic, but things are good.

My mom loves Silver Hills as much as I do. She sees Clara and Lane at least once a week, and she fits right in around here. She loves Sadie and Elle and Calista. Honestly, I think she knows more people than I do at this point. She's working at Rose & Thorn, the elegant restaurant on Jupiter Lane, and I'm shocked by the amount she makes in tips.

I love seeing her happy.

My dad is *not* so happy.

He hasn't come out here...yet...but he's started calling me regularly, wanting me to put in a good word for him with Mom. I tell him he's on his own there and that I hope she never goes back to him because she's doing so much better without him. That never goes over well. He hung up on me the last time.

Mom is obsessed with Henley. She says she's never met anyone like him and that I should hold onto a man who looks at me the way he does. She spoils him rotten every time he comes over and then goes to bed around eight thirty to give us time to ourselves, despite us telling her she doesn't need to rush off. He's spent the night occasionally, usually on the weekends, but I usually go to his place.

Things with Henley are...well, I can't even think about him without my heart flip-flopping, so I think it's safe to say that my feelings are only growing for the man. I'm ready for things to be out in the open soon—I've been the one still holding things back. If it had been up to him, the whole world would know by now, but I just needed to get through this school year for Cassidy's sake. She's doing amazing. Her reading has improved dramatically, and things are great between us, which has made me afraid to mess anything up.

But I think we'll be okay. I hope we will.

Henley wants to tell the girls tonight. His approach has been to not bring it up unless they did, while we've been exploring things between us, but we're past that point now. It's time to come out with it.

Sadie invited me to go with her and Caleb to see the Mustangs practice this afternoon, and I'll ride home with Henley. My mom's working the lunch shift today, so she can't go, but she hopes to make it another time. She gets downright swoony when she sees the five football players together.

"That's a lot of testosterone heaven right there," she says.

I'm watching when Sadie pulls into the driveway and I kiss Earl on the nose and set him down. He's gotten so big.

"I'll see you soon. Protect the fort for me, okay?"

Benson Boone is blasting when I get in Sadie's SUV. Caleb's little head is bopping. He waves excitedly when I see him, but it's nothing like the reaction I've seen him make when he sees Henley.

"Hi, Caleb!" I wave back, and say hello to Sadie.

"Are you ready for this?" she asks.

"I think so. Should I be nervous?"

"No, this is pretty chill. Some of the players' wives and girlfriends aren't as awesome, but there are enough that are." She looks over and smiles when she sees my outfit. I'm wearing a white cargo dress with teal wedges.

"Is this okay?" I ask, bringing my hair over my shoulder so it doesn't get smooshed. "I have a hard time doing casual."

"You always look stunning," she says.

"Thank you. So do you!"

"Thank you, but any style I have is thanks to my girls in Landmark Mountain."

"I love them." I met Felicity's sisters-in-law about a month ago and adored every single one of them. I wish they lived here, but they're near Felicity in Landmark Mountain.

"Right? You don't need any help in the style department, but I sure do. The media gave me a ton of crap about it in the beginning with Weston."

I stare at her. "Are you serious?" I look down at my outfit with new eyes.

"You'll be fine. They're going to love you, you hot little thing. And you and Henley have been so hush-hush that you're not even on their radar yet." She smirks over at me. "So, are you ready for everyone to know you're Henley Ward's girlfriend?"

I grin just hearing those words. I haven't really thought them or said them out loud, but I know that's how Henley thinks of me.

"I'm nervous but ready. I really only care about how the girls feel about it, and I don't know what we'll do if they're not happy." I make a face and look out the window.

I feel her hand on my shoulder. "Hey, don't worry. They love you. I saw the way they lit up when they saw you at the Pixie Pop-Up Market the other day."

"I hope you're right."

We get to the training facility and there are more people than I expected. I knew that this practice was open to the public too, but still…it's *crowded*.

We find seats up close and my heart ping-pongs around in my body when I spot Henley. Number forty-nine…when I asked him why he chose that one, he said he just really likes that number. Now I feel like I see the number everywhere and it symbolizes him.

Caleb loses his mind when he sees his dad and all his favorite boys. They all run by and wave, Weston coming over to kiss Sadie and Caleb, and Caleb jumps up and down. When Henley waves, Caleb yells, "UNCA HEN" at the top of his lungs, and my insides are exhibiting that same level of excitement at seeing him out on the field.

Henley pauses when he sees me. I can see him mouth the word *fuck* as he looks me over and I know the feeling because I'm in love with football tights. Pants. Whatever. Those tight things highlight the most perfect ass I've ever seen and I can't even look at him head-on without my eyes wandering down to his bulge. I've gotten to know my way around his body and it still takes my breath away, but seeing it showcased in this way does something to me.

I fan my face and Sadie laughs at me.

"Have you seen him in his uniform before?" she asks.

"No. And I should have asked for a preview instead of this being my first time."

She cracks up. "Little secret for you. I can't believe I didn't tell you before now, but you've got time to get one before the season starts. Wear his jersey to a game, and magical things will happen for you."

"I will get right on that," I assure her.

And then for the next couple of hours, both of us are spellbound by the men in front of us. I can't believe how much stamina Henley has. He's shockingly fast for how huge he is, and he catches every ball Weston throws his way. They work like clockwork together. I don't even know the game, but I can tell that Henley is really, *really* good.

He texts after he's run off the field.

HENLEY

I loved seeing you out there. Do you mind if I take fifteen to shower?

> Sure, take your time. It's a beautiful day and I've got a book.

I help Sadie and Caleb get to their vehicle and then go sit near the door Henley said he'd be exiting. He saunters out with Penn and Bowie flanking either side of him. I can just imagine my mom saying her *testosterone heaven* line. It's true. I've never seen men in real life who look like these guys, but Henley...he just does it *all* for me.

He's wearing grey sweats and a white T-shirt, and it's a close second to the football tights. My mouth waters, and from the way he's smiling at me, I think it must show.

"Damn, tiny dancer," he says when he gets near me. "You look so fucking sexy, I didn't think I was going to be able to play with you sitting out there like that."

My cheeks burn. He doesn't normally say things like that around anyone else, but today his eyes are practically burning with lust.

Penn and Bowie laugh.

"So this is why you fumbled a few times at the beginning of practice," Penn says.

"Yeah, I couldn't take my eyes off of this woman right here."

Bowie grins at me. "Good to see you, Tru."

"You too." I smile back.

"I personally love seeing Henley all out of sorts over you." Bowie pounds Henley on the back. "You're the only woman I've ever seen make him lose his cool."

"Shush, both of you," Henley says to them, but his eyes never leave mine. "Let's get out of here."

He stalks toward me and Penn whistles. They're still laughing as we walk away. Henley leads me toward the parking garage and when we're in his SUV, he turns to look at me.

"Can I take you to a place near here? It's beautiful, and I need my hands on you."

"Please," I whisper.

He drives about ten minutes into the foothills then turns and drives through a path lined with trees. When we get to the end, there's a lookout point and the view is beautiful.

"Is this where you come to make out with girls, Mr. Football Player?"

He grins, leaning over and unbuckling my seat belt. "Actually, no. I've been up here a few times, but I've never brought anyone.""

"Well, I'm honored." I giggle like a kid and then suck in a breath when he lifts me into his lap.

"You wore the perfect thing." His fingers are deftly lifting my dress.

"I didn't plan on doing this exactly, but it does feel providential."

He grins. I stroke the length of him over his pants.

"There's a condom in my pocket. Can you get it?"

I take it out of his pocket and tug his pants down, sliding the condom over him. He nudges my panties to the side and lifts me over him.

"So wet," he whispers.

"Watching you play was perfect preparation."

"Yeah?"

I nod, leaning my forehead onto his. "The tights are like foreplay, I swear."

He chokes back a laugh and leans in to bite my lower lip.

I sink lower and he hisses.

"God, you are exactly what I need," he says against my mouth. "Everything I want." He pulls back to meet my eyes. "Do you know that I'm in love with you?"

I freeze and stare at him. "You are?" My voice trembles.

"I didn't think I was doing a very good job at keeping it a secret."

I run my fingers over his lips and he kisses them.

"I'm in love with you too," I whisper.

He lets out a long breath and for a second we just sit

there, holding each other, with him so deep, I don't know where he ends and I begin.

He leans in to kiss me, and we kiss until our lips are swollen. When we start to move with each other, it's excruciatingly good. The kind of good that is so right it's almost painful.

His fingers tease me at the perfect tempo until I'm writhing against him, and as I start to crest over the edge, he hits deep in me with tiny stabs that help me fall the rest of the way.

"I love you, I love you," I pant.

He makes a sound somewhere between pain and elation, and his thrusts get wilder.

"Say it again," he says between thrusts.

"I love you, Henley." My eyes roll back with the sensation my words unleash from him. He hammers into me and it sends me flying.

Wave after wave, we both fall into the abyss together, and it is the best feeling in the world.

A loud chirp sounds near us and our lips break apart. I hear a car door slam and my mouth drops. Henley turns and curses.

"Sorry, baby." He lifts me off of him and I scramble to get back in my seat while he tucks himself into his pants.

An officer knocks on the window and Henley lowers it.

"Evening. Everything okay?" the officer asks. His brows gather and his eyes light in recognition. "Henley Ward, I'll be damned."

"Good evening, Officer. We're just enjoying the beautiful view."

The officer looks over at me and nods briskly. "It's a beautiful spot. But we get a lot of kids out here—they keep us busy, if you know what I mean."

"I can only imagine," Henley says. "We'll be on our way. I think we've seen our fill."

I fight the urge to laugh.

"You have a good night." The officer taps on the roof of the SUV.

"You too," Henley says.

When the window is up, we start laughing and can't stop the whole ride home.

CHAPTER THIRTY-ONE

GOTTA ROLL WITH IT

HENLEY

I pull up to Bree's house. She'd asked me to come to dinner tonight a few days ago and I'd said that was perfect because I'd hoped to talk to her and the girls tonight anyway.

Now that I'm here, I'm nervous, which is just crazy talk. I wish Tru was with me for this, but she thought it would be best if they heard about us first without her there. She's right, but I still want her by my side.

She told me she loved me.

I didn't have any doubts about how I feel about her, but hearing her say it back to me, it means everything.

It also means this has to go well with the girls.

I tap on the door and Bree is the one to open the door.

"Hey. How did you manage to beat Gracie out of answering the door?"

She laughs and there's something different about her tonight. She looks extra happy. "I might've been extra excited for you to get here."

My face contorts in surprise. "Okay. What's going on?"

"Dad!" Gracie yells. "Is that you?"

"Yep, it's me, peanut," I yell back.

"Come on back. I thought I might get a minute with you to myself, but they're so excited about the dessert we've got, they'll probably cram dinner down your throat if you don't eat it fast enough." Bree laughs and is already moving briskly toward the kitchen.

"Way to get me curious and leave me hanging," I call behind her.

She smiles at me over her shoulder and I grumble like I'm irritated even though I'm not. Nothing can wreck my mood tonight. Tru loves me.

I hug the girls and we sit down at the table.

"Why don't you pass your plate once you've got the noodles and I'll serve the sauce," Bree says.

"Everything looks great." I smile at Cassidy who's accidentally bumped into my foot.

"Audrey made the spaghetti sauce," Bree says, smiling at Audrey.

"Sign me up." I pass my plate to Bree and she pours the sauce on and puts three meatballs in the center.

"Thank you."

I take a few bites, commenting on how good it is, but

mostly wondering when I should come out with my news. The table jostles and our silverware rattles, which startles everyone. I look over at Bree and see how nervous and fidgety she's acting.

"You okay over there?"

"What? Yeah." She laughs. She makes a face. "I'm okay. Great, actually. I've just got something to tell all of you, and I guess I'm a little nervous."

We all stop and look at her. I set down my fork.

"What is it, Mom?" Cassidy asks.

Bree looks at her girls and puts her hand on her neck before she leans in. "Alex asked me to marry him and I said yes!"

There's silence for a few seconds and then I lift my glass to her. It's only water, but it'll still work.

"Congratulations! That's great news, Bree. Right, girls?" I add when they don't say anything.

"Congratulations, Mom," Audrey says, her smile sweet.

She clinks her glass to mine and everyone else does it too, a delayed reaction.

"Do we get to be in the wedding?" Gracie asks, perking up.

"I'd love for you to be in the wedding if you want to," Bree says. "All three of you."

She looks at Cassidy, who's twisting her cloth napkin as tight as it will go.

"Alex will never replace your dad, no matter what," Bree tells Cassidy. "But isn't it great to have two men in your life who care about you so much?"

When Cassidy finally looks up at Bree, she nods and smiles and it's like we all exhale at once.

"Congratulations," she says simply. But it's enough.

Bree relaxes into her seat and then for the rest of the meal, we talk about all things wedding.

"Alex wanted to be here tonight too, but I thought it'd be best if I told you first. Maybe we can have a little party to celebrate with him tomorrow night though," she tells the girls.

I personally wish he had been here tonight, and I hope that if…no *when* I get to this stage with Tru, that the girls will be farther along in their relationship with her than Alex is. But it's not my place to decide that. I know we're all just doing the best we can do and we won't always make the right call.

However, I'm certain the right call for me tonight is to wait to share the news about Tru. As much as I'm dying to tell them, I want Bree to have her moment and I don't want to pile onto the girls when this is already a lot.

There are messages from the guys when I'm heading home, all wanting to know how it went. They're the best, ready to celebrate Tru and me being official like we're all in high school.

I'm here for it…when it actually happens.

But on a whim, I message back.

> It didn't happen. Bree is engaged. I felt like that news held precedence. But I still feel like a party. Want to come over? Bring whoever you want…dates, kids, all the people. I'm going to see if Tru and her mom can come over. I need a distraction tonight. It's been a great day. And I want to end on a high note.

RHODES

Henley making a plan after eight o'clock…
count us in. Levi and I will be there shortly.
We won't stay long since he'll be crashing
soon, but we'll come say hey. Maybe Elle
too. She said she was heading out soon,
but she might be up for seeing Tru, her new
BFF. <Eye roll emoji> Just no pics.

Elle is a Mustangs cheerleader now, so she's not really supposed to be around us, but we're being discreet for her. She's our friend, but she's not going out with us in public anymore to ensure she keeps her job. We miss her, but it's exciting that she'll be out there this season.

BOWIE

Becca and I will be there too.

PENN

I'm with Sam right now. Is it okay if I bring
him over?

Of course. I can't wait to see the guy. It's
been too long.

WESTON

Sadie says she's in. And Caleb's probably
good for a little while, or I might call and see
if my mom would want to watch him. But if
she hears it's at your house and that
Stephanie's coming, she might want to
come too.

Everybody's welcome. We could put Caleb
in the portable bed if you want to spend the
night. Invite your parents. Come on.

WESTON

Okay, it's a party!

I get home and order a bunch of pizzas in case anyone hasn't eaten, and they start arriving at the same time as everyone else does. I let Tru know that the conversation with the girls won't be happening tonight after all, and she agreed it was best to let the girls digest the news about Bree and Alex first. Tru and her mom haven't gotten here yet and Weston and Sadie are going to be a bit late. Sadie's parents called right after Weston was talking to me and they're going to watch Caleb.

Levi is in rare form tonight. I think Rhodes imagined him falling asleep on the way or soon after he got here, but he is *wound up*. The little guy is one of the cutest kids I've ever seen. His curls are amazing, and his eyes are the color of amber, and they're always smiling like he's thinking about the punchline. He starts dancing when I turn on the music.

"SexyBack" by Justin Timberlake comes on. Rhodes lifts his eyebrows.

"You been holdin' out on me? I didn't take you for a Justin fan. I thought we were all about Britney."

"I didn't know it was on here," I admit. "But hey," I point at him, "get your sexy on."

He laughs and starts swiveling his hips back at Levi, who throws his head back and laughs as he tries to do the same moves.

"Go 'head, be gone with it," Rhodes sings.

And that starts a whole chorus of us dancing our asses off and singing at the top of our lungs. Penn slides across the floor in his socks, taking the lead. And I cover all the background vocals. Rhodes, for all his Justin judgment, and I know there are reasons—Tru's told me all about the Britney memoir—he also happens to know every word.

I'm sore from practice today, but it feels damn good to let

loose with my boys. We finish the song and high-five each other.

And then I hear the laughing.

Tru and her mom are standing there, laughing with tears rolling down their cheeks. Tru can't even get words out without laughing.

"That…was…" she starts and then cackles again.

Stephanie holds her hand to her chest, wheezing with laughter. "I have never seen anything like that," she says, "but oh, wow, life made."

"We didn't even have our boy West here to back us up. He's got some great moves too." I wink, and that sends them into another wave of laughter.

CHAPTER THIRTY-TWO

ONE WEDDING

TRU

As much as I love teaching, and I really, really do, summer vacation is my favorite thing in the world. I love the liberty of knowing that I have the whole summer to do whatever I want. In the past, I've always had other jobs during this time. I've waitressed, I've worked retail, but this summer I've decided I'm going to at least enjoy a few weeks with nothing. Maybe I'll get a job, but my house payment is reasonable. I'm getting paid enough to cover that and *not* work beyond the dance studio during the summer, and I really like spending the days with Earl or Henley...when he's not at practices. He's actually at practice most days now and exhausted if he stays up too late, so the occasional day off that I have with him is precious time.

I'm continuing to tutor Cassidy throughout the summer. I want her to feel confident when she goes back to school in the fall. She's improved so much and works hard to implement the strategies I've shown her to try when she struggles.

The next Saturday when Henley's dropped off the girls after dance, he talks me into going to Starlight Cafe. I'm hesitant because we still haven't told the girls, but he insists there's no harm in eating together.

"The girls had lunch plans with Bree and Alex today. They're busy. And you've gotta eat, my sweet...tiny dancer."

He turns those big brown eyes on me, and combined with that hopeful smile of his, I just can't resist.

We sit at a corner booth in the back, scrunched together in the center and closer than we should be, but again...I can't seem to resist anymore. A pile of food is spread out in front of us. We're sharing pancakes, a Greek omelet, and a fruit platter, and enjoying every bite, when he freezes.

"Okay, don't panic," he says, "but Bree and Alex and the girls just walked in."

"Are you kidding me? The one time I decide to go out with you in public and this happens?" I laugh incredulously, but I feel like crying.

"It'll be okay. Don't worry," he says.

He reaches out to squeeze my knee and then waves at them. They come over, hugging him and looking at me. Curious but friendly gazes. I can work with that.

"Hi, Miss Seymour," Gracie says first, and Cassidy and Audrey say hello as well. "What are you guys doing here?"

"Just getting a late lunch…or is this an early dinner?" Henley says.

"I didn't know you come here after dance," Gracie says to me.

"I don't usually, but I decided to today." I smile at her. "I love their pancakes any time of day."

"Me *too*," Audrey says.

Cassidy grins. "Same."

Okay, so far so good.

I've met Alex before, occasionally he picks up the girls from dance with Bree. He's a nice guy.

"Congratulations. I heard about the engagement," I say to him and Bree.

"Thank you." Bree smiles and holds up her ring finger, waving it. "It's official," she sings.

"I'm really happy for you guys," I tell her.

"I appreciate that," she says, and she looks pointedly at Henley. "*We're* happy to see you guys here together too. Aren't we, girls?"

She bumps Cassidy's arm and Cassidy startles and then rolls her eyes at her mom, but she's smiling.

"Yeah…yes." Cassidy looks at me and then her dad. "Yes, I am happy to see you guys here together."

"Really." Henley looks too pleased for words. "I'm glad to hear that. I didn't want to steal any of the engagement thunder the other night, but I was hoping to talk to you all about it then, the fact that I'd like to see Miss Seymour a whole lot more."

Cassidy snorts. "Do you really call her Miss Seymour?"

"No, never. Well, I did, uh, in the beginning," he stutters. "But not now. No." He runs his hand down his scruff and takes a deep breath, putting his arm around my shoulder. "But I do like Tru a lot and it's important to me to be upfront about that. She's not your teacher anymore, but she still wants to make sure you're okay with all of it, and so do I, but I assured her you would be." He looks at them and they seem to slowly jar out of the realization that their dad has his arm around me. One by one, they come over to hug me.

It's the sweetest thing and I get a lump in my throat.

"Thank you. This means a lot to me," I say when Cassidy hugs me last. "I hated upsetting you before, and...I don't want to make you uncomfortable in any way."

"I'm sorry," Cassidy says. "I shouldn't have ever made an issue about it. You've been great to me, and I just didn't want anything to change that."

"You don't need to apologize. I understand the conflicting feelings. But nothing will change how I treat you," I assure her.

"I believe that now," she says.

Now I get teary, but I start to laugh. She smiles while I dab my face.

"Sorry. I'm emotional and just really relieved," I tell her.

"So, are you guys gonna get married too?" Gracie asks.

Audrey elbows her. "Gracie!"

"One wedding at a time, how about that?" Henley says, laughing. "I'm just now getting her to Starlight Cafe with me."

His eyes meet mine and only the two of us know all the places we've gone with each other in the confines of his house and mine.

I wouldn't trade anything for the time we've had getting to know each other while we've stayed in our little bubble.

But to have the girls' blessing and to be out and about with Henley...I'm ecstatic about it. Henley and I exchange a derpy grin with each other and Cassidy sighs.

"It's still weird," she says, making a face. "But a good weird."

"How about we do something together the next time you're at the house? A fishing day or swimming...or both," Henley says.

"I'd like that," Audrey says.

"Can we go fishing right now?" Gracie says, doing a little dance.

"How about Monday? You're spending the day with me then already, right?" Henley says to the girls. "We might as well make a fun day of it." He looks at me. "What do you say?"

"That works for me." I nod and look back at the girls.

"Yay," Gracie says.

"Well, this is fun," Bree says. "We should go sit down before they get rid of our table. I'm happy for you guys." She winks. The girls and Alex start walking to the table and she leans in. "It's about time you 'fessed up. You've been all lit up for months now," she says to Henley. "Dead giveaway."

Henley's laugh is gruff and warms my insides.

"Go eat," he grumbles.

Bree laughs and walks away.

Henley and I look at each other for a few long seconds, the smiles uncontained.

"Well, we did that," he says.

"We sure did."

"You know what this means, right?"

"What?"

"We're official."

I laugh and he does too, pulling me in closer, his head against mine.

Later that night, after we've worshipped each other's bodies and have rummaged through the kitchen, we climb back into his bed. My contacts are out for the night, so I grab my glasses and pick up the romance novel I'm reading, while he writes in The Single Dad Playbook. I glance over, my heart thumping as I take in his profile. He's so gorgeous and he's mine.

"Whatcha writing about?" I ask.

"In a way, I'm writing about us and today."

I'm so curious, but I know it's something he only shares with the guys, so I'm thrilled when he says, "You want to hear what I wrote?"

"I'm dying to."

He grins and starts reading.

There are these moments as a parent when you'll know
you've taught them well.
When you see them use their manners with strangers.
When they do a chore without being asked.
When they say they're sorry for something they've done
wrong.
When you let them know you're dating someone and they
accept it with grace,
despite it being a challenge.
Soak in those moments.
There will be plenty of times you feel like you're blowing it as
a dad,
but kids will surprise you.
They know how to take the high road better than anyone.
They're resilient and smart and funny.
And when you show them that you respect them,
you'll see that reflected back when they look at you.
I live for these moments.
~Henley

.   .   .

He's surprised when he sees me wiping tears from my face.

"I'm so glad I know a man like you, a dad like you," I tell him. "There are many things I love about you, but the way you love them is right up there at the top."

He sets the book aside and I do the same with mine, and we collide, our bodies greedy as we consume one another.

The following Monday is gorgeous, as if the sky and weather and all wildlife conspired to get along and be as perfect as possible. We're out on Henley's dock. The girls and I are lined up in a row in our swimsuits, toes dipping in the water. Gracie carefully hands out our lures to match our swimsuits —no live bait because it makes her too upset to "murder a cricket" and the colorful lures are entertainment on their own. I'm given a bug-eyed red fish that has orange and red strings trailing after him and I hold it up to my red swimsuit.

I'm not wearing the sexy bikini I've worn here when it's just Henley and me, but my tankini set is cute. Red on top with a black and white polka dot bottom.

"Nice match," I tell Gracie.

She nods, pleased.

"I know we said no live bait..." Henley pulls out a container.

We all eye him suspiciously. He looks a little too excited and I don't think it's because we're all together.

"But I heard these are the best to catch rainbow trout..." He opens the container and it's *filled* with maggots. He jiggles it our way and we all scramble to our feet, screaming our heads off, me included.

He picks one up and touches my cheek with it and I scream louder, only to realize that oh, that felt very similar to rubber. He's laughing his ass off and I swat his arm.

"That's not real, is it?" I pant, my stomach in my throat.

"It's not real," he admits, still laughing so hard.

It's a good thing he's so damn cute.

Gracie and Audrey tentatively reach out to touch them and then pick them up when they're certain they're not real.

"That is so disgusting." Cassidy shudders and then gags.

Henley wipes tears from his eyes as he tries to stop laughing, but he's still far too pleased with himself.

"You'll pay for that," I say, smirking.

"Oh, I will, huh?" He comes up behind me, his hands on my waist, and I shoot him a look.

He freezes.

"What?" he asks under his breath.

"Not in front of the girls," I say, between clenched teeth.

I try my best to look like I'm smiling, but it's hard to smile and clench teeth at the same time.

"What? Don't touch your waist?"

"Don't touch me at all," I continue between gritted teeth.

He looks like he wants to laugh again, but he drops his hands and holds them up.

"Okay, whatever you say, but for the record, I think they would be okay with it," he whispers, a little too loud for my liking.

I shoot him another look and sit back down where the girls have gotten back in place. He puts the lure on our hooks and hands us our fishing poles. Cassidy has hers already, but Audrey and I are waiting for Henley to do ours, and Gracie is still playing with the lures.

"You're making me nervous with all those fish hooks," I tell her.

"Don't worry. Daddy tells me to be so careful too," she says.

"He's right about that, not about the maggots, but he's right about being careful."

She giggles. "That was terrible." She makes a face.

"It sure was." I lean toward the girls and whisper, "We're going to have to figure out a way to get him back."

"What do we do?" Cassidy asks, excitement in her eyes.

"I'm not sure yet, but I think it will come to us. Let's just watch for opportunities today," I tell them, and they all nod excitedly.

"What's going on over here? What are you guys doing?" Henley asks.

"Nothing," we all say.

It's his turn to look suspicious as he tries to figure out what we're up to. Later that night, I realize we're going to have to make our opportunity because the day has been flawless from start to finish. We've caught enough fish to eat for supper. We've swam in the pool, eaten till our bellies are full, and laughed more than I have in a long time. It's been the best day.

When Henley gets up to turn off the grill, I lean in and whisper, "Okay, here's what I'm thinking. When we go in for the night, we could stage jump scares around the house..." I look around and they nod in agreement. "Who wants to be behind the door in the kitchen?"

"I do," Gracie says.

"I'll hide in the closet by the stairs and jump out when he passes," Audrey says.

We all giggle quietly.

"I'll be in the bedroom," Cassidy says.

"Oh, this is all good. Okay, I'll be in the bathroom. And remember, we have to be quiet."

They agree, and I stick my hand out in the middle of the table and they pile their hands on top. In that moment, I get a wave of giddiness. Henley's girls are accepting me. I love being around them and I think they love being around me too...even knowing I'm their dad's girlfriend. I want to laugh and cry and jump in the air and dance and scream out the loudest *woohoo!*

But instead, I just smile at them conspiratorially. "All right, it's on."

By the time he comes back to the table, we've got our game faces on. I look at Gracie and she stands up with her plate.

"I think I'll go inside now. The bugs are starting to bother me," she says.

I'm impressed by how convincing she sounds.

"Is the citronella candle not working?" Henley asks.

"No, I think I got a bite," she says, grinning at me.

He looks at me to see what's so funny and when I'm just smiling, he shakes his head.

"Okay, I guess we can take it in," he says.

Audrey and Cassidy jump up faster than I've seen them move all day and they head inside.

"Wow, I guess they're all ready to go in." He looks toward the house in surprise.

"I think I will too. I kind of need to check on something I left in there earlier," I mumble.

I pick up as much as I can carry and hustle into the house. We each get in our places and when Henley walks in, I can hear one by one as they jump out and scare him, and he yells and cracks up each time. I'm trying so hard not to giggle in my place behind the bathroom door. I have to wait a while. I hear him calling me, but I don't answer. When I hear him startled by Cassidy, it takes everything in me not to giggle out loud.

"What is going on, you guys? Is this payback for the maggots or what?"

I cover my mouth and laugh. I almost miss it when the door starts opening, but just in the nick of time, I jump out and say, *ha!* He jumps so high and groans, laughing.

"It's like the first time should have been my clue, but you've all gotten me every time." He leans against the back of the bathroom door, breathing hard and laughing.

"You're just too innocent, Mr. Football Player," I tell him.

"Or are the four of you just up to no good? My kind of no good," he adds, putting his hands on my waist.

"Ah, ah, ah," I say.

"No little eyes are looking," he says.

"Not until later," I sing.

"Oh, you'll pay for that," he promises.

And he makes good on that promise after the girls go home.

CHAPTER THIRTY-THREE

IN A SPLIT SECOND

HENLEY

I jog out onto Clarity Field's sidelines. Colorado is still feeling a spike of heat even though it's the end of September. I'm tired and missing Tru and the girls after an intense week of practices, but I'm in the middle of a great game. It's halftime, we're up by fourteen, and Coach Evans just gave the halftime speech of a lifetime back in the locker room. We're pumped, and with good reason. Besides the loss to the

Vikings last week, we've won every other game this season. And I'm ready to make up for that loss tonight.

Tru is up in the suite with our friends and family and I look up there to see if I can catch a glimpse of her. She's wearing my jersey and it just does something for me. My family adores her. My parents have visited several times since we've been dating, and they prefer her to me. I don't blame them. I prefer her too. Pretty sure my girls feel the same. All three of them hog her when they're over, and she says she loves every second.

I only have one complaint: Tru is insistent that there is no PDA around the girls. I'm trying to change her mind about that, but she's stubborn. She more than makes up for it whenever we're alone though.

We have regular game nights with the girls now and I don't think I've ever laughed so much. It hit home one night when I dropped the girls off and Audrey said, "You smile a lot now, Dad."

I met her eye in the mirror and could tell her eyes were smiling.

"You think so?" Yeah, I'm cheesing right back at her.

Cassidy pointed at me, laughing. "You look like that all the time."

"Like what?"

"Like you're in lurve," she sang.

"I am," I said. "I *am*."

"TMI." Cassidy held her hands over her ears.

"I like lurve," Gracie said, laughing.

"Me too," Audrey said.

"Me three," I chimed in.

"Ugh, you guys are nauseating," Cassidy said, but she laughed, and when she looked over at me, she put her hand on my shoulder and shook me. "Tru's good for you," she said softly.

I don't think I've ever been any prouder or happier than I was right then.

Jeremy says I need to put a ring on it and coming from him, that's the highest praise. He's happily married, but after Bree and I divorced, he was all about me living the bachelor life. He's singing a different tune now that he knows Tru.

I'd be happy if I could convince her to move in with me. Her mom is doing great, moving forward with a divorce and fitting in to the Silver Hills life, but Tru is still hesitant to move out and leave her.

I'm more than ready. It just feels right when she's there. I glance up at the box again, my thoughts on getting caught with her in the rain a few nights ago. She was in jean shorts, not her typical attire, but she looked so damn cute in them, I hauled her onto my shoulders. Instead of wanting to run inside, she leaned over and kissed me. We ended up under the eave of the pool house, her jean shorts history, as we created a storm of our own. She was still hoarse yesterday from screaming out my name.

Fuck.

I swipe my hand down my face, trying to cover my grin. I can't think about any of that in these football tights, as she still calls them.

Liver and onions.

Curdled milk.

Roadkill.

Those sad puppy eyes on the heartbreaking ASPCA commercials.

Okay, dick crisis mostly averted.

"You ready?" Coach Evans asks.

"Born ready," I tell him.

"You're on fire out there tonight. Carry it on home," he says.

Weston gives us some last-minute directions as we huddle, and we pound each other on the back before we run onto the field.

Time to put our foot on their neck.

But a couple uncharacteristic miscues leave the door open. Arizona's offense seizes the opportunity and starts working their way back into the game. With time winding down in the fourth quarter, they throw up a prayer, and suddenly it's all tied up.

We run the offense back onto the field with just under two minutes left on the clock, determined to make a statement. Our two-minute drill is starting to click, and it feels so good. We've moved forty-some yards in just three plays and hardly eaten any time off the clock.

In the huddle, Weston calls me out. "Forty-nine, red, on three."

I've had two defenders on me the whole game, but they fall back when Penn takes the handoff and runs toward me. I'm already headed back the opposite way with a full head of steam when he pitches me the ball. It's a perfectly executed reverse.

By the time I hit the line of scrimmage, the defense is already beat, and I'm headed for pay dirt.

About ten yards from the goal line, out of the corner of my eye, I see the free safety desperately racing toward me, so I step it up, surging faster than ever.

And I get there.

I break into the end zone feeling like I could still run another forty yards, the adrenaline is pumping so fast.

I'm about to spike the ball and start the party, when I feel it.

I'm tackled from the side. The crowd is roaring too loud to hear the crunch in my knee, but I feel it, and I instantly know it's not good. A penalty is called on the other player, but it barely registers. The pain is blinding and when I'm unable to get up right away, I'm surrounded within minutes. Dr. Grinstead and Jimmy Scott, our head team physician and athletic trainer, are the first two faces I see when I roll to my back.

"What is it?" Dr. Grinstead asks.

"My knee," I croak out.

Jesus, this is bad. My eyes squeeze shut as I pray and curse and try to take a breath. This is so fucking bad.

I look at Dr. Grinstead and see the alarm on his face.

There's very little that has kept me down in my career. I've had my fair share of injuries, but I've been lucky.

I've also been a stubborn son of a bitch and walked off the field every single time.

This is different.

ACL tears are one of the things we fear most, and I'm pretty sure that's what just happened.

A stretcher comes out and it takes everything in me to not yell when they lift me up onto the cart. As they start rolling me out, I realize the entire team is surrounding me. I lift my head and look around, relief flooding me when I see the guys.

"Tell Tru and the girls that I'm okay."

Bowie nods. "We will."

"Love you, man. Please be okay," Rhodes says.

"You've got this," Penn yells.

Weston's eyes are intense as he grips my hand. "We'll be back to check on you as soon as we can."

As I'm taken out on the injury cart, the noise in the stadium builds to a roar. I hear my name coming from every direction. There is stomping and clapping and I close my eyes and let the sound fan the last flame of hope that I'll be back out on this field again.

CHAPTER THIRTY-FOUR

I DON'T LIKE THIS PART

TRU

The fear I feel when Henley doesn't get back up is indescribable. I'm still a newbie to football, but since the season began, I've been to every home game, including the ones during the preseason.

Every time he's tackled, my heart stops, but he always hops right back up, that grin visible from the field, and he brushes it off like it's nothing. Even though I can see later that he's hurting.

We've spent many hours in the hot tub to ease his aches and pains. The game is taking a toll on his body, but he never shows it...so when he stays down on the field for too long, I feel like I might collapse myself.

"What's happening?" Cassidy asks. "Why isn't he getting up?"

The girls and I clutch each other's hands and I pick Gracie up when she starts crying.

When the stretcher lifts him up and puts him on the cart, I study the screen to see if I can tell anything. His eyes are squeezed shut, but his hands are clenching.

He's not unconscious.

He's okay, he's okay, he's okay.

Please be okay.

They roll off the field and the noise is deafening.

"What should we do?" I look at Sadie. "Can I go down there? Can I take the girls with me?"

"I think so," she says. "I'll come with you. I don't know if they'll let us see him, but we can try."

I leave the suite with the girls and we rush through the back halls, Sadie leading the way. Timothy, one of the trainers, is outside the office when we get there. He motions for us to follow him.

"He wanted you to know he's okay. All of you," he says, looking at me and the girls.

"What happened?" I ask.

"I wish I knew more..."

"Can we see him?"

"He's with the doctor right now and if he has anything to say about it, you'll see him soon. He was more worried about you guys than anything."

Gracie buries her head in my hair and sniffles and my other hand grips Audrey's as we follow Timothy. I can tell we're getting close because of the crowd slowly gathering around the closed door. I've seen the way these guys look after they've just won a game and this is not it. They look gutted and it just adds to the apprehension I'm feeling.

My phone buzzes and I pull it out. Bree.

"I should take this. It's your mom," I tell the girls. "Hey, Bree."

"Is he okay?"

"I haven't seen him yet, but one of the trainers says he is. The girls are with me. I'll let you know what's going on as soon as I've seen him."

"Thank you. Hug the girls for me and tell Henley that Alex and I are praying for him."

"I will."

We hang up, and when it's time for us to go back, I rush to Henley's side. He grabs my hand and the girls take turns hugging him. We surround him, and I try to stay calm for everyone's sake, but inside, I'm still panicking.

"I'm okay. I'm okay," he says, but he looks awful.

His coloring is wrong. His forehead is clammy and the way he's squeezing my hand, I can tell he's hurting.

"What happened? I asked.

"They're saying it's most likely an ACL tear and that I may need surgery in a few weeks. After X-rays, we'll have a better idea. An ambulance is waiting to take me to the hospital, but I wanted to see you first." He lifts my hand to his lips and kisses it. I brush back his hair and lean down to kiss his forehead.

When I lean back, his eyes are intense.

"I'm so sorry you're hurting." I can hardly get the words out.

I'm sorry for more than his pain, although I hate knowing

he's hurting more than anything, but I'm also sorry for what this could mean for his career. That's the unspoken giant in the room.

Gracie whimpers in my arms and he reaches out to squeeze her arm.

"I'm okay, peanut," he says to Gracie.

He reaches out and motions for Audrey and Cassidy to come closer. They lean down to hug him again.

"Look at me. I'll be fine," he tells them.

They all cry and he puts his hand on Audrey's face. "Don't worry," he says. "My knee hurts a lot, but it's not the end of the world. Okay?"

"Are you going to be able to play football again?" Cassidy asks, through her tears.

He winces. "I don't know. I really don't know."

He meets my eyes and I see the fear and pain there. It kills me.

"We need to head out," Dr. Grinstead says. "You can meet us over at the hospital if you want."

"I'll be there," I say.

"You don't have to come," Henley says. "Dr. Grinstead says they'll most likely keep me overnight to run all the tests. I can have someone take me home tomorrow."

"I don't know who you think you're talking to, but I'll be there."

He swallows hard. "I love you, tiny dancer. I love all my girls."

He forces out a smile to the girls. I can tell by his breathing that he's in so much pain.

"We love you. I'll be there soon," I promise.

The girls want to go with me to the hospital, but after I call Bree again to let her know what's going on, we arrange a place to meet so she can get the girls. She says she'll take them over to the house to see Henley once he's home. They're not happy about this, but I do as Bree asks and then head over to the hospital. It's one of the things I'm learning is challenging about being the significant other of a parent...I don't have the final word.

I'm mostly okay with that, but in this situation, knowing how worried the girls are, I wish they were given the choice to decide whether they're at the hospital or not. But I'm going to trust that Bree knows what's best there.

I rush to the hospital and since Dr. Grinstead knew I was coming, I'm immediately taken to Henley's room. I recognize Jimmy Scott, but not the other handful of people in the room. No sign of Henley. They stop talking for a moment to look at me, their expressions grave.

"Hi, Tru," Jimmy says. "Henley's still getting an MRI and another couple of tests. He should be back soon."

I nod. "I'll be in the waiting room just outside."

I back out before they can say anything else, the need to bolt from the room too strong. I can tell by how devastated the men in this room look that what's happening with Henley is not good.

I want to ask them what this means for his career. What the chances are for a player who's had this injury. In my hurry to get the girls to Bree and to come here, I haven't had time to look anything up. It's just as well, I didn't need to be any more fearful than I already was. But now that I have time, I open my phone and what I read on there has me tearing up. When I hear people coming, I put my phone away and wipe my face.

Sadie and Weston are walking toward me and when I stand up to hug Sadie, I see my mom coming too. It makes me start crying all over again.

Sadie gives me a sympathetic smile when I pull away.

"Elle called on our way over. She's sending her love and wants you to call her if you need company—or anything at all —when you go back home. She was on her way here, but I told her she better not risk being seen with the players. Calista will be here soon."

"Thank you. I don't want Elle to risk it either. But I'm so glad you're here." I can hardly get the words out. I'm not used to having a support system like this.

"The guys are right behind us. They got stopped by fans. Sadie and I managed to sneak past," Weston says. "Have you seen Henley yet?"

"Only at the stadium. He's still having tests done."

When my mom reaches me, she wraps her arms around me. "How did he seem?" she asks.

"Like he's in so much pain," my voice breaks. I swallow hard and smile at her.

"He won that game," she says, shaking her head. "I've never seen anything like it."

"He's the best there is," Weston says. "I can't believe Anderson made such a cheap shot." His eyes are so sad when I look up at him. "I really hope Hen has more time to play—" He stops and swallows, crinkling his face. "I don't need to say things like that. He's going to recover and be one hundred percent."

It's what we all want to believe, but those statistics I just read are playing through my mind and Weston is more aware of the usual outcomes of this injury than I am. If wishful thinking and positivity can make it happen though, I want to do my part.

Sadie squeezes my hand and we all sit down. Bowie, Rhodes, and Penn gradually make their way to the waiting room and Calista is just arriving when Jimmy sticks his head in the door.

"Henley's in his room and he's asking for you, Tru," he says.

"Tell him we love him," Rhodes says, and they all chime in as I stand up and walk toward the door.

"And let us know if you need any food or anything," Calista says. "We can go pick something up."

"Thanks, guys. I'll keep you posted."

Henley's room is still full when I walk in and move toward his bed. I take his hand and lean in to kiss him. "How are you feeling?"

"Not my best day," he says, brushing my hair back.

He pats the bed and I try to sit there, but it's a tight spot and I don't want to hurt him. I opt for standing.

"It's what I thought—my ACL is torn. It's not good."

"I'm so sorry," I say softly. "What happens next?"

Dr. Grinstead clears his throat and we turn to look at him.

"We were just talking about it and it was too depressing. I wanted to see you instead." Henley grins, but I can tell it takes effort.

"Did they give you anything?"

"Yes. I'm okay."

"No, you're not."

He puts my hand up to his lips and kisses it. "Better now that you're here."

"We'll see how things look this week," Dr. Grinstead says. "What the range of motion is looking like after a few days…how Henley responds to physical therapy…and hopefully we won't have to do surgery, but if so, we've got the best of the best on standby, ready to get on the first flight when that time comes. We won't know for sure if that's our course of action for another couple of weeks."

It's still surprising to me what a different world it is for famous football players, especially since Henley is so down to earth, but he's treated like royalty everywhere he goes. Even now as we're talking, a pitcher of iced water and Gatorade are placed next to his bed, with a better-than-any-hospital-food-I've-ever-seen meal. Henley thanks the guy, who blushes furiously before backing out of the room.

"When can I get out of here?" Henley asks.

"Since there's no concussion or other internal injuries, we'll let you go home tonight, but you can't put weight on this leg, Henley," Dr. Grinstead says firmly. "Elevate it, ice it, stay on top of the anti-inflammatories. We'll see how it looks tomorrow. I can't stress the importance of you taking it easy...and not the way you usually *think* you're taking it easy when you've been injured..." He gives Henley a pointed look. "We want that swelling to go way down and we want you playing again. It's important you take this seriously."

Henley nods. "I'm taking it seriously, trust me."

I message everyone that Henley gets to go home tonight and they offer to bring food to the house, but I tell them we'll be okay. Henley doesn't have much of an appetite and I just want him to sleep as soon as he can. They stop by the room before they go and huddle around his bed.

"You gave us quite a scare," Bowie says.

"Yeah, don't ever do that again," Rhodes adds, putting his hand on Henley's shoulder.

"Name it, whatever you need, and we'll do it, Hen. Just say the word. Or have Tru tell us," Weston says.

"You won that game for us like the motherfucking star you are," Penn says.

They all get emotional then, these big, muscled football players pure mush, and I'm sniffling along with the rest of them.

They say their goodbyes, hugging me after they hug Henley, and within an hour or so, Henley gets to go home too. I don't even consider staying at my house tonight. I think I need to sleep by his side even more than he needs me to.

CHAPTER THIRTY-FIVE

SHADOWS GATHERING

HENLEY

"Are you not hungry?" Tru asks, eyeing the massive Reuben sandwich I've hardly touched.

"It's delicious, but yeah, can't seem to eat much," I say apologetically.

It's a Sunday afternoon and Tru and I are watching the game from home. It's a rare moment lately for us to have the house to ourselves. My parents and brother were here for a couple of weeks to help me with things, and my mom will be returning later this week. The girls left a little while ago for dress fittings. Bree's wedding is in early December, and it will be here before we know it. Stephanie's here a lot too, and I really love that woman.

When Tru's not at work, she and Earl have been here with me, and it's the only positive thing that's happened over the past few weeks. I'm still treating it as something temporary though. Because as much as I want her to move in with me, I don't want her to decide to do it just because I'm going through a hard time. But I love waking up with her by my side and going to sleep with her face being the last one I see.

It's been three weeks since my injury and it's been fucking hell. My knee hasn't improved the way it needs to and I'll be having surgery in a few days. The pain is rough but tolerable. I'm used to pain, but what I'm having the most trouble with are all the unknowns.

I didn't want to go out this way.

That's the thought that stays on a loop in my mind now. When I'm working with my physical therapist, when I'm unable to sleep in the middle of the night, when I watch my team on their way to losing their second game in a row…I want to know if I'll be given another chance to get out there and play again.

I wanted to go out on top. End this phenomenal career I've had on my own terms.

"Fuck!" I yell at the screen when Penn fumbles the ball.

Tru jumps next to me, and I put my arm around her, tugging her closer.

They call a time-out and I give up trying to make out what they're saying.

"I'm sorry," I say softly in her ear. "I need to chill the fuck out. It's harder than I thought to be on this side of things." I kiss her hair and she softens in my arms. "Mmm, you feel good, tiny dancer." I cup her breast and my dick stands to attention when her nipple pebbles. "I don't know how you've put up with me the past three weeks. I've been a bear."

She turns to face me and puts her hand on my cheek. "Your version of being a bear is so tame, Henley Ward," she says. "You haven't yelled at anything but the TV screen, you haven't thrown anything, you've put up with endless company and grueling appointments, all while being the sweetest man who ever lived. I don't know how you're not showing some meanness by now. My father would have ripped me and my mom to shreds every single day if he were going through something like this."

From the things she's told me about Allen, and the one-sided conversations I've heard her have with him on the phone since her mom left, it's enough to make me hate the man.

"I hope I never remind you of your father."

"There's no possible way you ever could."

I lean in and kiss her, groaning when she pulls away too soon.

"Don't you want to watch the game?" she asks, laughing.

"No," I mumble. "Yes. *No*." I lean in for another kiss. "Okay, I guess I do. But I miss you," I say against her mouth. "I don't want you to keep holding back from me."

We've messed around here and there, but we haven't had sex since I hurt my knee. Her refusal to hurt me is sweet but unnecessary. The need to make her feel good, to lose myself in her and not be able to the way I want, is driving me crazy.

She moves back to look in my eyes. "I'd never forgive myself if I did something to make your pain worse. Or to keep you from healing the way you need to."

"I feel no pain when you kiss me."

She smiles, her eyes going all melty the way I love. "And I want to keep it that way."

I groan again, but she points to the TV.

"They're back on."

I watch the game, but I slide my hand down the front of her leggings and my mouth waters when I find her wet. I tease her with my fingers, getting her close and then backing off, until she's squirming underneath me.

When our team loses the game, I pull my fingers out of her and lick them clean. "Tru?"

"Yes?" she pants.

"I'm going to stretch out on this couch and I need you to come over here and ride my face. Okay?"

Her cheeks flush and she nods. My dick bobs in victory. She stands and tugs her shirt over her head. I grin when her tits bounce and she smirks as she turns her back to me and lowers her leggings. She bends over, the flexible goddess that she is, giving me the most exquisite view, and I adjust my dick, cursing.

"You can't possibly know what you're doing to me, tiny dancer."

I tug her hand to face me and she shakes her head, surprising me by moving to sit with her back to me instead. Her ass is close enough to bite and so I do, and she looks at me over her shoulder, her full lips lifting in a seductive smile.

"This view is phenomenal, but my mouth is up here," I say, squeezing her perfect peach-shaped ass.

She ignores me, lowering my shorts and pulling down my boxer briefs until I pop out, my dick slapping heavily onto my stomach, hard and long past ready. When she leans down and takes me in her mouth, I choke back a hiss and pull her sweet lips to my face. She hums her approval around me, and I lose myself in her taste and the way she works me over.

I don't think about the pain or what comes next or anything but the way she flutters against my tongue and the way I want to get lost in her forever.

When she starts coming, her whimpers against me egging me on, my orgasm threatens to barrel through me. I spread her wide and lick her until she's limp against me. It takes supernatural effort to not lose my shit before I've satisfied her, but when her contractions on my tongue finally slow down, she doubles her efforts, her mouth hollowing out around me. She devours me and it is fucking earth-*shattering*.

I try to warn her I'm coming, but she doesn't pull back. It's so intense when I spill into her, when I feel her swallowing...I see fucking stars. She makes a hungry sound and I shoot another stream into her.

"*Fuck*, Tru," I croak when I can finally speak coherently. "So fucking good." I press my fingers to my eyes, my dick still twitching in her mouth. "I wish I could flip you over and fuck the sense out of both of us."

Her mouth slides off of me with a pop and she laughs, turning to look back at me.

"I must've not gotten you good enough if you're already thinking about more."

"You got me so good, my vision still hasn't fully returned. And I'm always thinking about more." My fingers trail down her back as she carefully climbs off of me.

The pain in my leg screams out, as if to say, *"How dare you forget about me, you filthy bastard?"*

My hands and jaw reflexively fist, but I keep my face trained on her, determined not to let her see my pain. Not now when she already worries too much that she's going to hurt me.

"We're going to make up for lost time when you're fully recovered," she says, bending down to kiss me.

I grab onto her hair and tilt her head, deepening our kiss until we're both breathless.

"I'm not waiting until I'm fully recovered to be inside you," I tell her.

She lifts an eyebrow. "Is that so?"

She bites her bottom lip and I lean in and tug it from her teeth.

"That's so," I say, my hands cupping her tits. I lean in and swirl my tongue around those pretty tips and she inhales a shaky breath.

"Henley," she whispers.

My dick jerks to life, ready for another round.

She pulls back. "Am I gonna have to go stay at my house?"

I pull my eyes away from her breasts and look at her in alarm. "You want to leave?"

She laughs and kisses me again. "No, you big oaf. I'm not leaving. But don't think I didn't see how you tried to mask how much you're hurting just now."

"Because we *stopped*." I say it with a smirk and a playful tone because I don't want her to know how fucking true it is.

But I don't try to stop her again when she starts to put her clothes back on.

The last thing I want to do is guilt my girlfriend into having sex or staying here if she wants to go home.

"Maybe you should go home tonight," I tell her after I'm tucked back into my shorts and sitting up. "Have a girls' night with your mom or Sadie and Elle and Calista...I'm good here and the guys said they'd stop by later."

Her lips part and she shakes her head. "I was teasing, Henley."

"I know, but...you've been here for weeks and you don't

have to stay here every night. Take a break. Go have some fun."

"Do you need a break from me?" Her forehead furrows in the center and I reach out to smooth it.

"Never. But go. Please. I'll be fine here." The more I say it, the more I'm convinced she needs to do this.

She frowns and looks around the room. She picks up a pillow that fell off the couch and puts it back in place.

"I guess I could use a trip to the house to grab a few sweaters now that it's getting colder."

"Okay, sounds good." I pick up the remote and turn the sound up when I hear them talking about the Mustangs.

Tru clears her throat and when I look at her, she seems lost. "Do you need anything before I go?"

"Nope. Just...go already."

She flinches as she's bending to kiss me. "Wow. Okay, call or text if you need me."

"I didn't mean anything by that." I shake my head. "I just don't want you worrying about me," I tell her.

She tries to hide it, but I can tell I've hurt her feelings. She leaves quickly and I feel like such an asshole. When I hear the front door close and her car start, my head falls back on the couch. And I'm not sure why now, but everything I've been holding inside for the past three weeks comes flooding out.

I message the guys.

> Hey, guys. I'm sorry for the loss today. And sorry to ask if we can do a rain check on hanging out. I'm worn out and I think I need to crash.

PENN

We miss you! You sure you don't need some company?

BOWIE

Rest. We can come over tomorrow.

RHODES

I hope you're okay, man. It doesn't feel right, not seeing you on game day.

> I miss you guys too. Let's catch up another day.

And then I message Tru.

> Hey, tiny dancer. I'm sorry. You didn't deserve my foul mood today. I'm gonna head to bed early tonight. I hope you're out doing something fun for a change. Let's talk tomorrow. I love you.

TRU

Sleep well. I love you.

I've been hovering over a dark place since the injury, but this is the first time I fully fall into it.

It's best that I'm alone for a while. I don't want Tru or anyone else to see me this way.

CHAPTER THIRTY-SIX

SHORT-LIVED

TRU

I had a horrible night. Earl got annoyed with how much I was up and down. I must have checked my phone a hundred times, and each time was more unsatisfying than the last. Nothing from Henley. No texts. No phone calls.

I'm trying not to worry, but after I ended up in my car crying when I left him yesterday afternoon, it's been hard to just shake that off when I'm not hearing anything from him.

I break down and text him.

> Good morning! Missed you last night. How are you feeling today?

> I hope you're catching up on sleep. Let me know how you're feeling...and if you're craving anything. I can bring it over during my lunch break.

When I get to school and still haven't heard anything. I text the guys, asking if they've talked to him.

RHODES

> He said he was going to bed early last night, so we didn't see him, and I haven't talked to him today.

BOWIE

> I texted him that I'd stop by on my way back from the gym, but I haven't heard anything.

WESTON

> Same. I told him Caleb and I were about to pick up something from Serendipity and asked if I could grab something for him and take it over.

PENN

> I'm actually at his gate now. Beau is seeing if he's available.

I text Henley again.

> I'm not used to you being so quiet. Everything okay? Are we okay?

> Maybe you had an appointment I'd forgotten about. I might stop by during lunch.

It's impossible to put it out of my mind while I'm teaching, but I try. I see Cassidy in the hall and ask if she's talked to him. She says she hasn't but that they're stopping by after school.

During my lunch break, I drive over and talk to Beau and Linc. Beau lets me through the gate, but there's no answer at the door. Henley had talked about having a key made for me, but we still haven't done that, and since I left yesterday thinking I'd be right back, I didn't bother taking one with me.

That afternoon after school, I'm starting to get a sick feeling.

> I've talked with the guys and they haven't heard back from you either. I'm worried, Henley.

When my phone dings, my hands are shaking when I pick up the phone, and I let out a relieved exhale when I see that it's Henley.

That relief is short-lived.

HENLEY
> I'm okay. I just need a little time to wrap my head around all of this. I need to work through some things on my own. I hope you understand.

I hope you understand? What does that even mean? I understand he's trying to come to terms with what's happening to him, but what is he *not* saying here? The last thing he said last night is that he loves me, but today he sounds so distant. Is he trying to break up with me?

I go home and cuddle with Earl while grading papers instead of going over to Henley's. After stewing over it too long, I finally text him back.

I understand you needing time to work through this, but I want to walk through this with you. I wish you wouldn't shut me out.

HENLEY

I'm the worst company right now.

I start blubbering and Earl looks up at me.

"Meow?"

"He's shutting me out when he needs me the most," I tell my cat.

Earl nuzzles his head under my hand and his next meow sounds like he's agreeing with me.

"When did you get so smart?" I sigh.

It just gets worse over the next few days. Henley's hardly talking to any of us, Bree and the girls included. He's never been like this before, and it's so out of character that no one knows what to do. His excuse is that he's taking some time to work through things and he doesn't want anyone affected by his foul mood.

We're all affected. I haven't been sleeping and the tears are coming way too often. The guys are stressed and we all feel helpless. The concern for him is only building at an alarming rate.

On day four, Bowie calls as I'm leaving the school. I pick up on the first ring.

"Hey, Tru. You doing okay?"

"Not really."

"I'm so sorry about that. What can I do to help?"

"Have you checked on Henley? I'd feel better knowing if he's okay."

"That's part of why I'm calling. I just remembered that Henley gave me a key to his place when I was having my house remodeled. I'd forgotten all about it and came across it just a few minutes ago. I'm going over there and checking on him, and I'll let you know how he seems, okay?"

"That's great. Please, let me know. And let him know I just want him to be okay. If he...if he doesn't want to be with me anymore, I'll...I'll deal with that, but I want to know he's okay."

"Tru..." Bowie's voice is soft. "He loves you. It's not that he doesn't want to be with you anymore. I think he's just...in a dark place."

"I don't know," I admit. "I think I have to accept that he might not want to be with me anymore."

"I'll talk with him."

"Okay. Thanks, Bowie."

I'm distracted during dance and Jacklyn lets me go a little earlier than usual. I stop by the grocery store on the way home, and later, my mom and I watch a movie. But my mind is on Henley.

I should've seen this coming with him. He's been quiet and withdrawn. The light in his eyes has dimmed and he's been in his own little world. I keep telling myself that this isn't about me, but I'd be lying if I said it didn't stir up old wounds.

Am I not enough? Is he not happy with me? The fears my dad instilled in me come to the surface at the worst times.

If he wants to end this, I need to know it.

CHAPTER THIRTY-SEVEN

WASHED UP

HENLEY

I get out of bed and hobble to my closet, in a hurry to get ready for practice, before I remember that it's not only evening and not time for practice, but I wouldn't be at practice anyway. I crawl back into bed and groan, hoping that I can go back to sleep and not have to deal with all the shit going on in my head.

Sleep is the only time my head is quiet, and even then, my

dreams aren't always playing nice. But it's still better than being awake and dealing with all the emotional junk.

I don't want to think about it. I don't want everyone else thinking about it either. I want everyone to go about their business and be happy, while I take a break from reality.

I'm *tired*. It's been a long road. All the sacrifices I've made to play this game....the ways my body has been wrecked, the times I've missed with my family, the way my life is not my own, but every detail is broadcasted on the news channels like I'm up for public consumption.

It's exhausting.

And as much as I've tried to keep this injury from consuming me, I think it's caught up with me.

When I fall asleep again, it's fitful, one nightmare after another.

"Henley?"

I turn to the sound and then feel my shoulder being shaken.

"Henley," I hear, firmer this time.

I open my eyes, blinking rapidly, and Bowie comes into focus. He's in my room, standing over me, and when he sees that I'm awake, he stands upright. My lamp is turned on and he glances around the room, wincing when he sees the disaster.

"So, this is how it is," he says.

I feel ashamed, like I've just been caught with my pants down in church or something.

I sit up and Bowie's nose twitches.

"Dude, when's the last time you showered?"

"I was going to shower soon," I tell him.

"Yeah, that's a good call." He starts picking up the pizza boxes, frowning when he feels how heavy they still are.

"Were you done with these or have they been sitting out for a while?"

"They've been sitting out a while, but I can get it. I said I would let you all know when I was ready to start seeing people…"

He looks at me and swallows hard. "Let me help, Hen."

I stare at him. "I'm fine, Bowie."

"Clearly, you're not."

He moves around the room, picking up my trash and taking it downstairs. When he comes back, he has a bag and he finishes picking things up. I move to the bathroom and take a shower, careful not to get my fucking leg wet. Bowie is in the kitchen when I'm done getting cleaned up, and it's a lot cleaner than the last time I saw it too.

"Thank you," I say quietly.

"It's the least I can do. You were there for me when I needed you. And there are so many people in your life who want to be there for you. I haven't been through what you're going through and I can only imagine how much it hurts, both physically and emotionally, but what are you fucking doing, man?"

I stare at him in surprise. Bowie doesn't raise his voice often, and when he does, it's on the field. He's never raised his voice at me.

But apparently he's not done.

"You have a woman who loves you. She would do anything for you, and she's worried sick about you because you've completely shut her out."

I look down at the floor. "I'm not what she signed up for. She's young and has her whole life ahead of her. She shouldn't be stuck playing nurse to some washed-up athlete."

"She couldn't care less what you do for a living. *You* are what she signed up for. And you can't decide for her what she needs and doesn't need. You're going to lose the best thing that ever happened to you if you don't get your head out of your ass!"

I stare at him in shock.

"And you think this is doing your kids a favor? This withdrawing bullshit? They don't need to see you be perfect Henley all the time. Your girls need to know that sometimes we fall, but what's important is how we get back up."

I slide my hand down my face. "I...I hear ya."

"You're not doing *anyone* any favors by acting like you don't need any help. You're only prolonging the healing process by isolating yourself and trying to do it alone. "

"I haven't wanted anyone to see me this way. I'm not used to sinking quite this deep into...this dark pit."

"Have you talked to Dr. Katie?"

"She's tried to set up several appointments, but no, I haven't yet."

He shoots me a withering look and I curse under my breath. Bowie doing the tough love shit is a hard-ass.

"It's why we have paid psychologists on the team, for times like these...and for a lot less than what you've been through. You like Dr. Katie, right? She's easy to talk to." Bowie lifts his eyebrows when I don't answer right away.

"Yeah, sure. She's easy to talk to. We've never gone super deep, but—" I let out a long sigh. "I guess it's time."

"I suggest you set up an appointment with her right away...see your girls...and your fucking girlfriend!" His cheeks get red as he glares at me.

"I didn't mean to make things worse. I just needed a couple days to think."

"And how have these four days of you thinking all alone gone for you?" He puts his hands on his hips and stares me down.

"Fuck. It's been four days?"

He nods.

Fuck.

I press my fingers over my eyes. "Thank you for checking on me. Did Beau let you in?"

"I still had your key from the time Becca and I stayed here. Beau and Linc have been letting your cleared list through your gate—we may have been acting more like you were expecting us than is really the truth," he admits. "But no, they'd never let anyone inside. I can tell they're worried about you too though."

I nod. "Okay, I'll take care of it."

He turns on my dishwasher. "Should we order some takeout?"

"Actually, I think I need to make a few phone calls."

"I'd leave you in peace to do that, but I want to stick around for a while and just make sure..." He grins for the first time since he got here, and I chuckle quietly.

"Suit yourself. Go ahead and order whatever sounds good to you then, and I'll get started on this." I wave my phone.

"I'm ordering enough for you too—you need to eat," he says as I walk onto the deck.

I wave over my head and hobble outside, trying to situate myself comfortably on one of the chairs.

I text Bree and the girls first.

> I'm sorry I've been so quiet this week. I haven't meant to hurt your feelings by shutting you out, but I know it's probably resulted in that. I've been dealing with some things and not in the healthiest way. I hope you'll forgive me for that. If you have time to come over tonight, I'd love to see you, or we can plan on tomorrow too. Or both. Love you all.

And then I don't hesitate to call Tru.

She picks up right away. "Henley?"

"It's me. I'm so sorry, tiny dancer. I've been trying to deal with all these feelings myself and ended up being a selfish dick in the process."

"It's okay," she says softly.

"No, it's not."

She's quiet for a moment. "I'm sad you thought you had to deal with it alone. But maybe I'm just not the one you need with you right now."

"I need you most of all," I tell her.

"Then let me in. Don't shut me out."

"Can you come over tonight? Better yet, move in with me."

She laughs. "I'll come over tonight."

"I can't wait to see you. I've missed you so much...I will do better."

"You don't have to be better than you are. I can walk through this with you."

"I love you. Bowie reminded me that I need to see the team's psychologist too, so I'll be doing that soon."

"That's a great idea. I love you, Henley. I'm really glad you called. I was afraid..." Her voice cracks. "I thought you might be breaking up with me."

My breath hitches. "No. You deserve better than me, but I'm not going anywhere. I almost lost sight of what is most important, but I won't make that mistake again. I promise you that."

CHAPTER THIRTY-EIGHT

I'LL HAVE WHAT HE'S HAVING

TRU

We've talked so much more since I've been back at Henley's, but it still hasn't been easy. For the past two nights, I've woken up in the middle of the night and he hasn't been in bed. I've found him in the living room watching old Mustangs games or just sitting in the dark.

But now that he's let me in, I'm not scaring off easily. He had an appointment with Dr. Katie and that helped, but it's not going to turn around overnight. I'm too worried about him to leave him alone again…not just about his recovery, but about his state of mind.

We're driving to the hospital the morning of the surgery, and it's still dark out. I glance over at Henley. He's staring out the window and looks so sad.

"Hey," I say quietly. We're at a stoplight near the hospital and he turns to look at me. I clench the steering wheel. "I love you no matter what."

He stares at me, his throat working as he swallows, and he reaches out and touches my face.

"I love you, Tru Seymour."

The light turns and I just want to keep looking at him, but I look at the road.

"I'm sorry I've been a lot to handle." His voice is scratchy and sleepy. "I'm afraid…"

I wait, my heart pounding with his words. When he doesn't say anything else, I glance at him.

"I'm afraid it's just gonna get worse," he adds.

"The pain?"

"This darkness I've been feeling. I don't want it to, but I can't seem to snap out of it."

"You don't have to snap out of anything. You're hurting, you're uncertain of what comes next…it's a lot to go through."

"It's pretty stupid when you think about it—it's just a game." He snorts and adjusts in his seat.

"Don't say that. It's not stupid at all. The game is your life."

I pull into the hospital parking lot and go around to the entrance that they told us would be more private. A few guards are lined up as promised, and there's a wheelchair waiting to take him inside.

I want to keep talking. When he's opening up like this, I don't want him thinking any of his feelings are foolish.

But his door is opened for him and everything moves quickly from there. He's whisked away, with a nurse telling me she'll come get me before he goes into surgery so I can see him. The exhaustion of the morning hits me when I reach the waiting room.

I feel little arms around me and startle, looking down into Gracie's big eyes.

"Hey!" I say in surprise, hugging her back.

Bree, Cassidy, and Audrey aren't far behind.

"Thought you might need this," Bree says, holding out coffee and a pastry. "Wyndham and Greer send their love."

"That's so sweet. Thank you." I hug them all and then take a sip of coffee. "Mmm, I'm usually at Luminary, so I forget how good Serendipity's coffee is too. I did need this…"

"How's he doing?" Bree asks.

"I'm worried about him." I meet her eyes and both of us fight back tears.

"I am too," she says. "Besides the girls, I don't think I've ever understood what it's like to be passionate about something until I started my business…and as much as I'm loving it, it's not even *close* to how much Henley has loved football. And he's really, *really* good at it." Her voice cracks and I reach out and squeeze her hand. "I've resented football over the years, but I would've never wished this for him."

"I keep hoping that it's not over. That he'll be fine after the surgery and—"

She shakes her head, her face crumbling a little more. "It's unlikely, you know…" She sniffs and wipes her face and the girls crowd around her, crying too. "I'm not making this any better, am I? We came to bring cheer and I'm bringing down the mood." She tries to laugh.

The nurse comes out and her eyes widen when she sees the five of us.

"We have a few minutes. Would you like to come back now?" She directs the question to me.

"Yes." I put my hand on Cassidy's shoulder. "These are Henley's daughters and his ex-wife. Can they come back to see him too?"

She pauses for a few beats and then nods. "We normally wouldn't let so many people back, but we're doing a lot of things we don't normally do this morning." She smiles warmly at the girls and motions for us to follow her. "There's really only time to say hi though."

I nod and we follow her to Henley's room. His eyebrows lift when he sees all of us.

"Well, this is a nice surprise," he says, smiling at them.

The girls are somber as they walk up to his bed.

"Mom says it's so early we're not even going to be late for school, but I don't really think we should go to school when you're having surgery," Gracie says, her braids bouncing around with her impassioned words.

Henley chuckles. "You're not getting out of school on my account, peanut."

"But if there were ever a time to miss school, this would be it," Cassidy says, her eyes welling up.

"I agree." Audrey sniffles.

"Hey, no tears, okay? You're gonna break my heart and that'd be worse than any knee problem. Come here." He holds his arms out and they fall into him, Gracie crying now too. "Hey, hey. Listen, it's just a silly ole surgery, okay? No big deal."

"But Mom says you might not play football again and that's really sad," Audrey says into his neck.

His mouth parts and his eyes meet mine and then Bree's. She shifts next to me.

"I'm sorry, Hen. I shouldn't have told them that until we know for sure," Bree says.

"Don't be sorry. It's the truth." He lifts Audrey's chin and she stares up at him. "Life might look a little different, but we'll still have each other, right?"

"Right," she says.

"Will you still be able to pick me up?" Gracie asks, her little voice pitiful.

"Yes. Not right after surgery, but yes, peanut."

"Girls, we don't have much time. They're gonna take Dad back any second to get him ready. Let Tru get in there," Bree says. She shoots me an apologetic look.

I smile to let her know it's not necessary. "I'm glad he got to see you this morning." I squeeze Cassidy's shoulder. "This is the happiest he's looked all week."

Henley reaches out for my hand and tugs me toward him. "I love you. I'm sorry I haven't been—"

I put my fingers on his lips and kiss his forehead. "No more apologies out of you, sir. You're the best man I've ever known."

The nurse comes in and raps on the door. "Okay, Mr. Ward, it's time to take you back."

"We love you. I'll be here when you wake up," I promise.

"Love you, Daddy," the girls say in unison and it makes us all laugh.

"I love you all so much." He's smiling as they roll him out of the room.

"I'm really glad you came. You made him so happy." I put my arms around the girls and we huddle together. When we make our way out of the room and into the waiting room, Bowie, Weston, and Penn are in there. They stand up when they see us and hug everyone.

Rhodes walks in a minute later with a drink carrier filled with coffees and sets it down.

"Hey, let me in there too," he says, and we do a huge group hug. "He'll be all right, you guys, but he's gonna need lots of these hugs when he's home."

"We're not going anywhere," I say.

"Yeah," the girls pipe up. "We're not going anywhere."

"Except to school," Bree reminds them, and they groan.

She assures them they'll see Henley later, and they head out.

Sadie and Caleb stop by for a little bit too, and playing with Caleb is a nice distraction while we wait.

It's almost two hours before the surgeon steps out.

"Tru Seymour?" she says.

I walk over to her. "That's me. Hi."

"I'm Dr. Cermak. Surgery went well. Henley's waking up and asking for you. Dr. Grinstead said you'd want to see him right away."

"I do. Thank you."

She's already turning to go through the doors, so I follow. I turn to look back at the guys, seeing all the questions they have, but Dr. Grinstead walks out and stays with them while I go to Henley.

Henley's eyes are closed when we enter the room, but when I sit down next to him, they open and he looks at me groggily.

But then his face breaks out into the biggest smile.

I smile back in surprise and take his hand. "Hey, you look so much happier than I was expecting."

"I am *so* happy to see you." His words slur, but even as he talks, I can hear the smile in his voice. "You are the most beautiful woman I have ever known." He lifts my hand up to his mouth to kiss it, but he misses. He laughs. "Oops. I dreamed about you."

"You did? When you were in surgery?"

"Totally dreamed about you in surgery," he says really fast...like he's trying to fight the slur.

I giggle and look back at the surgeon.

"He's feeling pretty good on those medicines, I think," Dr. Cermak chuckles. She starts to say something else, but Henley jumps in.

"I dreamed we were getting married. We were getting married on the dock by the water with the candlestick in the library," he says and then laughs.

When I've got my bearings back after laughing so hard, I say, "Well, *that's* funny since you haven't even asked me to marry you yet. *Not* that I expect you to yet." I hold up my hand when he opens his mouth, but he starts nodding his head so fast.

"I thought of that," he says. "I thought of that in my dream...that I have not asked you yet. And so, will you please marry me? Tru. Trudi...uh, Trudi...Tru Seymour. Dammit. I wanted to say your middle name. Eloise!" He snaps his finger. "Trudi Eloise Seymour, will you please marry me on the dock by the water with the candlestick in the library?"

"I kind of feel like we're playing Clue instead of having a real proposal." I lean in, unable to stop laughing. "Oh, how I love you, Henley Ward." I lean in and kiss him.

"Are you avoiding my question?" he says, still grinning against my lips.

"I *am* avoiding your question," I say emphatically.

"Because I'd rather your proposal not be whenever you're on...whatever this is you're on."

"But, I feel *so good*," he says. "So much love I can't even express it all," he slurs. "Tell her, Doctor, tell her I'm completely coherent."

"You're coherent, all right, but I'm not sure proposals are the smartest option during this recovery time. How about we talk about how your surgery went?"

"I don't really want to talk about that," Henley says. "It's not going to be good, is it? I'm thirty-six. I have a major ACL tear, and even though you're a genius doctor, I know it does not look good for me."

"Sadly, you're right...where football is concerned anyway," Dr. Cermak says, "but it's too soon to know that for sure. Let's keep a positive outlook and we'll see how everything heals. I'd feel better if you stayed the night, but I know you're not wanting to."

"No, I don't need to stay the night," Henley says, staring at me. "I want to be in bed with my fiancée." He grins his wide-open smile.

And I grin back in spite of myself.

Dr. Cermak chuckles. "This guy's a charmer," she says, looking at me.

"Yes, he is." I run my hands through Henley's hair and then pat his scruffy cheek.

I can't believe that even in recovery from a major surgery that could be ending his career, this man is still managing to make me happier than I've ever been. I don't know how that's possible, but he does.

Even though this mood he's in, or this high, I guess, will be fleeting. The gravity of what he's facing had caught up with him before surgery and will again, but for now he's happy and I want to keep him that way.

"I'll make sure he doesn't overdo it if you think he's okay to go home," I tell Dr. Cermak and then look at Henley, "but I really think if Dr. Cermak wants you to stay, you should and I'll stay with you."

"I'll sleep so much better in my bed, but I'll do whatever you think, Dr. Cermak." Henley nods at Dr. Cermak then winks at me.

I try not to crack up.

"If you promise to let this lady take care of you when you get home and not be on your leg *at all*, I guess you can go home," Dr. Cermak says.

"*Yes*," Henley says, sounding like one of his girls when they get excited about something.

"All right. I will come back in a little bit with discharge instructions…it's going to be really important that you follow them." Dr. Cermak looks at me then. "And important that you make sure he does," she reiterates.

"I will. And when I'm not there to do it, one of his daughters or teammates or family members or friends will fill in."

"There *was* a full room out there with guys who seem willing." Dr. Cermak smiles.

Dr. Grinstead comes in and he and Dr. Cermak nod at each other.

"Okay, great. Rest a little while and I will be back." Dr. Cermak taps the end of the bed and walks out.

"Dr. Grinstead!" Henley sings.

Dr. Grinstead looks at him and then me in surprise, and I laugh.

"He's feeling all the love right now," I say.

"*So* much love," Henley says, beaming up at me.

The guys come in to say hi, and Henley is just as dreamy-eyed with them.

"I love you guys," he says over and over. He points at Penn. "Even you. Especially you, pretty boy."

Penn beams. "I knew you did." He elbows Weston. "What did I say when we first became friends with these guys? I said I'm gonna win Henley Ward over if it's the last thing I do."

Everyone laughs.

"You've had my heart from day one. All of it," Henley says, laughing along with everyone else. "And you and you and you and you." He points to the rest of us.

"It's a fucking love fest in here," Rhodes says, wiping the tears from his face. "And I, for one, could not be happier about it. You're gonna be just fine, Hen. We'll make sure of it."

"Damn straight, we will," Bowie says.

They put their fists together and lift them up the way they do when they're out on the field, and my heart nearly bursts with love and relief and gratitude.

CHAPTER THIRTY-NINE

WITNESSES

HENLEY

I groan when I wake up. The pain in my leg is screaming, but the nausea overrides everything.

"Oh, shit." I sit up and look around, fumbling to grab the small wastebasket by the side of the bed.

Tru put it there a week ago in case I needed to throw away Kleenex or wrappers from the fruit snacks and nuts I've been eating. Thank God she did.

She rushes to my side as I'm emptying my stomach in the

trash. She makes concerned sounds and when I'm done and lean back, she looks at me with such compassion, my heart twists.

"I'm sorry you had to see that," I croak.

"What did I say about no more apologizing?" Her hand is tender as she brushes my hair back.

I don't remember what she said about apologizing and I feel too wrung out to ask her.

She sets the garbage can down and sits carefully on the bed. I grab one of the wrapped peppermints we keep by the bed and pop one in my mouth to get the foul taste out and so I hopefully don't gross Tru out any further.

"I'll take care of that in a sec. After we're sure you're not going to throw up again," she says, tilting her head toward the garbage. "You're not feeling so good, huh?" She makes a face. "There I go, stating the obvious."

"I'm okay. I guess I don't react that great to anesthesia."

I'd hoped they'd only have to do an epidural nerve block, but due to the extent of the injury, I was completely knocked out.

She studies my face and then bites her lower lip. I reach out and rub my thumb over her lip.

"You slept a while. I almost woke you up to take your meds, but you were sleeping so peacefully, I couldn't do it." She seems shy or nervous and when she glances up at me, her head still lowered, I put my hand on her thigh and squeeze.

"Thank you for being here. Where's my mom though? I thought she'd relieve you by now. It's a gorgeous day out there. You don't need to be stuck in this dark, dreary house."

Hurt flashes over her face. "There's nowhere I want to be but right here with you, Henley. Stop trying to send me away. I knew the proposal earlier was the drugs talking, but telling me to go out now and enjoy the day when you've just gotten out of surgery?" A choked laugh comes out of her and she shakes her head, standing up. "It's a little extreme." She picks up the garbage and starts walking to the bathroom. "I wasn't going to hold you to it anyway, don't worry."

She disappears into the bathroom and I stare after her, my head pounding. My eyes close as I try to piece out what she just said. She comes in a few minutes later and hands me the medicine I'm supposed to take with a glass of water.

I take it and look up at her. "Can you explain what you meant just now?"

Her head tilts and she bites the inside of her mouth. "You don't remember?"

"Remember what exactly?"

She laughs, but it's as if the humor takes a minute to catch up, and only later turns into a real one. Her eyes meet mine and she laughs again.

"What?" I say, smiling up at her.

"Do you remember anything from right after your surgery?"

"I remember being really happy to see you."

She snorts. "Yeah, you were. You weren't trying to get me to go on any outdoor excursions then!" She laughs and this time it's so hard, she has tears in her eyes.

She sits on the bed, facing me.

"What did I do?" I make a face. Now I'm nervous.

"You were on a love high...thanks to the anesthesia and meds, I'm assuming. Dr. Cermak and the guys got to witness it too."

"Fuck me. What did I say? They'll never let me live it down."

She presses her lips together, fighting her smile. "You confessed that Penn has had all of your heart from day one."

"*Fuck*," I say, laughing and then groaning because my

head is still not right. I rub my forehead. "What did you mean...when you said you weren't going to hold me to it? What was that about?"

"I'm not holding you to your post-surgery proposal." Her eyes are bright now and I'm just so damn happy to see her smiling again, I smile back at her, but I'm still confused.

"What kind of proposal?" My forehead creases between my brows and she reaches out and smooths it.

"Does *Tru. Trudi...uh, Trudi...Tru Seymour. Dammit. I wanted to say your middle name. Eloise*...ring a bell?"

Now when she laughs, I laugh with her.

"Uh...no. But I'm afraid to ask now."

She threads her fingers through mine. "It was a very funny and charming marriage proposal in front of your surgeon, who suggested it might not be the right time to propose...but you were having none of that."

"Shit." I reach up and slide her long, silky hair between my fingers. "I can't believe I don't remember any of that." My cheeks burn and she puts her hand on my cheek.

I lean into it.

"You were also weirdly attached to getting married on the dock by the water with a candlestick in the library," she barely manages to get out in one breath.

"That makes no sense. The marrying you part does," I hurry to add, "but I don't even have candlesticks in the library. Those things would burn the books in an instant."

"Right?" she agrees. "I don't know where the candlesticks in the library came in...with the dock by the water. Sounds like two totally different backdrops." She frowns. "You didn't marry Bree by the water or in the library, did you?"

"No, we got married in a church."

She wipes her forehead in exaggerated relief. "Whew. That earns you some points. Hey, how's your stomach feeling? Do you think you could eat something yet? Ginger ale, maybe?"

"Tru...are we...okay? I can't believe I proposed and don't even remember. I'm so—"

"*No apologies.*" She leans in and I hope to God I smell like peppermint and not vomit.

This whole *being knocked on my ass* business is already doing a number on me. I don't want to disgust my girlfriend too. Or wait.

"Did you say yes?" I ask.

She smirks. "You wish. No, I did not say yes, you sexy, hot fool."

My lips form into a pout without me even trying. "Well, that stings."

"If we ever get to that place, it'll be when you remember asking, and you'll have to see what I say then." She pokes me in the chest and I take her finger and bite it, which makes her yelp.

My mom knocks on the door then and walks in with a tray of soup and crackers.

"I thought I heard you awake in here," she says. "How's my boy?"

"Apparently I am making all kinds of declarations in my addled state," I say. "But otherwise, I'm doing all right."

"He threw up when he woke up," Tru tells my mom, which causes a round of Mom tutting and fussing and babying. Tru widens her eyes when I frown at her. "What? She'd want to know."

"Of course, I do. My poor baby," Mom coos. "Should we call the doctor?"

I lean my head back, groaning. Mom insisted on coming to help and I agreed so Tru wouldn't feel pressured to do anything, but she took off a few days of work anyway. I adore my mom and love the way she and Tru have bonded, but the two of them nursing me might send me over the edge. Especially when I feel like such shit company.

"No. I'm fine. You don't need to fuss over me, okay?" I tell my mom as she places the tray on the bed. "Dr. Grinstead will be stopping by later...in fact, I'll be bombarded with all kinds of help from the medical team over the next couple of weeks." I put my hand on Mom's arm. "I love you. Don't worry."

Her chin wobbles and she pats my hand. "How can I not? You scared us to death when you were clobbered by that player." She frowns. "Actually, I've been fearful every single game I've watched you play. This just feels like our worst fears are coming true. I know you love that game so much and it's been incredible, all that you've accomplished, but haven't you had enough now?"

I gape at her. "Whether I've had enough or not, I may not have a choice." She winces and I grab her when she starts to pull away. "I'm sorry, Mom. You're right. I'm just...I don't know what to say about it right now."

She nods. "I know, honey. It's a lot to take in. You've had such an amazing run. I just hate the toll it takes on your body." She lifts her hand when I start to say something. "I know you act like you don't bleed, but you *do*. There's no way your body can get bashed countless times and you not live with untold pain, day in and day out." Her chin wobbles again and I feel like shit for making my mom cry. "You do a really good job of hiding it and not ever complaining, but I'm your mother. I know you, and I'm ready for you to take care of yourself."

She pats my cheek and turns to go.

"Let me know if something besides soup sounds good.

I've got oatmeal raisin cookies in the oven that I should go check on."

"I can never resist your oatmeal raisin cookies. I love you, Mom."

She smiles at me. "I know you do. And I love *you*."

I eat a little bit of soup and Tru helps me into the bathroom. I think she can tell I need some time alone after that conversation with my mom. She sets out my toiletries where they're easier to reach and walks to the door. I'm not supposed to shower yet, so I won't be in here long, but I start by grabbing the toothpaste.

"I'll just be right in there if you need me," she says, motioning toward the bedroom.

"It's like I'm grieving the me I've been." It comes rushing out and Tru steps back in. "I'm not taking what my mom said lightly. Regardless of what anyone is saying about my future, I know that I'm either done now or I will be soon. I've gone longer than most players do at this level. I'm just not sure who I am without football."

She comes and stands behind me, wrapping her arms around me, as we stare at each other in the mirror.

"You're the man I fell in love with. You're the best dad I've ever known. You're the friend everyone can count on. You're smart and funny and successful because you're Henley Ward, and Henley Ward is a *good person.*"

She kisses my shoulder and I kiss her hair.

"You're going to figure the rest out. Your life isn't over, even if your football career might be. There's a lot more you're meant to do." She smiles up at me and I wrap my arms around her, hugging her tight.

"I don't know what I did to deserve you, tiny dancer."

"Think about all the things I just told you. I'm the lucky one."

"We'll have to agree to disagree on that."

CHAPTER FORTY

SHAPES AND SIZES

TRU

Between school and dance and taking Henley to PT when I can, the days fly by. Henley is trying so hard to be his normal, cheerful self, but I can see the toll it's taking on him. He has circles under his eyes and even when the guys are over, it's almost as if he's hanging back from conversation, an onlooker instead of one of the ringleaders.

One thing that hasn't changed is his desire for me...unless it's that he wants me even more. Trying to have sex without hurting him has been challenging and comical and the high-light of all of this.

I've been on top a lot. In bed, on the couch, on the shower bench. We've tried it all, and he says he's frustrated with not being able to do all he wants with his body, but when it comes to sex, he is loving every second of seeing me ride him.

I have no complaints whatsoever.

He's stopped trying to force me to get out of the house. I think he knew I wasn't going to stand for one more thoughtful *get out and enjoy this day* conversation. But this cheerful front he's trying so hard to portray is almost worse.

We stop by my house to pick up a few things and my mom hugs us when she walks in.

"Why don't we just pack everything?" Henley asks.

My mom laughs. "When *are* you going to give in and move in with Henley?" she asks.

I make a face. "You too now, huh?"

"Can you please convince her to move in with me while I go to the bathroom, Stephanie?"

My mom's still laughing as he walks out. "He's pretty convincing. What's holding you back?"

There's a knock at the door and I walk toward it.

"Were you expecting anyone?"

"No." She shakes her head and tries to look out the window.

I open the door and there stands my dad. My eyes narrow on him. "What are you doing here?"

"Is that any way to greet your father?"

"Seems like you wanted the element of surprise since you didn't let anyone know you were coming." I fold my arms and he shoots me an irritated look.

"It's cold out here, Trudi. Let me in."

I turn back and my mom nods at me, so I open the door wider.

My dad saunters in like he doesn't have a care in the world. He's a good-looking man, and he knows it. He turns his most charming smile on my mom and I wait to see if it's going to work on her.

"You look beautiful, Stephanie," he says, moving toward her.

He reaches out to hug her and she holds up a hand before he can.

"We don't need to hug," she says. "If your daughter wants a hug, that's a different story, but I don't need one from you. What are you doing here, Allen?"

"Come on, Stephanie. How long are we going to play this game? I've said I'm sorry. What more do I have to do to prove that I want you back?"

Her lips flatten. "Not a damn thing. Because I don't care if you want me back. I said I was done and I meant it."

His nostrils flare and he takes a closer step. "It's sad that you think you're better off without me. No one's going to want your sorry ass at this age."

"Dad!"

My mom laughs and when her eyes fill with tears, I brace myself because when he makes her cry, I always cry. It also usually means she's about to soften. He makes her cry and she caves.

"The only thing sorry about my ass is that I put up with yours for so long. I have no idea why I thought so little of myself that I didn't stand up to you sooner, but you know what?" She moves in closer to him and gets in his face, her finger pointing in time with her next few words. "Every minute away from you has been the best time of my life. I wish I'd left you *years* ago. I also wish you'd work to have a relationship with your daughter, but as it is, you don't deserve her either. I'd suggest you get the message and go work on yourself for a while. It won't bring me back, but it just might salvage things between you and her." She looks at me. "If you even want that, Tru. I wouldn't blame you if you didn't."

"I'm her goddamned father. It's not like she has another option here," my dad yells.

Henley limps into the room. His eyes land on me and he exhales in relief before they settle on my dad. The expression on his face is unlike any I've ever seen on him. Cold and fierce.

"It's your *honor* to call Tru your daughter," Henley says. "A privilege, *not* a right. One that you should cherish until your dying day because you've got such a special daughter here."

"Who the hell are you?" Dad snaps.

"I'm Henley, Tru's boyfriend, partner, man…fill in the blank. And it's only because you're her father that I don't wipe the floor with you for talking to your daughter and her mother like you just did."

I smile despite the tension in the room.

My dad swallows hard.

"You ladies okay?" Henley asks, looking at me and then my mom.

"Allen showed up out of the blue and I was just leaving," my mom says. She looks at my dad pointedly. "I hope you brought the divorce papers and signed them. There's no sense in prolonging this."

"We need to talk about this, Stephanie," he argues.

"I'm done talking about it. *Sign the papers.*" She leaves the room and a minute later, I hear her pulling out of the driveway.

There's an awkward pause as we all stand there, no one knowing what to say.

"You and your mom sure are in a big hurry to get rid of me," Dad says.

I lift a shoulder. "You haven't exactly made being around you an enjoyable experience."

"It was a mistake for me to come here." My dad's face is red, the vein in his forehead popping.

"Feel free to see your way out."

He huffs out a disbelieving breath and walks to the door.

"Sign the papers!" I say to his back.

The door slamming is his response.

Henley puts his hand on my cheek and looks at me with concern.

"I'm okay." I sag into Henley and he puts his arms around me, holding me tight.

———

"How about we get takeout from Starlight Cafe or Rose & Thorn tonight?" he suggests on our way to his house. "Or The Fairy Hut…"

It's almost seven o'clock on a Friday night and Jupiter Lane is bustling.

Black and silver wreaths line every lamppost and there are pumpkins and ghosts and witches and skulls everywhere we look. Silver Hills makes Halloween the classiest I've ever seen it. The color theme is mostly silver, black, and green with more white pumpkins than orange. I've always loved Halloween in every look, so I'm here for all of it, but this is a really fun and gorgeous take on it.

"What sounds good to you?" I ask.

"I'm not really hungry."

He hasn't had much of an appetite for a while now.

"I wish we could think of something that sounds good to you," I say.

"I'm such a fucking downer all the time," he mutters. "I don't know why you keep putting up with me."

"Hey. You are not. You're going through a hard time. I want you on your bad days and your good days, and everything in between."

He doesn't say anything and when I look at him again, he's starting to smile.

"What?" I ask.

"That sort of sounded like a wedding vow to me."

The only thing I have to throw at him is a napkin from the car, so it sort of flutters his way with no punch.

"Shush," I tell him.

"Oh shit!" he says.

I jump and try to focus on the road. "What?"

"I can't believe I've forgotten the pumpkins. Do you mind if we stop by the store to pick some up? It's almost Halloween and I haven't even done the pumpkins. The girls will be disappointed if we don't do them together like we do every year." He sounds both disappointed and excited.

I turn into the grocery store parking lot, chasing after whatever makes him excited right now.

"What do you do to the pumpkins?"

He grins. "You'll have to wait and see. They'll be pricier here, but Nelson's Pumpkin Patch is probably picked over by now." He's reaching for his crutches before I've fully parked, and I put my hand on his arm.

"Why don't you let me go pick them out? You've done too much today already with PT and then that episode with my dad."

"I'll be okay."

I stare him down and he sighs.

"Okay, but there needs to be a variety of sizes. I like some round, plump ones and tall, skinny ones in there too."

I laugh at that. "Okay. Round, plump, check. Tall, skinny, check." I look back at the pile of them outside the store. "Do you want them to be orange or white?"

"Surprise me."

Oh, he's so cute.

He gives me some cash and I shake my head, not taking it from him.

"Don't argue with me, Tru."

I roll my eyes and take the money.

"How many are we talking? Three? Five?"

He gives me a look like *Surely, you jest.* "Two dozen."

My mouth falls open. "Twenty-four pumpkins."

He nods, bright-eyed like a little boy, and I'd buy a hundred pumpkins to make him look like this.

"Okay! Twenty-four surprise pumpkins coming right up."

"I need to help you get them in the—"

I hold up my hand. "Don't you dare. We are not going to undo all your hard work with a pumpkin excursion."

He laughs and leans his head back on the seat. "Fine. I don't like it, but fine."

I lean over and kiss him and he hums.

"Now *this* I like a lot…" He deepens the kiss and my insides turn to jelly.

His hands are wandering fast, and I have to pull myself away so we're not caught by another officer.

As I'm shopping for the perfect pumpkins, I come up with what might be a great idea if I can pull it off. Since Henley's accident, it's typical for me to hear from not just my new girl-friends, but all of Henley's friends throughout the day. They text him to see how he's doing and then they text me to see how he's *really* doing.

I text everyone while I'm waiting in the checkout line.

> So...I didn't discover until now just how much Henley loves Halloween. With everything going on, I don't think he even realized until tonight that it's almost here. What if we had a surprise Halloween party at his house next week? Everyone dress up. You can come after you've taken the kids trick-or-treating or we'll have plenty of treats for them at the house...what do you think?

The yeses start rolling in right away, first from Penn and then Sadie and Elle, and by the time we get home with all of the pumpkins, I've heard from everyone, and they're all in.

Over the next week, Henley and the girls make the cutest pumpkins I've ever seen. They have doorknob eyes, metal drawer pull mouths, nuts and bolts noses, squiggly screw hair —you name it, every hardware appliance or tool or old piece of scrap metal that can be spared is used to make pumpkin faces. When he's done with one, he names them, and every time the girls come over, they want to meet his new creations. Gracie talks to Betty and Charlene, her two favorites, like they're her new besties.

The diversion has been good for him and while he works on them, I tell him I'm decorating his house and yard for Halloween, so our new pumpkin family can feel at home. I carry over the color theme from town—black, white, and green—except we have the orange pumpkins in the mix too.

The girls know about the party, and they've been so excited about it, helping with the decorating and working on Henley's costume. Bree even contributes extra pampas grass she's not using for her wedding and says she and Alex will stop by the party.

On Halloween morning, Henley's in the kitchen when I leave for school.

"You look cute," he says, when I lean down to kiss him.

I'm going low-key with a witch's hat and spider earrings, so I can save my better costume for later.

"I'm not used to the girls taking care of my costume. Have you seen what they're working on?"

I nod, unable to hide my grin. "It's gonna be good, don't worry."

It's a fun day at school. The kids are more chatty than usual because of all the candy they're getting in every class. But I manage to reel them in when it counts.

Bowie takes Henley to his PT appointment so I can finish getting things ready for tonight, and my mom comes over to help. Bree drops the girls off not long before Henley is supposed to come home, and she can't get over how great the house looks.

"If you ever need a job, you could always come work with me in the wedding business," she says, pointing at me before she gets in her car.

"I'm honored you'd even consider that," I tell her, pleased.

The plan Henley *thinks* is happening is that after Bowie drops him off, Henley will dress up and sit by the front door passing out candy, while the girls go trick-or-treating. And then we'll hang out with them for a little while afterwards.

When he gets home, the girls are already dressed up in their monster outfits, and they giggle as they lead him to his room to show him the costume they got for him. I go get ready in another bathroom, piling my hair high around a cutoff two-liter bottle. It's giving *Bridgerton* vibes, but this look came out long before the idea of *Bridgerton* was conceived. I angle a mirror to look at the back and laugh at how high it is. My dress is green, rather than the typical white usually worn with this costume, but the style is so similar to the movie that it'll still be obvious.

The girls peek into the bathroom.

"Oh my God, you look amazing," Cassidy says.

"Wow," Audrey says. "So cool."

"I want that hair next year," Gracie says.

"Do you think he has any idea about the party?" I whisper.

"Not at all. He's ready and we told him you'd be there in a second."

The girls move out of the bathroom and run downstairs and when I step into the hall, Henley is opening his bedroom door. We stare at each other and start laughing.

"You look perfect," I tell him. "Frankenstein has never looked so good."

"Are you the *bride* of Frankenstein?" he asks, lips quirking up. He stares at my hair in awe and then down my body.

I hold my hand up. "No, no. Not the bride. I'm the *girl-friend* of Frankenstein. Let's not get ahead of ourselves."

I still haven't stopped teasing him about his proposal...I probably won't ever stop.

His head falls back as he laughs. "We will have to remedy this," he tells me. "You look like a bride to me."

My heart never fails to lose its mind when he says things like that.

"Look at you though." I laugh when he walks toward me. "This costume works perfectly with your brace. You don't even have to fake the stiffness...it's built in. And the girls did an amazing job on your makeup. I'm impressed."

He laughs. "Yes, they did. I'm guessing you helped them with this idea? Because it is pretty perfect for what I'm going through." He points to the bolt coming out of his head and we laugh.

"We might have brainstormed together."

His hand grips my waist and he tugs me closer. "Come here." His fingers trace over my blood-red lips. "I love these red lips. Gives me all kinds of ideas for later."

"These red lips are game," I say, pulling his finger into my mouth and sucking it.

He hisses in a breath.

Something clatters downstairs and we both freeze.

"Everything okay down there?" he calls.

There's a long pause and I hold my breath, wondering if the surprise is blown.

"Yes, Daddy. Everything's fine," Audrey calls back.

My body relaxes and I hope that we've taken long enough getting ready that everyone has gotten in place by now.

"Should we go hand out candy?" I touch his smoothed-down hair, laughing at how stiff it is.

"Let's do it."

We walk downstairs and the lights have been turned off, so there's only the glow of the twinkle lights from outside.

"Why is it so dark down here?" Henley asks.

When we reach the foyer, the lights come on at the same time as the music, and everyone is standing there, all dressed up in their Halloween costumes. Rhodes is a mummy, and Levi is a ninja. Elle is Audrey Hepburn in *Breakfast at Tiffany's*. Bowie and Becca are pirates. Penn is Batman and Sam is a Colorado Mustang. Calista and Javi are Beauty and the Beast. My mom is a teddy bear. Everyone looks *phenomenal*. But Weston, Sadie, and Caleb win the prize for most creative costumes…Weston is Colonel Sanders, and Sadie and Caleb are the chickens.

"Boo!" They all yell.

Henley holds onto my hand and the wall and once he's caught his breath, he starts laughing.

"Holy shit, are you all trying to kill me?" He clutches his heart and everyone laughs.

Penn reaches out and bumps his fist. "Did we really manage to surprise you?"

Sam is beside Penn, and Henley bumps his fist next.

"Looking good, Sam," he says.

Sam flushes and then stares at Cassidy with adoration. The few times I've seen him around the girls, it's obvious he's starstruck by Cassidy. From what I can tell, Cassidy is clueless about his crush.

"Dad had no idea…did you?" Cassidy says, turning to smirk at Henley.

"That you guys were creating this elaborate surprise behind my back?" He bops her nose and turns to me, his eyes warm. "No idea."

He tugs me closer and leans in.

"You're just full of surprises, aren't you?" he says under his breath.

"Trying to do my part to keep you hopping, Henley Ward. And that smile looks really good on you."

The party is a success. Henley laughs more than he has in so long, and when we crawl into his bed that night, he sighs and turns to look at me.

"You make everything better, Tru," he says.

"That's how I feel about you too."

"So, how long did Frankenstein and his girlfriend date before they got married?" He nuzzles into my neck and his fingers trail up between my legs.

"You'd have to ask him," I say, already heating up from his touch.

I kiss him before he gets a chance to say anything else, too hungry for him to think about what's next...

Except *this,* right here, right now.

"I'm ready to move in with you if you still want me," I tell him.

His eyes widen and he grins. "Really?"

"Really."

"What made you decide that?"

"I don't want to hold back from you for another second. Hearing the regrets my mom has for holding onto my dad all those years...I don't want to regret a single thing. I want to be with you. Wasting a minute missing out on this beautiful thing we have because of fear or being cautious...I trust you. I trust our love. I don't have anything to be afraid of when it comes to choosing you."

He lowers his forehead to mine. "This is the best news ever...the only thing that would be better is if you'd become my bride." He grins, already knowing how I'm going to react.

"One of these days, I'm going to surprise you and say yes."

"I'm living for that day." His hand drops to my hip and he kisses me until I'm one limp noodle. "I'm living for *all* the days that you're by my side."

"We're forever, Henley."

CHAPTER FORTY-ONE

SUBMERGED

HENLEY

I'm finishing up with Dr. Grinstead when Coach Evans knocks on the door and pokes his head in.

"How's it going?" he asks, looking between Dr. Grinstead and me.

"I'll let Henley answer that," Dr. Grinstead says.

"I'm feeling stronger all the time, but there's more inflammation than we'd like," I tell him. "Jimmy is ready to up the intensity of my workouts soon, but we're waiting to see if this knee starts looking a little better." I lean forward.

Coach Evans sighs. "We're in trouble, Ward. We can't seem to get back on our feet without you."

"I'm sorry, Coach. It kills me that I left the season hanging, believe me. I'm willing to do whatever I can on the back end, though…if that means working one-on-one with Cal or being at the practices. I don't know if that would help or not, but we can try it."

"Yeah, I think that would be good. Both of those options," Evans says.

As I drive home, I decide I'll bring it up with the guys tomorrow. We're having Friendsgiving—dubbed by Sadie and Tru—at our place this year. Thanksgiving still isn't for another couple of weeks, but the game schedule got in the way since the Mustangs have a game that day.

The guys have avoided talking about football with me. I can understand why—I've been a moody bastard since the injury. I've been dealing with my own shit, trying to work through the reality that things are going to be different for me now. I haven't been ready to say it out loud just yet, but I don't think I'm going back to football.

I don't know for a fact that I'm done, but I've got a strong feeling that's the way this is going, and I'm trying to listen to my body and do a better job of taking care of it.

My headspace is getting better, slowly but surely, and now I want to do what I can to help my team.

Even if I'm not playing with them anymore, I'll always care about what happens to them.

"How did it go?" Tru asks when I walk into the kitchen.

Stephanie walks in and waves at me happily.

"Hey, Stephanie. You two haven't stopped cooking, have you?"

Stephanie turns and goes back to the garage, probably to grab something from the fridge out there.

"No, we missed you though," Tru says, laughing. "We'll let you pick up where you left off." She winks, and I swat her backside.

We've been cooking a ton, getting ready for tomorrow.

"I'll get right to it." I nuzzle her neck until she squirms.

"What did Dr. Grinstead say?"

"That there's still more inflammation than he'd like, but he's glad my mobility is so much better."

"You proved that last night when we had sex right here on this island," she whispers, turning to kiss me. "And this morning when you had your way with me in the shower."

"I loved every second of both of those times...but I also miss you being on top," I say, kissing down her neck.

"We will revisit my top positions very soon," she says.

"Since you don't call me Mr. Football Player anymore, I'd like to put the nickname Oh, God, Right There into consideration."

She giggles but then puts her hands in my hair and looks up at me.

"Does it make you sad that I don't call you that anymore?"

"When you say my name with such heat in your voice, nothing else matters. You know I'm yours, right?"

"Yes. And I'm yours," she says.

She stands on her tiptoes and I kiss her, only pulling back when I hear Stephanie coming in.

Later that night, we're exploring more positions. I thrust deeply into her, dragging her thigh around my waist, when I turn and pull her on top of me.

"Fuck me like you mean it, tiny dancer."

"I mean it, I mean it," she pants.

"I love you so much," I tell her.

"I love you too. It's so good, Henley."

"I know, baby. I want to spend the rest of my life doing this with you."

"Oh, God, Right There, harder!" she cries.

I laugh, but it quickly turns into me groaning out her name as we both sail into oblivion together.

We did Friendsgiving last year at Weston's and it's become a tradition. I'm riding high in the gratitude department right now, and these people are the reason why.

Cassidy, Audrey, and Gracie are watching a movie with Becca and Sam. Caleb keeps going back and forth between the movie and seeing what we're up to.

"Where are Rhodes and Elle?" Bowie asks.

"They said they were coming an hour ago. I'm not sure what happened to them, but I've texted to see if they're okay," Tru says, reaching past me to pick up her phone.

"Maybe they *were* coming..." Penn says, wiggling his eyebrows.

"In our dreams." Calista laughs, clinking glasses with him. "Bernard has been sniffing around Elle again, and I'm so over him it's not even funny. He wants her back and he just can't let it go."

When Rhodes and Elle show up about ten minutes later, the tension is *thick*. If there was any action going on between them earlier, it's over now. In fact, I'm pretty sure they're fighting, which is maybe a first in the history books.

None of us know what to do with an angry Rhodes and Elle. They're both as easygoing as it gets. And in all the years

I've known them, I don't think I've ever seen them angry with each other.

Tru, Sadie, and Calista get up and hug Elle. I watch Tru lean toward Elle. Tru says something that makes Elle laugh and Elle's shoulders lose some of their stiffness. Tru feels my eyes on her and smiles at me. God, I love her.

"What's going on with you and Elle?" Weston asks Rhodes.

He sighs and runs his hand over his face. "I don't want to talk about it. I'm so fucking worried about the game this weekend and now Elle is..." He shakes his head. "Yeah, I can't talk about it."

"It's okay," I tell him. "Tonight's about being grateful and having fun and not being so fucking serious."

Rhodes nods. "I can get behind that."

The girls wander back over and find places to sit. We're spread out in the living room, and I love having everyone together, talking and laughing. This is what life is all about, this right here.

"Hey, can I say something?" I say, clinking my water glass with my dessert fork.

Everyone turns to look at me.

"I wanted to let you all know that I couldn't have gotten past these last couple of months without you. I've been a lot to deal with, but none of you have ever made me feel that way. You've dealt with my moods and hauled my ass to appointments and tried to fill any cravings—" That gets a laugh because they've all tried to think of things to feed me. "I might still have bad days, but I think I'm coming out of the tunnel. And there's no one I'd rather do life with than all of you. You're my safe place. Everyone in this room has become my family, and I just want all of you to know I appreciate you."

I lift my glass and they lift theirs back to me.

"We love you," Bowie says.

"I love you too. Every single one of you."

When everyone's gone home for the night, it's just Tru and me. We hold hands as we walk to our room. After we've brushed our teeth, she turns on the shower and I follow her in there.

She looks at me, eyes shining so bright.

"Come here," I tell her.

She grins and I put my arms around her.

"Thank you for an amazing day," I say."

She turns and points at the bench. She pushes me lightly, so that I'm sitting and then she straddles me, not putting her weight fully on me, but so her slit slides over me. I'm already aching for her and she gasps when she feels just how much.

"You like that?"

"So much," she says.

She rubs against me, and I dip into her slick heat. She's on birth control, so we stopped using condoms a while ago, and I love the luxury of fucking her without any barriers. It still takes my breath away when I enter her without anything between us.

I lift her off of me and set her back on the seat, grinning as I stretch my leg out and sit in front of her. Perfectly lined up with her goodness. The water pounds on my hair and I go in with everything I've got. Her moans get louder as I lick her. I don't have the patience to make her wait for it tonight. I'm relentless, barely coming up for air. My fingers do some of the work along with my tongue, but when I suck her tight bud and don't let go, I get the reward I'm after. She bucks against my face and I think I'd be happy drowning if it meant I'd go like this.

CHAPTER FORTY-TWO

A DIFFERENT PICTURE

TRU

I hustle around Silver Hills Community Theatre a few nights later, arranging flowers in the vases set up in the lobby and making sure the dance programs for our recital are lined up neatly. When a few stray dancers giggle in a corner nearby, I turn with what I hope is a patient smile and herd them back to the area where they're all supposed to be waiting.

Henley stops by to say hello to Cassidy and Audrey, and

he kisses me on the cheek, which causes another round of titters throughout the room.

"You look so beautiful tonight," he whispers in my ear.

I press my hands to my cheeks, trying to cool them down when he leaves. When I turn back to face everyone, I laugh at their wide-eyed expressions.

I overhear one of Audrey's friends ask if her dad and Miss Tru are getting married and my heart overflows when Audrey says, "I hope so."

Jacklyn stays out front to greet everyone, and when she comes back half an hour later, she looks around, beaming at all of us.

"The theatre is completely full," she says. "Are you ready to go out there and dance your hearts out?"

"Yes!" Everyone cheers.

"Our special guests are sitting in the front row and they will come up on the stage right before the last song. Stay in your places and no talking during that time, so we won't have any extra distractions. Okay?" she asks.

"Yes, Miss Jacklyn," they sing.

I suppress my laugh and help everyone line up, and the evening gets underway.

It's a magical night. When we get to the last piece, the dads, and in some cases, the moms, come up on the stage to dance with their kids, and I look at Henley to see how he's doing. He smiles as Bowie moves into place to dance with Cassidy, and Rhodes goes to stand by Audrey.

My eyes fill with tears even though Henley appears to be fine. I wish it could be him up there with his girls.

When we knew he wouldn't be able to do the dance, Rhodes offered right away. Cassidy had asked Alex to dance with her, but he said he had two left feet, so Bowie stepped in to fill Alex's place.

The crowd is delighted to see their beloved football stars performing. The phones are lit up all over the place, recording. They dance to "Don't Worry, Be Happy" and it's flawless. Rhodes and Audrey are in the middle and they steal everyone's hearts when he dips Audrey back. She's laughing when he lifts her up and the audience erupts in applause. Henley wears a proud papa smile and snaps pictures along with the rest of the parents.

My cheeks hurt from smiling.

I chat with people on their way out and am standing with Elle, Calista, and Sadie when Henley and all five of the guys walk up. Cassidy and Audrey are in the center of them, getting doted on, and the photographer for the event motions for them to go stand in front of the winter wonderland backdrop for a photograph. Sweet smiles are snapped first and then silly faces, and when they're done, Henley calls us over to take a huge group shot with them. Sadie moves next to Weston, and I move next to Henley. Elle and Calista stand on Rhodes' side, and I don't miss the tension that's still between Elle and Rhodes. I really need to ask her what's going on there.

Suddenly, a woman calls Elle's name and we all turn to look at her. Elle steps out of the group and goes over to talk to the woman. A few more pictures are taken, but I keep watching Elle and the woman because it looks like Elle's getting a stern lecture.

"Who is that?" I ask Calista.

"Lisa Harper, the cheerleader director of the Mustangs," she says quietly.

Rhodes curses under his breath and then apologizes to the girls.

"That's Lisa Harper? I've seen her at dance events before. I think she has a niece with the company. Is Elle okay?" I ask.

"It's the stupid rules for the cheerleaders, I bet," Rhodes says. "Elle's not supposed to be at any event that we're attending."

"But she's our family friend," I say, confused. "Surely tonight doesn't count?"

"It doesn't matter," he says. "It all counts."

Elle has told us she's not supposed to be seen with the players outside of team-sanctioned events, but with this being an event for Cassidy and Audrey, and her being my friend too, it never crossed my mind. And since she's broken the rules already by being at our house before, I guess I didn't think it really mattered.

"I hope she's okay," I say. "Can you keep me posted, Calista? I have to go make sure all our things are cleared out."

She nods and I hug everyone, thanking them for coming.

Henley finds me a little later and leans against the doorframe as I grab my coat. When I walk near him, he clasps my hand and then lifts our hands up high as I twirl around.

"Look at you, having the moves even when you're still healing from surgery."

He tugs me against him and I slide my hands up his chest and around his neck.

"We'll dance again, I promise," he says, leaning his forehead against mine. "I don't know if I'll get to play football again, but I *refuse* to miss out on dancing with you."

I swallow the lump that rises in my throat. "I want you to have everything you wish for, Henley. Football, no more pain, dancing the night away…everything you dream of, I want that for you." A tear drips down my face and his thumb swipes it away.

"I do have everything I've dreamed of," he says. "I've

found a love I never thought I'd have…with you. My girls love me and still put up with me," he laughs, "and the guys and their kids are still a huge part of my life, which is how I hope to keep it. Everything else feels…well, way down the list in terms of importance. *You* are what I dream of." His voice is gravelly and another tear slides down my cheek. "Damn, tiny dancer, you're breaking my heart. Do you have any idea how happy you make me?"

I hold my fingers up close together. "A little bit. Because you make me so happy."

"I'm going through this crazy transition where life is looking different and I'm making my peace with it. I didn't want to put you through my mess, but…" His smile grows and that mischief in his eyes is back. "Those nights without you were what felt like hell on earth. Once you let me know you're not going anywhere, I knew I didn't need another day out on that field to be happy. You and me. Our family and friends. That's all I need."

I stand on my tiptoes and kiss his cheeks and the side of his lips on either side.

"I."

Kiss.

"Love."

Kiss.

"*You.*"

Kiss.

"Henley."

Kiss.

"Ward."

When I finally kiss him full on the mouth, he's more than ready for me. He growls into my mouth, deepening the kiss. We kiss and kiss, our bodies suctioned together as close as we can get. I break away, panting, and smile when I see the desire in his expression.

"Take me home, Tru Seymour. I don't want to stop kissing you."

"*Home.* I love that plan."

EPILOGUE
THE FULL GAMUT

HENLEY

We lost the game yesterday. We're at Luminary in our private room, the mood somber. The Single Dad Playbook sits in the middle of the table.

"You're looking good these days, man," Rhodes tells me.

"Thanks. I'm feeling good," I tell him.

"Are you really?" Bowie asks. "Your leg's feeling better?"

I pause. Because the truth of the matter is, my leg is still giving me fits every damn day.

Bowie's face clouds. "You don't have to answer that."

"No, it's okay. I wanted to talk to you guys about all of this," I say.

Weston leans in and so does Penn.

"Are you asking Tru to marry you?" Penn asks.

I lift my shoulder, grinning. "We're getting there. She's almost completely moved in."

"That's great," Weston says.

"What did you want to talk to us about?" Penn asks.

"Coach asked me to start working with Cal, and I'll be coming to the games. I don't know if it'll help, but we're going to try. I feel like my injury broke the flow, and I hope I can do something to get you to trust yourselves again. We all know your skills are the best out there, we just have to get you believing it again."

"I love everything about this," Rhodes says after a long pause. "I hate being out on that field without you. Honestly, just seeing your face out there feels like it will boost all of us."

"Agreed," Bowie says.

"This is great," Weston says. "And I love that you'll be working with Cal too. He's good, but he's not you."

"What is the doctor saying about you?" Penn asks, looking down at the table. I'm surprised by the emotion in his eyes when he looks up at me.

"Dr. Grinstead wants me to be hopeful about a full recovery, but guys...we know it's a long shot, right? And I'm slowly making my peace with that. I wasn't at first...but the longer I have to sit with it...and the more my leg continues to be an issue, the more I think I need to let it go. I had a great run, and if it's really over for me, I'm so glad I got to finish out my career with the four of you."

They stare down at the table. Rhodes wipes his eyes and there's sniffling from Penn too.

"Fuck, guys, you're gonna make me lose my shit." My voice cracks and I groan. "Open the fucking playbook. I need to read something encouraging. Or funny. Or anything to not weep like a baby." I let out a choked laugh and they join me with their own sappy ones.

Bowie passes me the playbook and I open it to the last few entries.

When Caleb realized I couldn't magically
turn his bedroom into a forest the way he saw on his favorite
movie,
he looked at me with different eyes.
And I thought, wow, if he's looking at me like this already,
he's in for a world of disappointment.
I had to tell him dads don't have magical powers.
I'll love him and take care of him and our love will be magical,
but only because it's real and true and unconditional.
Of course, he doesn't fully understand this yet.
But I hope I can keep convincing him.
~Weston

I look at Weston and smile. "You'll convince him. The way he looks at you, he fully trusts your love."

"Last night, he asked if he was marrying Sadie too." Weston snorts. "I think he believes we're all getting married."

We all crack up at that.

"February will be here before you know it," Penn says. "I can't believe you're getting married." He shakes his head. "The end of an era."

We laugh again and I keep reading the book.

Sam gave me a card at Friendsgiving.
He told me to read it when I got home, so I did.
And I'm glad I did.
He said I've changed his life.
I cried like a fucking baby.
I get it now, you guys.
I get why you torture yourselves with having kids.
~Penn

Penn's sheepish when I look at him.

"It was a moment of weakness," he says, smirking. "I take it all back. He texted me today asking what I could tell him about Vaseline. The kid is not old enough for all this, I swear. One of the boys in his foster home keeps it by the bed and Sam wants *me* to tell him why. I'm not cut out for this."

"You are totally cut out for this," Weston says, laughing. "But I'm glad it's you and not me."

Henley's knee injury has inspired a lot of talks with Becca.
She doesn't understand why this happened and gets so sad
when she doesn't see Henley in the games anymore.
When I told her sometimes good things come to an end,
I didn't know it would start a whole tangent of questions:

Would I stop loving her?
Would Lucky Charms stop having the marshmallows?
Will her bed break in the middle of the night when she's
sleeping?
It's been endless.
So I've started to tell her that an ending
always makes room for a new beginning,
and I'm sticking with that.
~Bowie

I don't even realize I'm crying until a napkin is shoved my way.

"Thank you," I mumble, wiping my eyes and nose. "I think I'm making room for a new beginning."

"Dammit. I didn't know this was going to be the week we all bawl our eyes out," Rhodes says. "Here. Read mine."

Levi has an obsession with booties.
Last week at the grocery store,
he saw Mrs. Lyson in leggings,
and he went over and told her that her booty had a baby.
I don't know what to do with this.
~Rhodes

I laugh until I cry.

"How do you guys know what I need?" I wipe my face again. "Every damn time."

"You guys are good for the soul," Rhodes says.

We all pipe in our agreement.

"Well, I'm gonna get home to my girl." I get up and they do too.

We hug each other and walk out together, feeling a thousand times better than when we came.

Want more Henley and Tru? Click here!

https://bookhip.com/QRHFDMP

For Rhodes' story
pre order Reckless Love Here!
https://geni.us/Recklesslove

RECKLESS LOVE COMING SOON!

Prologue
The Night We Met

RHODES

Then

I heard her laugh before I ever saw her. A wild, unabandoned burst of sound that managed to still be delicate. I turned to find the face to that laugh and when I did, I tried not to gawk. She was beautiful with long, black hair, dark brown eyes, and cherry red lips…dressed in an oversized dress that went all the way down to her ankles.

Somehow she still made that dress look sexy.

I was about to go introduce myself, when a guy walked up to her and handed her a red Solo cup. I frowned when she took it without hesitation, and I moved in closer when she looked disgusted after a sip.

Doesn't she know you don't take a drink from someone without seeing where it came from?

But the next second, I relaxed, laughing to myself when she handed the cup back to the guy and shook her head like it wasn't for her. He downed it in three huge gulps and then burped loudly. A slight flicker of distaste crossed her face before he took her hand and led her through the crowd to dance.

I found myself looking for her throughout the night, but people kept coming up to say hi, and every time I saw her, she was still with that dude. He was getting sloppier by the second, and the later it got, the more she looked like she wanted to escape. A bunch of us were out by the bonfire and the guy sat on the ground next to her chair as she stared into the fire. Next thing I knew, he tried to pull her out of the chair, his voice rising to an obnoxious whine.

"Come on, I'll take you home," he said.

"I'll get another ride," she said.

"Come on, I'm fine, Elle. Let's go."

"No."

I stood up and was there to block his path when he tried to walk away with her.

"Hey, man, can I give you a lift home?" I put my hand on his shoulder and he swayed into me.

He held onto my arm to keep him standing. "Nah, I got it."

"Well, why don't you stay longer? The party's just getting started. Here, why don't you stretch out on this chair?" I led him to an open lounge chair and helped him sit.

He stretched out his legs and leaned his head back. "Thanks, man. I'll stay a little bit longer."

Within seconds, his eyes closed and his mouth gaped open as he fell asleep.

"You're good," the girl said as we looked down at him. "I've been trying to hide his keys from him for the past half hour, but he was onto me."

"Looks like he'll be out for a while. You okay?"

She turned and looked at me directly for the first time, and damn, I liked her smile.

"Much better now, thank you. I was trying to step out of my comfort zone...go to my first college party, say yes to Logan since he's asked me out every day for two weeks straight...but I have horrible luck with guys and next time I think I'll just stay in my dorm room." She laughed that tinkley laugh and it made me feel warm all over.

"Aw, now, let's not make rash decisions like that," I said. "Come on, let's turn this around. Why do you have horrible luck with guys?"

"Uh...because they either cheat on me...or put me down...or get drunk and pass out on the first date." She laughed.

"Damn. Guys are assholes, what can I say?" I crinkled my nose. "How about you tell me what would make your first college party experience better? It's my first college party too, by the way." I leaned in conspiratorially. "Did you try the JELL-O shots?"

She laughed again and I wanted to keep that coming.

"So JELL-O shots aren't just a college myth?" she asked.

"Nope. They're very real. Come on. I'll show you. There are even different flavors."

"Well, anything has got to be better than the beer I tried earlier."

I laughed at the face she made. "You don't like beer?"

"Turns out not at all. I didn't know that until tonight either, but—" She lifted a shoulder.

"You tried it for the first time to have the full college experience," I finished for her.

"Exactly." She grinned. "It's not like I'm new to *every-thing*...but a lot of things." She made another face, and I couldn't stop smiling.

"I'm Rhodes, by the way." We walked into the house and into the kitchen.

"I'm Elle. Nice to meet you."

"You too."

"Do you know who lives here?" she asked. "Logan told me who was throwing the party, but I forgot the name..."

I paused and give her a sheepish smile. "I actually live here with a few guys, but Shep is the one throwing the party."

"Wow, it's a really nice place."

A few girls walked up and I could tell what was coming next by the way one girl's mouth parted when she saw me.

"Oh. My. *God*. You're Troy Archer's son, aren't you?" she asked.

"I am," I said, glancing at Elle.

Elle's eyes widened. Fuck. I wanted a little more time to get to know her before she found out who I am. It inevitably made people weird around me.

"And isn't Amara your mother?" the other girl asked. "She's so beautiful. And your dad is *so* hot."

My eyes narrowed when she reached up and touched my hair. I'd been growing the curls out for a while, but that didn't mean I wanted just anyone touching it.

"I can't get over your eyes. So *unusual*," she said, moving even closer.

I took a step back and her hand dropped from my hair.

In my opinion, my hazel eyes weren't that unusual with a blond-haired, blue-eyed dad who was white, and a black-haired, brown-eyed mom who was Black, but I didn't bother saying that. I looked at Elle and lifted two JELL-O shots.

"Red or blue?" I asked.

"Red, please," she said.

"Excuse us, ladies," I said to the girls. They still stared at me like I was an exhibit as I motioned for Elle to follow me.

I leaned in toward Elle's ear. "Want to see a fun part of the house?"

"Where is it?"

"The roof."

Her eyes widened and I hedged.

"It's safe, I promise. And it's not the highest part of the roof, it's just off of my room, but we can go out my window and pretend to be gargoyles, checking out the party from up above."

She snorted but looked hesitant for a moment.

"We can tell your friends where you're going in case you're worried about going to the roof with me."

"Maybe if I had any friends." She giggled. "I don't really know anyone but Logan and look how that turned out. I'm not worried about going with you. I'm just not the best with heights. I mean, I probably *should* tell someone where I'm going, but you feel safe."

I lifted my eyebrows. "Not what everyone would think when they see me coming."

She giggled again and it was so fucking cute. "You *are* ginormous. But have you seen your dimples? I could be wrong, but I think I read somewhere that guys with dimples are harmless."

I smirked. She was adorable and I liked how she seemed exactly the same as she did before she heard about my famous parents. Don't get me wrong, I'd benefited from having a movie star father and a supermodel mother my entire life, growing up in a mansion in LA and going on fancy trips all over the world, never lacking for anything.

Except anonymity.

But people knowing who I am wasn't the worst thing, I guessed.

I just never knew for sure who wanted to get close to me for *me* and not my parents.

I started walking toward my room and she stayed close.

"I hadn't read that about dimples before, but you're safe with me," I said over my shoulder.

When we got to my door, we walked in and I went straight to the window, opening it. I turned, and Elle was looking around my room and then paused near my bookshelves. She rubbed her arms as she shivered.

"Do you need a sweatshirt?"

"Yes, please. I'm from Colorado, so I'm used to colder weather than this, but Palo Alto at night is chilly to me, for some reason."

"I grew up in Southern California, so it's chilly here for me too."

I grabbed one of my Stanford sweatshirts and handed it to her.

She pulled it over her head and beamed up at me. "Much better."

"I don't believe you don't have any friends. You're so nice and smart and cute."

Her cheeks flushed. "I'm pretty sure my roommate thinks I'm the biggest nerd she's ever met, and she's not wrong," she said.

I grinned and climbed out the window, stepping aside to make sure she got out safely.

"Can nerds dance like you do? I don't think so," I told her.

She looked at me in confusion. "You saw me dance?"

"Uh, is it creepy to admit that? Earlier...with Logan. You're good."

"Thanks. I love to dance. *Love* it. That's what got me to this party...I wanted to dance."

"You could be a cheerleader. Stanford's cheer team is pretty great." I motioned for her to sit on the ledge next to me and she did, both of our feet dangling from the roof. The sounds of the party drifted up there, but it was slightly muted. "I guess you've already missed the cutoff for this year. But you should try out in the spring."

She looked at me with an odd expression and my eyebrows lifted.

"What?" I asked.

"I'm actually on the team. I guess I look quite a bit different when I'm off the field."

I grinned. "You don't wear your crop top everywhere you go?"

She laughed and shook her head. "I'm still trying to get used to that." She scrunched up her nose. "Wait...you're on the football team, aren't you?"

"Yep. Sure am."

"Oh, gosh. I totally should have known that."

I chuckled. I hadn't heard anyone say *gosh* in a long time.

"I've been so nervous about doing all the right steps that I'm not paying close enough attention to the game yet," she said. "But I know you're a big deal!"

"I do all right." I shrugged.

I just signed another NIL deal this morning. I was doing more than all right.

She laughed at my cocky grin.

"Tight end's my thing." I tilted my head in a slight bow.

"It totally makes sense, now that I think about it. You're so tall and you have muscles on top of muscles." She laughed when she heard me laughing but didn't seem embarrassed. I liked how she said what she thought. "You're nicer than most jocks I've met. Well, I guess I haven't met that many, but... you're definitely nicer."

"I'm not that nice. It's you bringing it out in me," I admitted.

She let out a derisive sound. "Right. And why would I bring that out in you?"

"You haven't acted any different since finding out who my parents are," I said, ticking off my fingers. "You seem very genuine and down-to-earth."

Her shoulder bumped mine. "That's such a kind thing to say. See? You can't tell me you're not that nice." She sighed contentedly and looked over at me, her eyes crinkling with her smile. "I didn't know I was going to make a friend tonight."

My heart both warmed and cracked a little. I didn't think I'd ever had such a fun conversation with a girl and I'd certainly never been friend-zoned before. But the thought of having her as a friend suddenly seemed like the best possible option. I didn't just want a hookup with this girl and then never see her again, and the thought of starting out our freshmen year of college in some sort of relationship didn't seem smart or realistic.

I bumped her shoulder back. "I've really needed a friend," I told her.

Her face softened and she gave me that smile that felt like it was shining from the inside out. "Me too." Her lips puckered and her eyes narrowed as an idea formed. "We should make a pact."

"Okay," I drew the word out. "What would this pact be?"

"That this will be a legit friendship...we'll talk like this always."

"Okay."

She snapped her fingers and pointed at me. "Oh, and that we won't let anything come between us...not other guys or other girls or love. Just pure friendship for the rest of our days." She laughed. "Or at least throughout our four years at Stanford..."

I nodded. "I can agree to all that. Should we shake on it?"

"I think we should."

She held out her hand and I took it, shaking firmly.

"That settles it. Friends forever," I said.

Now if I could just lose this crush on my newfound best friend.

Chapter 1
Off-Kilter

RHODES

Now

I look in the rearview mirror and smile at Levi. He's bopping his head to "Training Season" by Dua Lipa. I blame Weston Shaw for getting my son hooked on this...as my fingers tap to the beat on the steering wheel.

"We see Elle?" Levi asks.

And damn. My three-year-old isn't the only one missing Elle. I can't stop thinking about her.

Last night, before I ran off of Clarity Field, my eyes scanned the crowd for Elle Benton, my best friend in all the world. She was still on the sidelines, looking better than any cheerleader has a right to look, and her dark brown eyes burned into mine.

The anger was still there, glaring back, and it's killing me.

I thought there was nothing I hated more than losing.

Okay, there are other things that suck too.

Like it's the worst when Levi is sick. He's a happy little guy and it takes a lot to get him down, but when he's sick, those sad eyes make me want to cry.

Or it's rough when his mother, Carrie, tries to use a new angle of manipulation on me yet again, or when I'm benched with an injury.

I intensely dislike all those things.

Being on a losing streak after being the first team to ever win three consecutive Super Bowls in a row doesn't help.

It has me feeling more off-kilter than I have in a long time.

Not fucking good. But *especially* not good when everything else is also going wrong.

Henley, another best friend and the most incredible wide receiver I've ever had the honor of playing with, was injured this season and most likely won't be playing again.

We've been practicing so hard trying to make up for Henley being out, I haven't even had time to get laid.

Well…if we're going for full disclosure here, I was off my game even before Henley's accident.

Normally, I'm the chillest guy I know. I like to have fun,

not take anything too seriously, and enjoy life with my son, my guys from the team, and Elle.

But things being weird with Elle…now *that* is more than I can take.

I honestly didn't know we were capable of a fight anymore. We became best friends during our freshmen year of college and that bond has only gotten stronger over the years.

I wish we could talk all night right now, like we did that very first night.

I barely get a spare minute with her these days.

Clara, my favorite barista and owner of Luminary Coffeehouse, holds up my matcha latte when I walk in, and I kiss her cheek.

"And here's a chocolate milk for Mr. Levi Archer!" she says, leaning down to give him his drink in a sippy cup.

"You're the best, Clara. Thank you." I glance down at Levi and tilt my head toward Clara.

"Thank you, Miss Clara," Levi says, leaning in to hug her legs.

I grin at Levi and he takes such a long swig of his chocolate milk, he has to take a gasping breath when he's done.

"Oh, you are so welcome, sweet little man." Clara beams at my little boy.

"Are we the last ones to get here?" I ask.

"I haven't seen Henley yet," she says. She takes another look at me and frowns. "You doing okay? You don't seem yourself this morning."

"When are you guys gonna get it together?" Marv calls across the coffee shop.

Marv and Walter are the two grouchos who are at Luminary anytime the doors are open. They love football and they love complaining about everything we do wrong, even when we're doing everything right.

During a dismal 5-8 season, we're giving them plenty of material.

I wince and look at Clara. "Not my best day, no."

"No trash-talking in my shop," Clara tells Marv, her hand on her hip.

Marv grumbles to Walter but listens to Clara. Everyone loves Clara, even Walter and Marv.

"Hopefully we're gonna get it together by Sunday," I tell Marv.

I lift my matcha, thanking Clara again, and Levi and I head back to the room where my guys are waiting. My teammates, Bowie, Henley, and I started meeting regularly to talk about dad life, and it sort of grew into hanging out with my best friends and talking about *everything*.

Bowie has a daughter and Henley has three, so we had plenty to cover. Weston and Penn started showing up because they wanted to hang out with us, but then Weston became a dad and Penn started mentoring a kid, so the Single Dad Players now consists of five of us. We write shit in The Single Dad Playbook, and hanging out with these men has become some of my most treasured times, outside of the football field.

There are fist bumps all around. Levi goes around the table, saying hi to everyone, and stops when he gets in front of Caleb, Weston's son. Levi plops down in front of Caleb with his toys and hands him a toy he knows Caleb likes.

"Good job, Levi. I love it when you share." He hasn't always been the best at sharing, so I make sure to praise him a little bit for it.

"What have I missed?" I ask.

"Not much," Bowie says, leaning his elbows on the table.

I'm saying, "We look old this morning," when Henley limps in. He's still recovering from ACL surgery and he turns and acts like he's going to walk back out of the room when he hears me.

I jump up and tug him in, laughing when he pretends to hit me in the gut.

"If I can't talk about how old I feel, you can't either. And only one of us can be depressed at a time. Last time I checked, that was me," he says.

He's grinning as he says it, but he's right. I wouldn't want to be dealing with what he is for anything.

"I thought you were feeling better," Penn says, eyebrows puckering in concern.

"I am, but it's not a joyfest overnight or anything. And that game last night…" He looks around at us and sits down, stretching his bad leg out to the side.

We all groan.

"I need to drink this tasty beverage before I go there yet," I grumble.

"How are negotiations going for you?" Weston asks.

"Pretty good." I nod. "Sounds like they're trying to get everything I wanted."

"That's awesome, man," Henley says.

"Okay, then let's talk about what's going on with you and Elle and the way she looked at you at the game last night," Bowie says.

"Elle?" Levi echoes, standing up to see if she came into the room. He goes back and sits down when he realizes she's not here.

I give Bowie a pointed glare and he returns it with a contrite one.

"You noticed that, huh?" I say under my breath.

Bowie lifts his shoulder as if to say, *Who didn't?*

"Hard to ignore those daggers," Weston says.

If these guys noticed, who else did?

"You think anyone else noticed?" I look around at each one of them.

"I doubt it," Penn says. "It's just because we know you guys. So what's going on? You were weird at Friendsgiving too...and at the dance recital."

"Are we really saying Friendsgiving when the girls aren't around? It's just so..." I sigh.

"We do Friendsgiving now and we own it," Weston says, laughing.

"I love doing it, it's the *word* that I never thought I'd be saying..."

They all laugh.

Weston elbows me. "Out with it. If it were one of us not talking about our mess by now, you'd be all over us. Spill."

I groan and pick up a napkin, twisting it. "I don't know where to begin, I guess. When she told me she wanted to be a cheerleader for the Mustangs, I was all for it. She loves to dance...she was the best cheerleader on our college team. She has that IT factor that makes everyone want to get another look at her. I mean, you've all seen her. She's *fucking* gorgeous," I whisper the F-word since Levi and Caleb are here. "She belongs out there, and she needed something to boost her confidence. She's spent her whole life trying to fit into the box her parents wanted her to be in...she deserves this time. But she's busier than she's ever been. And you guys know we're skirting the rules even hanging out at all, with the no-fraternization policy between us and the cheerleaders. But it's *me and Elle*. Everyone knows we've been best friends forever."

Thirteen years is a *long* time.

"Can't the rules be bent a little?" Penn asks.

I tilt my head and make a face. "I thought so. But since she got on the team, we've hardly seen each other. We've hung out at Henley's and at each other's houses a couple of times, which is technically prohibited, but come on! It's ridiculous to think that we'd cut off ties with each other just because she's a cheerleader on the team."

I scowl at the floor.

"Elle doesn't think it's so ridiculous," I add. "She's been adamant that we can't be seen together, ever, and she came *this* close to not showing up at Friendsgiving. She'd come over the night before upset, and we drank a little...and..." I pause, still unable to meet them in the eye because again, it's *me and Elle*.

"The anticipation is killing me," Bowie says.

"Same, bro. What happened?" Penn pounds on the table.

I clear my throat. "Well, one thing led to another, and..."

The room is silent. I look up at them and they're staring at me in shock before they all start speaking at once, demanding to know what happened.

"We kissed," I admit, wincing. *And a little more than that*, I think but don't say.

"Why are you making that face? Was it bad? Did it feel wrong?" Henley leans in, disbelief on his face.

"No, not even a little bit. It was all kinds of right."

Pre Order Reckless Love Here!
https://geni.us/Recklesslove

ACKNOWLEDGMENTS

Writing is a solitary experience a lot of the time, but it also takes a village. I'm overwhelming grateful for mine...with this book more than ever!

All my love and thanks and unending gratitude to the following people and then some, in no particular order: Nate Sabin, Greyley Sabin, Indigo Sabin, Kira Sabin, Kess Fennell, Nina "Georgie" Grinstead, Christine Estevez, Natalie Burtner, Katie Friend, Laura Pavlov, Catherine Cowles, Kim Cermak, Emily Wittig, Christine Bowden, Tosha Khoury, Amy Jackson, Courtney Nunness, Kalie Phillips, Gracelyn Szynal, Savita Naik, Claire Contreras, Kim Gilmour, Katie Robinson, Jacob Morgan, Savannah Peachwood, Connor Crais and Ava Erickson (I forgot to thank Connor and Ava in Mad Love and they were BRILLIANT), Christine Miller, Sarah Norris, Kelley Beckham, Valentine Grinstead, Josette Ochoa, Meagan Reynosa, Ratula Roy, Amy Dindia, Megan Cermak, Charlie Grinstead, Tarryn Fisher, Winston, Troi Atkinson, Phyllis Atkinson, David Atkinson, Destini Simmons, and every single reader and reviewer...THANK YOU WITH ALL MY HEART!

And to my family and friends who don't read my books but help me without even knowing it, I love you.

ALSO BY WILLOW ASTER

The Single Dad Playbook Series

Mad Love

Secret Love

Reckless Love

Wicked Love

Crazy Love

Landmark Mountain Series

Unforgettable

Someday

Irresistible

Falling

Stay

Standalones with Interconnected Characters

Summertime

Autumn Nights

Kingdoms of Sin Series

Downfall

Exposed

Ruin

Pride

Standalones

True Love Story

Fade to Red

In the Fields

Maybe Maby (also available on all retailer sites)

Lilith (also available on all retailer sites)

Miles Apart (also available on all retailer sites)

Falling in Eden

The G.D. Taylors Series with Laura Pavlov

Wanted Wed or Alive

The Bold and the Bullheaded

Another Motherfaker

Don't Cry Over Spilled MILF

Friends with Benefactors

The End of Men Series with Tarryn Fisher

Folsom

Jackal

FOLLOW ME

JOIN MY MASTER LIST...
https://bit.ly/3CMKz5y

Website willowaster.com
Facebook @willowasterauthor
Instagram @willowaster
Amazon @willowaster
Bookbub @willow-aster
TikTok @willowaster1
Goodreads @willow_aster
Asters group @Astersgroup
Pinterest@willowaster